Someone had ransacked th
contents scattered across the
pans, and broken glassware and dishes. Drawers had been yanked
out and tossed aside, appliances swept from the counters. Not a
single package of food remained on the pantry shelves or in the
refrigerator. Whoever had trashed Marlene's kitchen had taken
the time to open boxes, bags, and canisters and dump all the food.
Everything from raisin bran to frozen broccoli florets to dried
pasta peppered the room. A dusting of flour and sugar lay over
everything like newly fallen snow.

Acclaim for the Anastasia Pollack Crafting Mysteries

Assault with a Deadly Glue Gun

"Crafty cozies don't get any better than this hilarious confection...Anastasia is as deadpan droll as Tina Fey's Liz Lemon, and readers can't help cheering as she copes with caring for a host of colorful characters." – *Publishers Weekly* (starred review)

"Winston has hit a homerun with this hilarious, laugh-until-your-sides-hurt tale. Oddball characters, uproariously funny situations, and a heroine with a strong sense of irony will delight fans of Janet Evanovich, Jess Lourey, and Kathleen Bacus. May this be the first of many in Winston's Anastasia Pollack Crafting Mystery series." – *Booklist* (starred review)

"A comic tour de force...Lovers of funny mysteries, outrageous puns, self-deprecating humor, and light romance will all find something here." – *ForeWord Magazine* (Book-of-the-Year nominee)

"North Jersey's more mature answer to Stephanie Plum. Funny, gutsy, and determined, Anastasia has a bright future in the planned series." – *Kirkus Reviews*

"...a delightful romp through the halls of who-done-it." – *The Star-Ledger*

"Make way for Lois Winston's promising new series...I'll be eagerly awaiting the next installment in this thoroughly delightful series." – *Mystery Scene Magazine*

"...once you read the first few pages of Lois Winston's first-in-series whodunit, you're hooked for the duration..." – *Bookpage*

"...madcap but tough-as-nails, no holds barred plot and main character...a step above the usual crafty cozy." – *The Mystery Reader*

"...Anastasia is, above all, a JERSEY girl..., and never, ever mess with one of them. I can't wait 'til the next book in this series..." – *Suspense Magazine*

"Anastasia is as crafty as Martha Stewart, as feisty as Stephanie Plum, and as resourceful as Kinsey Millhone." – Mary Kennedy, author of the Talk Radio Mysteries

"Fans of Stephanie Plum will love Lois Winston's cast of quirky, laughable, and loveable characters. *Assault with a Deadly Glue Gun* is clever and thoroughly entertaining—a must read!" – Brenda Novak, *New York Times* best-selling author

"What a treat—I can't stop laughing! Witty, wise, and delightfully clever, Anastasia is going to be your new best friend. Her mysterious adventures are irresistible—you'll be glued to the page!" – Hank Phillippi Ryan, Agatha, Anthony, and Macavity award-winning author

"You think you've got trouble? Say hello to Anastasia Pollack, who also happens to be queen of the one-liners. Funny, funny, funny—this is a series you don't want to miss!" – Kasey Michaels, *USA Today* best-selling author

Death by Killer Mop Doll
"Anastasia is a crafting Stephanie Plum, surrounded by characters sure to bring chuckles as she careens through the narrative, crossing paths with the detectives assigned to the case and snooping around to solve it." – *Booklist*

"Several crafts projects, oodles of laughs and an older, more centered version of Stephanie Plum." – *Kirkus Reviews*

"You'll be both surprised and entertained by this terrific mystery. I can't wait to see what happens in the Pollack household next." – *Suspense Magazine*

"The book has what a mystery should...It moves along at a good pace...Like all good sleuths, Anastasia pieces together what others don't...The book has a fun twist...and it's clear that Anastasia, the everyday woman who loves crafts and desserts, and has a complete hottie in pursuit, will return to solve another murder and offer more crafts tips..." – *Star-Ledger*

Decoupage Can Be Deadly

"*Decoupage Can Be Deadly* is the fourth in the Anastasia Pollock Crafting Mysteries by Lois Winston. And it's the best one yet. More, please!" – *Suspense Magazine*

"What a great cozy mystery series. One of the reasons this series stands out for me as a great one is the absolutely great cast of characters. Every single character in these books is awesomely quirky and downright hilarious. This series is a true laugh out loud read!" – Books Are Life–Vita Libri

"This is one of these series that no matter what, I'm going to be laughing my way through a comedy of errors as our reluctant heroine sets a course of action to find a killer while contending with her eccentrically dysfunctional family. This adventure grabs you immediately delivering a fast-paced and action-filled drama that doesn't let up from the first page to the surprising conclusion." – Dru's Book Musings

"Lois Winston's reluctant amateur sleuth Anastasia Pollack is back in another wild romp." – The Book Breeze

A Stitch to Die For

"*A Stitch to Die For* is the fifth in the *Anastasia Pollack Crafting Mysteries* by Lois Winston. If you're a reader who enjoys a well-plotted mystery and loves to laugh, don't miss this one!" – *Suspense Magazine*

Scrapbook of Murder

"This is one of the best books in this delightfully entertaining whodunit and I hope there are more stories in the future." – Dru's Book Musings

"*Scrapbook of Murder* is a perfect example of what mysteries are all about—deft plotting, believable characters, well-written dialogue, and a satisfying, logical ending. I loved it!" – *Suspense Magazine*

"I read an amazing book recently, y'all — *Scrapbook of Murder* by Lois Winston, #6 in the Anastasia Pollack Crafting Mysteries. All six novels and three novellas in the series are Five Star reads." – Jane Reads

"Well written, with interesting characters." – Laura's Interests

"...a quick read, with humour, a good mystery and very interesting characters!" – Verietats

Drop Dead Ornaments

"I always forget how much I love this series until I read the next one and I fall in love all over again..." – Dru's Book Musings

"*Drop Dead Ornaments* is a delightful addition to the Anastasia Pollack Crafting Mystery series. More, please!" – *Suspense Magazine*

"I love protagonist Anastasia Pollack. She's witty and funny, and she can be sarcastic at times...A great whodunit, with riotous twists and turns, *Drop Dead Ornaments* was a fast, exciting read that really kept me on my toes." – Lisa Ks Book reviews

"*Drop Dead Ornaments* is such a fantastic book...I adore

Anastasia! She's clever, likable, fun to read about, and easy to root for." – Jane Reads

"...readers will be laughing continually at the antics of Anastasia and clan in *Drop Dead Ornaments*." – The Avid Reader

"I love this series! Not only is Anastasia a 'crime magnet,' she is hilarious and snarky, a delight to read about and a dedicated friend." – Mallory Heart's Cozies

"It is always a nice surprise when something I am reading has a tie in to actual news or events that are happening in the present moment. I don't want to spoil a major plot secret, but the timing could not have been better...Be prepared for a dysfunctional cast of quirky characters." – Laura's Interests

"This is a Tour de Force of a Murder/Mystery." – A Wytch's Book Review

"A series worth checking out." – The Ninja Librarian

"I flew through this book. Winston knows how to make a reader turn the page. It's more than a puzzle to solve—I was rooting for people I cared about. Anastasia Pollack is easy to like, a good mother, a good friend, and in a healthy romantic relationship, the kind of person you'd want on your side in a difficult situation." – Indies Who Publish Everywhere

"Lois Winston's cozy craft mystery *Drop Dead Ornaments* is an enjoyable...roller-coaster ride, with secrets and clues tugging the reader this way and that, and gentle climbs and drops of suspense and revelation to keep them reading." – Here's How It Happened

"Anastasia is a take-charge woman with a heart for her family—even her ex-family members who don't (in my opinion) deserve her kindness... What I like best about Anastasia is how she balances her quest for justice with the needs and fears of her family... I can't wait to read more of her adventures and the progress of her relationship with her family and her boyfriend." – The Self-Rescue Princess

"...a light-hearted cozy mystery with lots of energy and definitely lots of action and interaction between characters." – Curling Up By the Fire

"I thought the plot was well thought out and the story flowed well. There were many twists and turns...and I enjoyed all the quirky characters. I was totally baffled as to who the killer was and was left guessing to the very end." – Melina's Book Blog

"(Anastasia's) wit and sarcasm lend a bit of humor to this cozy, and the story kept me intrigued right up to the end." – The Books the Thing

Handmade Ho-Ho Homicide
"Handmade Ho-Ho Homicide" is a laugh-out-loud, well plotted mystery, from a real pro! A ho-ho hoot!" – *Suspense Magazine*

"Merry *Crises*! Lois Winston has brought back Anastasia's delightful first-person narrative of family, friends, dysfunction, and murder, and made it again very entertaining! Anastasia's clever quips, fun stories, and well-deserved digs kept me smiling, and reading the many funny parts to my husband...does that count as two thumbs up in one? What a great journey!" – *Kings River Life Magazine*

"Once again, the author knows how to tell a story that immediately grabbed my attention and I couldn't put this book down until the last page was read.... This was one of the best books in this delightfully lovable series and I can't wait to see what exciting adventures await Anastasia and her friends." – Dru's Book Musings

"This was such a fun quick read. I can't wait to read more of this series." – A Chick Who Reads

"The story had me on the edge of my seat the entire time." – 5 Stars, Baroness Book Trove

"Christmas, cozy mystery, craft, how can I not love this book? Humor, twists and turns, adorable characters make this story truly engaging from the first to the last page." – LibriAmoriMiei

"Take a murder mystery, add some light-hearted humor and weird characters, sprinkle some snow and what you get is *Handmade Ho-Ho Homicide*—a perfect Christmas Cozy read." –5 stars, The Book Decoder

A Sew Deadly Cruise
"*A Sew Deadly Cruise* is absolutely delightful, and I was sorry when it was over. I devoured every word!" – Suspense Magazine

"Engaging Drama! Brilliant! *A Sew Deadly Cruise* earns 5/5 Upgraded Cabins. Winston's witty first-person narrative and banter keeps me a fan. Loved it!" –*Kings River Life*

"The author knows how to tell a story with great aplomb and when all was said and done, this was one fantastic whodunit that left me craving for more thrilling adventures." – Dru's Book Musings

"The combo of investigating and fun makes for a great read. The author does a good job of keeping the killer a secret. Overall a fun read that cozy fans are sure to enjoy." – Books a Plenty Book Reviews

"Winston has a gift for writing complicated cozy mysteries while entertaining and educating." – Here's How it Happened

Books by Lois Winston

Anastasia Pollack Crafting Mystery series
Assault with a Deadly Glue Gun
Death by Killer Mop Doll
Revenge of the Crafty Corpse
Decoupage Can Be Deadly
A Stitch to Die For
Scrapbook of Murder
Drop Dead Ornaments
Handmade Ho-Ho Homicide
A Sew Deadly Cruise
Stitch, Bake, Die!

Anastasia Pollack Crafting Mini-Mysteries
Crewel Intentions
Mosaic Mayhem
Patchwork Peril
Crafty Crimes (all 3 novellas in one volume)

Empty Nest Mystery Series
Definitely Dead
Literally Dead

Romantic Suspense
Love, Lies and a Double Shot of Deception
Lost in Manhattan (writing as Emma Carlyle)
Someone to Watch Over Me (writing as Emma Carlyle)

Romance and Chick Lit
Talk Gertie to Me
Four Uncles and a Wedding (writing as Emma Carlyle)
Hooking Mr. Right (writing as Emma Carlyle)
Finding Hope (Writing as Emma Carlyle)

Stitch,
Bake,
Die!

LOIS WINSTON

Cover design by L. Winston

ISBN:978-1-940795-55-3

DEDICATION

This one's for Shelley, whose friendship means more to me with each passing day.

ACKNOWLEDGMENTS

For taking the time to answer my numerous medical, legal, and police procedural questions, a special thanks to Nora Spinaio; D.P. Lyle, MD; Judy Melinek, MD; M.L. Kelso; Teresa Reasor; Patricia Bradley; Allison Brennan; Wesley Harris; and Wally Lind.

And as always, special thanks to Donnell Bell and Irene Peterson for making sure I dot all my "i's" and cross all my "t's".

ONE

"Solve any murders over the weekend?"

Cloris McWerther, AKA *American Woman* food editor and my best friend, entered the break room as I helped myself to a cup of coffee, my second since arriving at the office half an hour ago. It was one of those mornings. I scowled into my mug. "Monday morning gallows humor? Definitely not appreciated, especially today."

"Uh-oh! Do tell."

I glanced at the large bakery box she clutched in her hands. "Only if you're about to bribe me. And it better include chocolate."

She quirked an eyebrow. "Or?"

"I refuse to take responsibility for my actions."

Cloris shoved the box into my outstretched arms. "In that case, take the entire dozen. I don't want to be charged with accessory to whatever crime you're contemplating this morning. Or worse yet, wind up your victim."

"Smart woman." I placed the box on the table and lifted the lid to reveal twelve chocolate éclairs. I grabbed one and took a huge bite. An explosion of raspberry pastry cream mamboed around my mouth, mingling with chocolate ganache and sending my taste buds into gastronomic bliss.

After rinsing the mouthful down with a swig of coffee, I said, "I'm nominating these for a Nobel Peace Prize."

"I don't think they give Nobels for food," said Cloris, helping herself to an éclair.

"Well, they should. If given a choice between these and war, peace would reign supreme."

Cloris consumed the éclair and helped herself to another. I forced myself to exert massive self-control as I stared longingly at the remaining nine éclairs. Superior metabolism is Cloris's superpower. No matter what she eats, she remains a Size Two. Me? I probably gained three pounds staring into the box.

"So?" she asked.

I nibbled at the remainder of the éclair in my hand. Best to make the pleasure last as long as possible. "My Lucille reprieve ended yesterday. She's back home."

Cloris frowned as she pushed the bakery box toward me. "When dealing with the mother-in-law from Hades, one éclair is never enough."

I definitely deserved to lose myself in éclair heaven, but with a courage I normally lacked, I shook my head and slid the box back to her. If I caved, I'd regret my weakness when I stepped on the bathroom scale tomorrow morning. Besides, with a wedding on the horizon, I should be eating escarole, not éclairs.

"Are we talking general Lucille belligerence, or something specific?"

"No point boring you with details. You've heard it all before in one form or another. Let's just say the reprieve was far too short, and she spent yesterday making up for lost time."

When my husband, Karl Marx Pollack, so named due to his mother's communist convictions, died suddenly in Las Vegas a little more than a year ago, Lucille Pollack became my permanent houseguest and albatross—along with her French bulldog Manifesto. The dog's ill-tempered disposition most likely the result of his political moniker. I've yet to meet a commie with a pleasant personality, and thanks to my mother-in-law, I've met far too many.

If I could, I'd set Lucille up in an assisted-living facility. Unfortunately, thanks to a well-hidden gambling addiction, Karl left me in debt greater than the GNP of the average Third World nation.

My name is Anastasia Pollack. I'm a widowed mother of two teenage boys, a women's magazine crafts editor, caretaker to a Shakespeare-quoting parrot, and ever since Karl's death, a previous member of the middle class and reluctant amateur sleuth. Don't ask me how many dead bodies I've stumbled across. I've lost count. Seriously.

Lucille had spent the last three weeks convalescing at a rehab center, the result of a car accident that saw the demise of a misguided assassin. Said assassin had taken it upon herself to eliminate several people she deemed problematic to me and my family, including my fiancé's father, my mother's ex-husband, and a boorish misogynist. We believe Lucille was her next intended target.

Cloris left the remaining sinful confections in the break room for nine lucky coworkers. Coffee cups in hand, we headed down the corridor to our cubicles, which lay across the hall from one another. Before we arrived, we heard our names called from behind.

We turned to find the ever-efficient Kim O'Hara, our editorial director's assistant, waving to us. As usual, she held a stack of file folders cradled in one arm, her phone clutched in her other hand as she held it overhead and continued waving. A curtain of straight auburn hair whipped around her face as she race-walked toward us, Manolo Blahnik's clicking a staccato beat along the terrazzo floor.

Half-Chinese, half-Irish, Kim had lucked out in the gene lottery, inheriting the best features from both branches of her family tree, but unlike our self-absorbed fashion editor, Kim was as sweet as she was gorgeous. When she caught up to us, she said, "Naomi wants to see you both, ASAP."

"About?" I asked, fighting back the trepidation growing inside me. Although the best of friends, Cloris's work and mine rarely overlapped, and with our monthly staff meeting still two weeks away, we certainly hadn't forgotten to show up for an issue planning session. For the life of me, I couldn't imagine why Naomi wanted to see both of us at the same time unless we were about to be fired.

Rumors concerning major editorial changes constantly whipped around the office at 5G speed. We'd had several upheavals since the hostile takeover that had absorbed us into Trimedia a few years ago. With so many magazines on life-support, I immediately expected the worst. I glanced at Cloris and saw the same thought reflected in her eyes.

Kim merely smiled cryptically as she shrugged and said, "You'll have to ask Naomi."

"Spoken like a true acolyte," said Cloris.

Kim chuckled as she zipped past us on her way to carry out her next task.

"Never let it be said that Kim allows any moss to grow under her designer stilettos," I said, amazed at her ability to stay upright in five-inch heels as she jogged down the hall. "I'd twist an ankle before I managed two steps."

"You and me both." Cloris took a deep breath and exhaled with a rush. "I suppose we'd better see what Naomi wants."

A minute later we stood outside the office of our editorial director. Cloris raised her hand and rapped twice. From the other side of the door we heard Naomi call, "Come in."

We found Naomi Dreyfus seated behind her desk. She waved us forward, directing us to take the two seats that faced her.

Naomi had recently turned sixty, but you'd never know it by looking at her. Statuesque and regal with emerald green eyes and silver hair always styled in an elegant chignon, she gave off an aura of old money and finishing schools. She reminded me of Grace Kelly—back before the former actress-turned-princess had added the menopause pounds that robbed her of her waist. At sixty, Naomi still maintained her girlish figure, not to mention her flawless, wrinkle-free complexion.

She offered us a warm smile as we settled into the chairs. I took that as a positive sign. If you're about to be canned, you might receive a malicious smirk from the boss, but a friendly smile? Not likely.

Without any chitchat-filled prelude, Naomi got right to the point. "Are either of you familiar with the Stitch and Bake Society?"

"I think so," said Cloris. "Aren't they a women's social group similar to the one where members wear purple and sport red hats?"

Naomi nodded. "Similar but different. The Stitch and Bake Society began several years ago when a recent retiree realized she'd spent her entire life as a single, workaholic executive and now had few friends and fewer pastimes to occupy her days."

I stole a quick glance at Cloris and caught her eye. I could think of dozens of activities we'd enjoy if only we had both the free time and funds of a financially well-off retiree.

Naomi continued, "She remembered how her mother, grandmothers, and aunts had always enjoyed needlework projects and baking, activities she'd deemed as old-fashioned and a waste of time."

"Why make what you can easily buy?" asked Cloris.

"Exactly."

"That's not why people pursue hobbies," I said.

"You and I know that, but she didn't," said Naomi. "Anyway, out of boredom, she took a few classes and found herself falling in love with the very hobbies she'd eschewed her entire life. Through social media, she connected with other retired professional women in similar circumstances and eventually founded an organization devoted to women exploring these shared passions in their golden years."

"Are we giving them a write-up?" I asked.

"More than that. The organization has grown to include chapters across the country. The New Jersey chapter is holding their first mini-conference next week, a three-day event at the Beckwith Chateau Country Club."

Cloris whistled under her breath. "These ladies are definitely not getting by on only their IRAs and Social Security checks."

"Not by a longshot," said Naomi. "Of course, it doesn't hurt that Marlene Beckwith is president of the New Jersey chapter."

"Nothing like having well-placed friends," I said. Marlene's family owned the most exclusive country club in the state. Rumor had it membership was by invitation only, and if you needed to ask the initiation fee and annual cost, you couldn't afford to join.

"*American Woman* has agreed to be one of the sponsors," said Naomi, "which leads me to both of you. Along with hosting speakers, as part of the festivities they're holding a baking competition and a needlework show. The two of you will each give a one-hour talk once a day and also judge the two competitions."

"Which three days?" I asked. "Are we talking giving up a weekend?"

"Tuesday through Thursday," said Naomi.

"That's a relief," said Cloris.

"Something doesn't add up," I said. When Naomi raised an eyebrow, I continued. "This conference is scheduled a week from tomorrow, and they're just now requesting speakers, judges, and corporate sponsorship? Most conferences take a year to plan and execute."

"Most conferences don't have Beckwith resources behind them," said Naomi. "But you do have a point. It does seem odd the way this was thrown together so suddenly."

"Not to mention," said Cloris, "if they have Beckwith backing them, why do they need our sponsorship?"

"For the publicity we'll give them in an upcoming issue," said Naomi. "We're not supplying any funding, only corporate merchandise, like the tote bags and other publicity items left over from last year's consumer show at the Javits Center."

"Still, it would have been nice to have more time to prepare," I said. "Judging a cooking and crafting competition doesn't require planning. But working up three one-hour presentations will take hours, if not several days."

"Not to mention the three days we'll be away from the office not getting our regular work done," added Cloris.

"Exactly," I said, glad Cloris had broached the subject.

"Would it help if I comped you both three days?" asked Naomi.

"Definitely," said Cloris, "given that we'll have to work nights to meet our deadlines."

"Overtime would be preferable," I said. The way to this impoverished craft editor's heart is always through her depleted bank account.

Naomi grew silent as she weighed her options. On the one hand, she was aware of my financial situation. On the other, I was aware of the magazine's financial situation. Finally, she clasped her hands on her desk and said, "I'll see what I can do. No promises."

~*~

"You think she'll come through with the money?" asked Cloris a few minutes later as we made our way back to our cubicles.

"Hard to say. I guess it depends on how much her discretionary fund was slashed in this year's budget."

"At least we've got three comp days if nothing else."

"All in all, not a bad negotiation." Yet I still couldn't help wondering why an organization would throw together a conference with so little prep, not to mention scheduling it for March. Even though the conference began on the first day of Spring, historically, New Jersey had suffered through some of its worst snow storms the end of March. If one hit the day of the conference, the chapter would wind up hosting an event devoid of attendees.

"Unfortunately, I can't even think about the conference right now," said Cloris. "I'm spending the day mentoring culinary students at the local vo-tech." She glanced at her phone. "I have to leave shortly."

"My day is already booked," I said. "I've got a photo shoot this morning and an interview with a breakout Etsy crafter this afternoon. We'll have to start brainstorming tomorrow morning."

Cloris made a face. "Which leaves us one less day to get everything done before next Tuesday."

~*~

I arrived home to find that my mother-in-law and several of her Daughters of the October Revolution octogenarian comrades had taken over my dining room table. In assembly line fashion, they folded neon yellow flyers and stuffed them into envelopes that others then sealed, labeled, and stamped.

I glanced at the stack of flyers, curious to see if they were planning yet another protest regarding who-knew-what in Downtown Westfield or preparing to flood Congress with a massive letter-writing campaign on the topic of your-guess-is-as-good-as-mine.

One of Lucille's minions noticed me and smacked her hand on top of the stack of flyers. "This is private business!"

I shrugged, having satisfied my curiosity. The over-the-hill commies were launching a fundraising campaign to finance their next tilting-at-windmills cause du jour. Good luck with that. Whatever the project, if past efforts were any indication of future success, they wouldn't raise enough money to cover their printing and mailing costs.

Previously, Lucille thought nothing of helping herself to my office equipment and supplies. In true communist fashion, she believed what was mine (or anyone's) was hers. Yet the philosophy never extended in the opposite direction. Go figure. But with Zack now living in the house, the apartment above the garage was once again an office, one we now shared and kept under lock and key. Problem solved.

"You need to remove all of this before dinner," I said with a nod to the mess covering my dining room table.

Harriet Kleinhample, Lucille's second-in-command, tore her attention away from her folding and scowled at me. "We won't be finished by then."

"Too bad," I said. "And before you assume otherwise, you're not invited to stay for dinner."

"I've already invited them," said my mother-in-law in a voice that brooked no defiance.

"Then I suggest you make other plans. I don't have enough food to feed five extra mouths tonight."

One of the other women glared at me. "Lucille is right. You're not a very nice person, Anastasia."

I glared back. "You have fifteen minutes to clean up and clear out."

Contrary to communist propaganda, I'm actually a very nice person. Just ask anyone besides my mother-in-law and her fellow rabblerousers. Or the various killers I've had a hand in catching. Or the identity thief who preyed upon my elderly neighbor. Or the kidnappers in Barcelona who mistook me for someone else. I wouldn't expect any of them to think kindly of me. But Lucille? If not for me, she and her dog would reside in a homeless shelter. You'd think that would count for at least an occasional kind word. It hasn't so far, and I doubt it ever will.

With virtual daggers shooting toward me, I exited the dining room, walked into the kitchen, and stared at the slow cooker on the counter. Could I trust the Bolshevik Brigade not to help themselves to dinner? Probably not. Instead of heading to the apartment, I texted Zack and the boys that I was home and needed their help.

Then I released Ralph from his cage. "What should we do about these unbidden guests?" I asked him.

He squawked once, lifted his wings, and took flight. As he flew into the dining room, he channeled the Duke of Bedford, "*Unbidden guests are often welcomest when they are gone. Henry VI, Part One*, Act Two, Scene Two."

The women jumped from their seats and made a mad dash for the coats they'd piled onto my living room sofa, their shrieking drowning out Ralph. You'd think I'd unleashed the Kraken instead of a housebroken African Grey parrot with a knack for situation-appropriate quotes from The Bard of Avon.

After the last Daughter of the October Revolution had fled, my mother-in-law hoisted herself out of her chair and waved her cane at me. "You did that on purpose!"

Yes, I had.

"Did what?" asked Nick, ambling into the house, Mephisto, one of our nicknames for the commie dog, close on his heels, Alex and Zack bringing up the rear.

My two sons and my fiancé took in the apparent standoff and formed a protective phalanx around me. Ralph, spying his favorite human, flew to Zack and settled on his shoulder.

Outnumbered, Lucille's mouth tightened. She turned her attention to her dog. "Come to mother, Manifesto."

Devil Dog refused to budge. At some point over the last few months, he'd transferred his allegiance to Nick.

Lucille stomped over to Nick and grabbed the leash out of his hands. "Give me back my dog!" When she yanked on the leash, the dog responded by sitting on his haunches. Nick bent down and unhooked the leash from the dog's collar.

"He doesn't want to go with you," said Alex, stating the obvious.

Drawing her eyebrows together and narrowing her gaze, Lucille pounded her cane once, then pivoted and clomped toward her bedroom.

Zack kissed me hello, then motioned to the coat I still wore. "You staying?"

He grabbed the coat as I slipped it off my shoulders. "Just one of those days. I was hoping to come home to a drama-free house."

Alex snorted. "Really, Mom? In this house?"

"Well, at least a house with only one belligerent Bolshevik."

A sudden loud crash brought further conversation to a halt.

TWO

The four of us rushed down the hall toward Lucille's bedroom. We entered to find her, hands on hips, glaring at the spot where her cane lay on the floor in front of the closet door. Shards of pottery from a broken lamp peppered the carpet.

"What happened?" I asked.

She turned and jabbed a finger in my direction. "I'll tell you what happened. You're a lousy housekeeper. I walked in to find a rat in my room. A giant rat!"

Zack, the boys, and I glanced around the room. I saw no evidence of a rat. No droppings. Nothing gnawed.

I also didn't see Mephisto.

My house was built in the nineteen-fifties. Every so often a mouse makes its way through a crack in the foundation, which is why I keep mousetraps in the basement. When this happens, Mephisto usually stands guard over the trap and growls to alert us of the intruder.

"Where did it go?" asked Zack.

Lucille pointed toward the closet. I breathed a sigh of relief. Mice could slip through the smallest opening, but there was no way a rat had scampered under the tiny space between the bottom of the closet door and the floor. Let alone a *giant* rat.

Nick raced from the room and returned a moment later with a baseball bat. He stood primed to swing as his brother approached the closet.

Zack reached for the bat. "Let me have that."

Zack positioned himself in front of the closet. Nick picked up Lucille's cane and stood at the ready in case Zack missed. Not that Zack would miss.

Alex swung the door open. Nothing happened. Not a rat nor a mouse raced from the closet. Just a small dust bunny, swept into the room by the woosh of moving air.

I raised an eyebrow at my mother-in-law. "A giant rat?"

In typical Lucille fashion she refused to back down, segueing her rage from the imaginary rat to the real, albeit extremely small, ball of dust. "None of this would have happened if you cleaned the house more often."

Granted, I never claimed to be Suzie Homemaker, but my home was always relatively clean, no thanks to Lucille, who never lifted a finger. Rather than offer a rebuttal, I said, "Maybe it's time for cataract surgery."

Lucille yanked the cane from Nick's hand and pounded it on the carpet. "There's nothing wrong with my eyes!"

"Tell that to the giant rat," said Nick.

I pierced him with a Mom Look, shook my head, and muttered, "Not helpful."

~*~

After dinner Zack and I escaped to the apartment above the garage while the boys loaded the dishwasher and cleaned up the kitchen. While Zack poured us after-dinner drinks, I collapsed onto the sofa and let out a huge sigh. "I'm a terrible person."

"I disagree."

"I have evil thoughts running through my head."

Zack quirked an eyebrow. "About Lucille?"

"None other."

"Are you contemplating acting on any of them?"

"Only if I could get away with it, and we both know, with my luck, that would never happen."

He handed me a glass of Baileys splashed over ice and settled in beside me. "Good to know. I don't relish the thought of having to visit you with a thick glass partition separating us."

"Maybe I should take up yoga or meditation."

"In your spare time?"

"And as Ralph would say, 'Ay, there's the rub!' Except he'd know the act and scene."

"Not to mention the play."

"Duh! *Hamlet*. I'll have you know I aced AP English in high school."

"Hmm...brains *and* beauty. Looks like I hit the jackpot." He leaned over and kissed me, taking care not to spill our drinks.

A knock at the door ended our romantic interlude. "Mom?"

"Come in, Alex."

Once inside, my son said, "Looks like Grandmother Lucille may have been right."

I jumped to my feet. "What! We have a rat in the house?"

"No, but there was a mouse. After we cleaned up the kitchen, Nick and I checked the traps in the basement. We found a dead mouse in one of them."

"How dead?" I asked.

He stared at me as if I'd grown a second head. "Dead is dead, Mom."

I shook my one and only head. "Of course. What I meant was, could you tell how long the mouse had been in the trap? It's strange that Mephisto didn't pick up the scent."

"He's getting old," said Zack. "Maybe he's losing his sense of smell."

"That's a dog's greatest sense," I said. "If he's lost that, what's next? Incontinence?"

"Let's hope not," said Zack.

"Anyway," said Alex, "Nick and I took care of Mickey's relative and set another trap."

I wrapped him in a mom hug and gave him a squeeze. "You're a good son."

"I know."

I chuckled. "Don't let it go to your head."

He wriggled out of my arms. "Gotta run. Chemistry test tomorrow."

I rejoined Zack on the sofa. "I hate that house."

"All houses occasionally have problems with vermin."

"It's more than that. The house was shabby minus the chic when Karl talked me into buying it. He promised we'd renovate, but every time I brought up the subject, he'd rattle off a litany of excuses as to why we should wait. Of course, now I know the real reason."

"We could move."

I stared wide-eyed at him. "You know I can't afford a new house, not with a boatload of debt still hanging over me."

Although a series of unfortunate events, some of which had

nearly cost me my life, had led to several financial windfalls over the past year, a substantial chunk of Karl-induced debt still remained unpaid. My credit rating was toast. No bank in the country would issue me a mortgage.

"I can."

I sighed. "Are we going to have that discussion again? You're not responsible for the mess Karl left me. I won't allow you to assume that burden. Besides, there's another consideration."

He offered me a quizzical look. "And that is?"

One of the reasons I'd acquiesced to buying the mid-century rancher was the apartment a previous owner had added above the detached garage. Until overwhelming debt had forced me to rent it out to Zack, the apartment had served as my studio. "I doubt we'd find another property with a detached apartment. Do you really want all your photography equipment, not to mention your *other equipment*, in the same house as Lucille?"

Zack nodded. "Valid point." He knew by *other equipment* I referred to deadly weaponry, which I believed had something to do with the secret agent life he denied leading.

"Maybe we can work out some sort of compromise," he said.

"And what would that be?"

He shrugged. "I'll give it some thought and let you know what I come up with."

That sounded vaguely suspicious to me, but I decided not to pursue the topic further. Besides, I'd learned to overlook the cracked Formica, peeling linoleum, and carpets that pre-dated my birth. However, I couldn't overlook the commie camped in what used to be Nick's bedroom. And that wouldn't change, no matter where we lived.

Instead, I changed the subject and told Zack about next week's

Stitch and Bake conference.

He tapped his index finger on my forehead. "This vertical wrinkle that suddenly appeared tells me there's more to the story."

"Just that it seems odd to me. I've attended dozens of conferences over the years. I know you've been to your share. Have any, even local ones, ever been thrown together at the last minute?"

He shook his head. "The ones I attend are planned at least a year in advance."

"Exactly."

"And you're thinking there's more to this last-minute event than meets the eye?"

"Wouldn't you?"

"I would…if I didn't know that Beckwith Enterprises is hemorrhaging money."

My jaw dropped. "How in the world do you know that?"

"It's no secret. Vernon Beckwith is overextended. His pharmaceutical company lost a huge class action lawsuit several months ago. At the same time, his newest cancer drug was recently pulled from trials due to major side effects. The bad press generated from both of these has negatively impacted his other businesses. Consumers are boycotting his over-the-counter products. I wouldn't be surprised to learn membership is way down at that exclusive country club of his. The guy is teetering on financial ruin."

"I had no idea, not that I've had time to read a newspaper lately. Still, I don't see the connection between all of that and a hastily thrown together conference."

"Don't you?"

I pondered for a moment. Then it hit me. "If Marlene came up with the idea for the conference and convinced the chapter to hold it at Beckwith Chateau, she'd drum up some needed revenue for the business."

Zack nodded. "It's probably a drop in the bucket, but at least she's helping the bottom line. I doubt the Chateau hosts many events in the middle of the week in the middle of winter. And even the most diehard members aren't hitting snow-covered, frozen links."

Which not only raised my suspicions but begged the question, did Marlene Beckwith really offer the New Jersey chapter of the Stitch and Bake Society a huge discount, or did she simply manipulate the quoted expenses to make it appear so?

~*~

The next morning I told Cloris what I'd learned about Beckwith Enterprises from Zack the night before. "I'll get out my violin," she said.

"Let's make it a duet."

After a quick trip to the break room, we began brainstorming ideas for the three hour-long workshops we'd each present at the conference. Since neither of us knew the skill levels of the attendees and had been given no directions beyond the number and length of the workshops, we were at a bit of a loss.

"Naomi must have contact information," I said. "We really need to know parameters. Are we to do lectures? Demonstrations? Hands-on presentations?"

Cloris nodded. "The last thing we want to do is bore them to death with information they already know."

I picked up my phone and dialed Naomi's extension. Kim answered, and when I asked for Naomi, she said, "She's in a meeting upstairs. Anything I can help you with?"

I explained my reason for calling. "Marlene Beckwith," she said. "Along with being the chapter president, she's also the conference coordinator." Then she immediately rattled off a phone number without taking time to look it up. This didn't surprise me. Kim had a head for numbers. And just about anything else.

I thanked her, hung up, and dialed Marlene's number. Since I was calling from our offices, I was hoping Trimedia would pop up on her phone display, and she'd answer. Sure enough, she picked up on the second ring.

"Marlene Beckwith."

"Hello, Marlene. This is Anastasia Pollack calling from *American Woman Magazine.* I have our food editor Cloris McWerther here with me. We'd like to discuss the workshops you want presented at your upcoming conference."

She huffed out what sounded like a sigh of annoyance before saying, "I can spare you a minute or two. I'm rushing off to a fitting. What do you need to know?"

"For starters, the type of presentations you'd like. Is there anything you had in mind?"

"And also the skill levels of the women who will be attending," added Cloris.

"Skill levels range from rank beginners to high expertise," said Marlene. "As for presentations, I expect visuals. If you plan to give a talk, include plenty of examples."

"What about demonstrations?" asked Cloris.

"Such as?"

"Perhaps some icing and decorating techniques?"

"I suppose we need something easy for the beginners. I've already arranged for a supplier to provide sets of piping bags and tips for the goody bags. The attendees can use those, but you'll need to bring miniature cakes or cupcakes for them to work on."

Cloris and I exchanged raised eyebrows at both her derisive tone and demand.

"However," Marlene continued, "I want to learn how to make a geode cake. And dessert imposters. Do those for the other two workshops."

"In an hour?" asked Cloris.

"Is that a problem?"

"As long as I can present a slideshow. I certainly can't create either cake in an hour."

"Why not?" Marlene's voice grew demanding. "I see it done all the time on baking shows. They're only an hour long."

"The shows might be an hour long," explained Cloris, "but the contestants have hours to complete their cakes."

"Fine." She huffed out her annoyance. "As long as you bring a finished cake with you for each workshop."

It was a good thing we weren't on a video call, given Cloris's expression at the moment, as well as the word she mouthed.

"And for the needlework workshops?" I asked, cutting off any further conversation between Marlene Beckwith and my extremely annoyed fellow editor. "Would your members like a talk on the history of samplers or quilts?"

"Samplers. Although, I doubt I'll learn anything new. I'm not interested in quilts. And make sure you have plenty of examples for your talk."

I pulled the phone from my ear and offered it a salute. Then I said, "I'll put together a slide presentation. Do you have any suggestions for the other two workshops? Would the attendees like to learn counted cross stitch?"

"I suppose that's acceptable for the beginners as long as you provide kits."

Acceptable? I glanced over at Cloris and saw her rolling her eyes.

"I want to learn something new," continued Marlene.

"Did you have anything in mind?"

"Either hardanger or silk ribbon embroidery. And you'll need to provide kits for those as well. Now, is there anything else, ladies?"

"The number of attendees you expect," I said.

"Plan for a hundred." And with that she severed the connection.

"Lovely woman," said Cloris through gritted teeth. "She obviously believes the world revolves around her."

"She's a Beckwith. It comes with the territory."

"Karma's going to catch up with that woman when Beckwith Enterprises goes belly up."

"One can only hope," I agreed. "As for me, I'm more interested in Naomi coming through with that overtime. Three comp days certainly aren't enough for the extra work we both have between now and the start of the conference next Tuesday. Especially since I can't even start right away."

"Why not?"

"I first have to contact manufacturers for product, and it will probably take at least two or three days for me to receive everything. But before I can even do that, I have to come up with projects."

"What about the stock you have in the supply closet? Can't you design projects around the needlework supplies you have on hand?"

"I don't have nearly enough of anything for two hundred kits."

"At least you can start on the slideshow in the meantime."

"The slideshow is finished. The reason I suggested it was because I had already given a History of American Samplers presentation to the Embroidery Guild last year and a History of American Quilts talk at the American Folk Art Museum a few years ago."

Cloris clapped her hands together and bowed. "I applaud your sneakiness, O Brilliant One. Unfortunately, I'm in much worse shape."

"Why is that?"

"I've never made either a geode cake or a dessert imposter, and they're both incredibly complex."

"Can you cheat?"

"How?"

"Buy them."

She shook her head. "Not if I have to include step-by-step photos."

"With all your contacts, can't you arrange to have a bakery make the cakes with you photographing each step?"

Cloris grabbed me in a suffocating bear hug. For a Size Two, she had incredible upper body strength. "Anastasia Pollack, you are an absolute genius!"

Too bad I didn't have an equally brilliant solution for my own time crunch.

"I'll start calling some of the local bakeries and caterers I've showcased in previous issues," said Cloris. "Since March isn't a big wedding month, fingers crossed that I'll find a cake artist with time to create one, if not both cakes."

"Promise them free promo in the write-up you'll do in the

magazine about the conference and workshops."

"That will help. I'll have to pay for the cakes, though. They're not cheap. I just hope Naomi will allow me to expense the cost."

"Define not cheap."

"Large cakes can run into the hundreds. Wedding cakes? They can run into the thousands, depending on the number of tiers, complexity of the design, and reputation of the cake artist."

"Yikes!"

Cloris shrugged. "They're labor-intensive. I'm hoping I can get small cakes for under a hundred dollars each."

I wished her luck as she headed into her cubicle, then turned my attention to designing a beginner cross stitch pattern for the first of the two needlework kits. I decided on a simple sampler design using traditional motifs and an alphabet, which would tie in nicely with my talk. The piece would be worked on fourteen count Aida cloth and utilize only full cross stitches, no half or quarter stitches, no backstitching, and no French knots. I also limited the color palette to seven shades of floss. Easy-peasy. And I'd be able to stitch up a sample in under five hours.

For the more involved kit, I immediately eliminated silk ribbon embroidery. The craft, although popular for a time back in the nineteen-nineties, had never really caught on. Few U.S. suppliers still carried the specialty ribbon, and I certainly didn't have time to place an overseas order.

Choosing Hardanger, a form of embroidery that originated in Norway, where it was used to embellish women's caps, aprons, and linens, made my life much easier. And easier was definitely better, considering the ticking clock. The stitches, a combination of counted thread, drawn thread, and cutwork techniques, create geometric patterns. The color palette was traditionally monochromatic white or ivory, with the embroidery floss closely matching the color of the evenweave fabric.

The trickiest and most difficult part of Hardanger embroidery involves cutting away portions of the fabric after the stitching was complete. With a hundred attendees, I suspected somewhere between twenty and fifty percent would ruin their work at the cutting stage. I didn't relish dealing with the anger and frustration that would inevitably ensue.

For that reason, I decided the workshop would consist only of practice pieces. The women would take home their kits to stitch at their leisure. And because I'd wait until the third day to teach the Hardanger workshop, I wouldn't be around to receive the brunt of their anger when they accidentally destroyed hours of intricate work.

I especially wanted to be far from Marlene Beckwith should she screw up her needlework piece. Judging from our recent phone conversation, I suspected Marlene possessed a temper that rose to Vesuvian proportions.

Once I had a general idea of my designs for both projects, I placed a call to a floss and fabric company headquartered in New Jersey. As an incentive for supplying me with the materials as quickly as possible, I offered to include promo materials about their various product lines in each kit.

The company jumped at the free promotion and agreed to expedite the order. I'd have everything by Thursday morning. Of course, I would have preferred tomorrow, but there's a whopping difference between next-day and second-day shipping fees. At least I had enough floss and fabric in my own stash to begin stitching one of the projects this evening.

THREE

A week later, Cloris had her purchased geode and dessert imposter cakes, plus 120 naked cupcakes she'd baked for her hands-on decorating workshop, along with several tubs of buttercream frosting.

I had my completed needlework samples and kits, and we both had our slide shows loaded onto our laptops. Luckily, the day dawned without the threat of snow, but with on-and-off mixed precipitation predicted for the next two days, we decided to bring everything with us the first morning. Yesterday Cloris had called the Chateau and been promised secure cold storage for the baked goods and a locked storage area for my kits and samples.

Since her car was larger than mine, Cloris offered to drive, and being Cloris, she arrived at Casa Pollack with two extra-large cups of coffee and two enormous apple spice muffins. Zack loaded my cartons into the back of her SUV, and after a quick kiss goodbye, I settled into the passenger seat for the forty-minute drive to Beckwith Chateau.

"Have you ever been to this place?" Cloris asked as we ate our breakfast while sitting in rush hour traffic on the Garden State Parkway.

"No, you?"

"Once. The richest girl in my high school held her Sweet Sixteen there and invited the entire class. The place is mind-boggling. Vast grounds with a formal English garden, multiple ponds, a stable, riding paths, golf course with a separate clubhouse, indoor Olympic-size pool, even a helipad."

"Helipad?"

"You wouldn't want all those rich people to fly their private jets into Teterboro or Newark Liberty, then have to sit in notorious New Jersey traffic, would you?"

I placed a hand to my heart. "Perish the thought!"

"The main house contains thirty luxury guest rooms," she continued, "each the size of half your house. It was built in the early twentieth century by some local industrialist as a country retreat."

"A Beckwith?"

She shook her head. "No, Beckwith's grandfather bought it from the industrialist's heirs after he died in the thirties. Beckwith's father turned it into a private country club about forty years ago and added several cottages for himself and his family."

"Cottages?"

"In name only. Anyway, Beckwith Chateau is now considered the most exclusive and sought-after venue in the country for private events."

"I'm guessing you didn't remember all this from a Sweet Sixteen party you attended nearly thirty years ago."

Cloris laughed. "Of course, not. I Googled the place last night."

When we pulled up to the entrance of Beckwith Chateau, we were greeted by two parking attendants and a bellhop with a rolling cart. All three appeared to be in their early twenties and had the bearing of armed forces cadets. Their blue-gray, gold, and black uniforms, clean shaven faces, and short haircuts added to the military academy image. One parking attendant quickly rounded the SUV and opened Cloris's door. The other opened mine.

"Welcome to Beckwith Chateau," said the attendant, whose polished brass nameplate identified him as Justin. He offered me his hand as I stepped from the vehicle.

After handing her valet key and a tip to the other attendant, Cloris directed the bellhop as he unloaded the SUV. She pointed to the boxes with the baked goods. "I was told arrangements have been made for these to be refrigerated."

The bellhop, whose nameplate read Tanner, nodded. "You're Ms. McWerther and Ms. Pollack?"

"We are."

He waved toward the cartons containing my kits. "And are these the items for our secure storage room?"

When I indicated in the affirmative, he said, "I'll take care of everything for you, ma'am."

I reached into my jacket pocket where I'd earlier placed a few bills and handed him a gratuity. "Thank you, Tanner."

He nodded as he tapped the brim of his cap and placed the bills in his pocket without stealing a glance at them. "Thank you, ma'am."

Justin swung open the Chateau door. I wasn't expecting what greeted us once we stepped inside. Beckwith Chateau was unlike any country club I'd ever seen. Instead of entering a public reception area, we stepped into what appeared to be someone's home. An extremely rich someone's home.

Handcrafted Spanish tile covered the floor of a long foyer leading toward the back of the Chateau. Wainscotting and wide crown molding, baseboards, and window and door trim were a deep, polished mahogany. Venetian plaster filled the remainder of the walls. A latticework of wooden beams crisscrossed the ceiling with three crystal chandeliers spaced along the length of the wide corridor.

Hidden off to the left of the entrance I spied a closed door with a bronze plaque labeled Office, but Tanner directed us down the hallway. We passed columned archways to our left that opened into a series of connecting rooms with cozy seating areas and fireplaces. Artwork and shelves of books lined the walls. Clusters of older women sat on overstuffed sofas and chairs grouped around the fireplace. Some worked on stitching projects as they chatted. Others sipped from delicate china cups while eating tea cakes.

A second archway opened onto another hallway that branched off to the right. Beyond that archway a series of French doors opened out onto an immense patio. Our hallway eventually opened up onto a domed rotunda with a wide circular staircase on one side. Additional archways around the circumference of the rotunda framed more corridors leading to other parts of the Chateau.

"Your registration table," said Tanner, sweeping his arm in the direction of a black skirted conference table off to one side of the rotunda. A decorative banner attached to the skirt read Stitch and Bake Society. A table to the left held filled tote bags emblazoned with the Trimedia logo and a list of our various magazines.

Several older women, engrossed in deep conversation, hovered off to the side, a few feet from the table where a woman sat in scowling silence. A younger woman, holding a clipboard stood slightly off to the side behind the seated woman. She wore a Chateau uniform of crisply starched white oxford shirt, blue-gray pencil skirt, and navy blazer trimmed with thin gold piping along the lapels.

When we approached the table, the seated woman quickly pasted a faux smile on her face. "Are you here for the conference?"

She was a stocky woman with an obviously dyed jet-black beehive and the recipient of at least one too many facelifts. Her two-piece Mondrian-inspired jacket and dress paid homage to Carnaby Street, circa nineteen sixty. I was curious to see if she'd accessorized with white go-go boots. Too bad the skirted table blocked my view of her legs and feet.

"We're your judges and workshop speakers from *American Woman*," I said. "I'm crafts editor Anastasia Pollack, and this is food editor Cloris McWerther."

"We're so glad you could join us," said the younger woman, reaching across the table to extend her hand and offering us a sincerely friendly smile that reached to her twinkling cerulean eyes. I pegged her at somewhere north of thirty but not too far north. "I'm Rhetta Margolis, Beckwith Chateau's head concierge, and this is Marlene Beckwith, the president of the Stitch and Bake Society."

"And conference chair," added Marlene in the same haughty voice she'd used when we spoke on the phone.

"Yes, my apologies," said Rhetta. Her smile remained but her features had grown pinched, and the sparkle fled her eyes. "And conference chair." She checked our names off a list on her clipboard, then handed us each a blue pocket folder, labeled with our name, and a tote bag.

I glanced at the list of names on the clipboard, surprised at the small number. "Are these all the attendees?" I asked.

"Yes," said Rhetta. "You'll find your nametags, a schedule, facilities map, and other information within the folders."

I turned to address Marlene. "You had indicated we should prepare for a hundred attendees. There are only twenty-five names on that list."

"We had some last-minute cancelations," she said.

"Three-quarters of your attendees canceled at the last minute?" asked Cloris.

When Marlene tightened her lips and stared at Cloris without answering, Rhetta said, "Extenuating circumstances."

Short of a major disaster or blizzard, I couldn't imagine any extenuating circumstances that would cause three-quarters of the attendees to drop out at the last minute. Besides, my phone would have alerted me to a major disaster or imminent blizzard, and I'd received no such alerts. However, I did notice the gaggle of women had abruptly ended their conversation and now focused their attention on us.

I decided to change the subject. Pointing across the room where Tanner still stood with the cart, I said, "We need to set up for today's workshops and have Tanner store the remainder of our cartons and the cakes."

Marlene's brow wrinkled. "Who's Tanner?"

"The bellhop?" I answered, again nodding in Tanner's direction.

"Beckwith Chateau does not employ bellhops," she said with enough disdain in her voice to indicate a major faux pas on my part.

When is a bellhop not a bellhop? If he dresses like a bellhop and acts like a bellhop, how is Tanner not a bellhop?

Rhetta stepped in to explain. "We refer to those staff members as butlers. Tanner is our latest Employee of the Month. If you need anything, just ask him."

Cloris and I both nodded as Rhetta continued speaking. "Your workshops will be at nine-thirty in the Bordeaux Room, Ms. Pollack. After a half-hour break, Ms. McWerther's workshops will take place in the Avignon Room. Lunch will be served buffet style in the Chartres Library at twelve-thirty."

"And how will the judging be held?" I asked.

"The needlework will be on display around the perimeter of the Grenoble Ballroom, which is behind the double doors to your right." She waved in the direction of a set of massive mahogany doors, currently closed. "Dinner will be served in the ballroom each evening at six. Once everything is set up, you have until lunch on Thursday to examine the pieces and choose the winners, which will be announced at dinner that night."

"And the baking competition?" asked Cloris.

"That will take place in the Rouen Conference Center throughout the three days. A series of elimination rounds, each beginning at two o'clock and lasting two to three hours, will whittle the contestants down after the first and second rounds. The finalists will take part in the third round. More information is in your packet."

"So we're eating cake and pastries before dinner each night?" I asked.

"Since when did you have a problem with that?" asked Cloris. I laughed.

"Judging will take place after dinner," said Marlene, finally speaking.

When she didn't expound, Rhetta once again stepped in. "The two of you will sit at a separate table away from the attendees, enabling you to speak out of earshot. You'll each receive a sampling of every entry. The remainder of the desserts will be served to the attendees each night."

"Let them eat cake," I said, but when I noticed Marlene looking anything but amused, I took a cue from her and cleared my throat. "I suppose we'd better get set up."

Once Cloris and I headed back to where Tanner still stood beside the luggage cart, he led us down one of the corridors that branched off from the rotunda. Our workshop rooms were situated across the hall from each other. We pointed out which items we'd need for today's workshops with the remainder placed in one of the hotel's industrial refrigerators or a locked storage room.

As Tanner began to unload, Cloris said, "Given the temperature in here, I think it's best to refrigerate the cupcakes and buttercream until I need them at eleven."

"No problem," he said. "I'll bring them to you a few minutes before the start of your workshop."

"Nice kid," said Cloris as Tanner pushed the luggage cart back toward the rotunda.

Setup for my workshop this morning consisted of plugging my computer into the projector and pulling down the screen at the front of the room. Afterward, I texted Zack and the boys to let them know I wouldn't arrive home until after dinner. Then I took a seat at the table in front of the room and opened the pocket folder to read through the information about the conference.

A cream-colored, deckled-edged linen envelope, embossed in

gold with the Beckwith Chateau logo, partially peeked out from one of the pockets. I slipped it out and flipped it over to find my name computer-printed on the front in a font that mimicked calligraphy.

But it was what I discovered when I opened the flap and removed the contents that sent my Spidey senses tingling from my desperately-in-need-of-a-haircut head to my desperately-in-need-of-a-pedicure toes.

I stuffed the contents back into the envelope and shoved it into the pocket folder. Cloris joined me a moment later. "Is it me?" she asked. "Or do you get a weird vibe about this conference?"

"It's definitely not you," I said. "And the vibe began the moment Naomi handed us this assignment. It accelerated at warp speed from the moment we entered the rotunda. And it just got a heck of a lot weirder."

She raised an eyebrow. "Meaning?"

I glanced at the wall-mounted clock at the back of the room. We still had fifteen minutes before the start of my talk, but early birds would probably begin drifting in soon to grab the best seats. "Did you take a look at the contents of your pocket folder yet?"

"No, why?"

"Go get it."

She scurried across the hall, returning seconds later with her own folder. "Got it."

"See if you have an envelope inside."

"This?" she asked, waving another Chateau envelope.

"Open it."

As she pulled out the single folded sheet of heavy paper and flipped it open, five one-hundred-dollar bills fell to the floor. Cloris stared mouth agape at what was written on the stationery, then at the bills, and finally at me. "Someone is trying to bribe us?"

FOUR

"Certainly appears that way," I said.

Cloris held out her hand. "Let's see your note."

I pulled my envelope out of the pocket folder and removed the letter, leaving the money, while Cloris scooped up the Benjamins that had fallen to the floor. Then we compared our notes. "Different names," I said. "Letitia Cramer on yours and Georgina Malloy on mine."

"Yours is probably entered in the needlework competition and mine in the baking competition."

"I was under the impression all attendees were entered in both competitions."

"Me, too."

I studied the two sheets of paper. "Given that both are written on Chateau stationery, use an identical font, and include the same amount of money, it appears they came from one person."

"Or two people conspiring together?" asked Cloris.

I pondered on that for a moment. "Highly unlikely. If you were going to bribe someone, would you want anyone else to know?"

"No way. The other person might snitch."

"Or blackmail you."

"So what are you suggesting, Sherlock?"

"I think it's more likely that whoever slipped these envelopes into our packets wants to eliminate her competition."

"Devious. But why? It's not like we're judging the Oscars or even a Food Network baking competition. This is just a local chapter. I doubt the winners receive much more than a cheesy trophy, a dozen roses, and bragging rights."

I nodded. "True, it's highly unlikely they're competing for a huge grand prize."

"Even if they were," said Cloris, "aren't these women all former executives and professionals living the good life on cushy pensions and investments?"

"That's my understanding, based on what Naomi told us." I considered that for a moment, then said, "Maybe this is more about a ruthless need to win at any cost."

"Or revenge?"

"Another possibility. After all, hell hath no fury like a woman scorned."

"But how would the briber know we'd play along? It's not like she'd have any recourse if we brought this to the attention of the organization."

"Or pocketed the money but didn't comply with the terms of the bribe."

Cloris's eyes widened. "You're not seriously suggesting we do that, are you?"

As much as I could use an extra five hundred dollars, I'd never stoop to something so despicable, and Cloris knew that. I raised both eyebrows and pointedly stared at her. "Really?"

She chuckled. "Just checking."

I waved the notes in the air. "However, the person who sent these doesn't know that. She's taking a huge gamble either way."

"Only if the notes are somehow traced back to her, and I don't see how that's possible."

"True, it's not like we travel with a fingerprint kit."

"Or know how to use one," she added.

"Hey, don't you know you can find directions for anything on YouTube?" I'd once learned how to pick a lock with a paperclip, discovering a treasure trove of diamonds in a lockbox. Too bad I couldn't keep them, but the evidence did help send a killer to prison.

"If we had a kit," said Cloris. "Which we don't, so what do we do? Tell Marlene?"

Out in the hallway I heard chatter, along with heels clicking on tiles, as a group of women approached. I glanced at the clock. "No time now. We'll have to wait until after our workshops."

We quickly stashed the envelopes into our pocket folders. Cloris took a seat off to the side while I prepared to greet my workshop attendees.

Within a few minutes, the Bordeaux Room filled with twenty-four brightly dressed septuagenarian and octogenarian women, many in outfits reminiscent of the sixties and seventies. I noted every style from Mary Quant psychedelic print shifts to floral bellbottom pants and folk-embroidered blouses, not to mention a plethora of tie-dye. Like the women who wore purple outfits and red hats, these retirees sported attire that boldly announced they had paid their dues and were now free to slip the restrictive bonds of corporate conformity.

As they took their seats at the conference tables that stretched in double rows across the width of the room, I tried to read nametags, hoping to identify Letitia Cramer and Georgina Malloy. I struck out. Some of the women hadn't bothered to wear their nametags. Others had attached them to their waistbands or inserted them into holders that hung from their necks. When seated, the women in the rows in front of them blocked my view.

I glanced at the clock. I was still missing one person, the organization's president and conference chair. "Looks like Marlene has been held up," I said. "I'll give her another minute before we begin."

"Don't bother," said a petite woman in the third row. She wore a T-shirt that proudly proclaimed *Make Love, Not War*, which I'm sure she had never worn to the office back in the day. Her nametag, which she wore pinned below the collar of her T-shirt instead of looped around her neck, identified her as Joy.

When I raised an eyebrow, she added, "She's not coming."

Cloris and I exchanged a quick glance before I asked, "Oh? Why is that?"

"I overheard her tell Rhetta she's not wasting her time, that she already knows all there is to know about the history of samplers."

"I see."

"Don't take it personally, dear," said a woman in a pink boucle two-piece suit and matching Jackie Kennedy pillbox hat. "Marlene considers herself an expert on everything."

"She tells us so all the time," added a third woman, seated next to the first woman.

Nearly everyone either nodded or murmured in agreement. I'd already formed my own negative opinions of Marlene Beckwith, but even though I had questions galore about her, my workshop was no place for the dishing of gossip. Still, from what I'd observed so far, I suspected there was little love lost between the president and her flock of stitchers and bakers.

"In that case," I said, picking up the projector remote and clicking to bring the introductory slide up on the screen, "if one of you ladies seated in the back would be so kind as to flip off the overhead lights, we'll begin."

~*~

An hour later I basked in the standing ovation I received at the end of my talk. "That went well," said Cloris as the attendees scurried off in a rush to beat each other to the ladies' room.

"My presentation, yes, but this conference gets more peculiar by the minute."

"Anything in particular ratcheting up your weirdness meter another notch?"

"Absolutely. Given how the membership feels about their president, how did she get elected?"

Cloris shrugged. "Maybe no one else wanted the job."

That was certainly often the case on PTA and other volunteer committees where I'd served. People make excuses as to why they can't take the lead or shoulder more responsibility. But these women had either broken through the glass ceiling or at least forced serious cracks in it at a time when most women had little or no power in the workforce. That took serious commitment and ambition.

I pointed this out to Cloris, ending by saying, "These women are used to calling the shots. I find it hard to imagine they've suddenly turned into passive sheep in their retirement."

"Maybe they're tired of doing it all and are happy to sit back and enjoy themselves while someone else does the heavy lifting for a change."

"I see Marlene more as someone who directs people to lift for her than doing any work herself. Besides, if your theory is correct, why the resentment we witnessed?"

She shrugged again. "Maybe they regret their decision. One of them will have to step forward to run against her when her current term is up."

"Depending on the chapter bylaws, that could be several years."

"That's their problem, not ours."

Since we had half an hour before the start of Cloris's workshop, we headed for the Chartres Library to grab some coffee. We found Rhetta helping herself to a cup.

"How did your talk go?" she asked me after greeting both of us.

"Very well. I received a standing ovation." Then I added, "I was surprised Marlene didn't attend."

When Rhetta made no effort to comment, I continued, "A matter has come up that we'd like to discuss with her."

Rhetta knit her brows together. "What sort of matter?"

When I hesitated, she continued, "Along with being head concierge, I'm also Marlene's personal assistant. I handle most matters for her."

I chalked that up to another strange circumstance, although perhaps not so strange for a family-run establishment where the family lives on the premises. Hopefully, Rhetta was well-compensated for pulling double-duty.

I glanced at Cloris. When she nodded, I said, "Is there someplace we can speak in private?"

Rhetta's eyes widened. "It's that serious?"

"We believe so."

"Let's head to my office."

Cloris and I quickly grabbed cups of coffee and followed her. Once seated in the small office near the Chateau entrance, we handed Rhetta the envelopes we'd received. "We found these in our packets," I said.

Her jaw dropped when she opened the envelopes and saw the contents. "Definitely serious," she said. Her brows drew together, and she chewed on her lower lip.

"Are these two women significant contenders for winning the competitions?" I asked.

She pulled her attention from the notes and asked, "Why?"

I pointed out the many coincidences of the two envelopes and their contents. "There are two possibilities here," I continued. "Either these women are attempting to bribe us, or someone is setting them up in order to eliminate what she perceives as her stiffest competition."

"I see your point," said Rhetta. "We can't assume Letitia and Georgina are behind this."

"Exactly," said Cloris. "What do you suggest?"

Rhetta glanced at her phone. "It's nearly eleven. Your workshop is about to begin." She stuffed the notes and money into the two envelopes, then stood. "The board is meeting during lunch. I'll handle this."

She walked us to the door but remained in her office after we departed.

"That should be an interesting board meeting," said Cloris as we headed to the Avignon room for her decorating workshop.

I agreed. "Too bad we can't morph into spiders under the table."

We found Tanner waiting in the Avignon room. A luggage

cart held the gallon buckets of buttercream frosting and the boxes of naked cupcakes. "Where would you like everything?" he asked.

Cloris directed him. When he'd finished, he said, "Is there anything else you need?"

"I'm not sure we'll use up all the frosting," said Cloris. "Would you mind coming back in an hour to return the leftovers to the refrigerator?"

"No problem, ma'am." He tapped the brim of his hat and exited as the first women began to arrive.

Cloris greeted her workshop attendees and directed them to spread out across the paper-covered conference tables, giving each of them plenty of room to work. As they took their seats, I removed the individually boxed naked cupcakes from the cartons and began distributing them.

After introducing herself, Cloris asked the women to retrieve the complimentary frosting kits from their tote bags. "Today you'll learn several advanced icing techniques using buttercream. And because last minute extenuating circumstances prevented so many of your members from attending today, you each have four cupcakes to practice on instead of one."

"You thought there would be a hundred people at the conference?" asked the woman dressed in the floral bellbottoms and embroidered peasant blouse. I sidled closer to where she sat in order to read her nametag, which identified her as Wanda. "Who told you that?"

"Marlene Beckwith."

I scanned the room and noted Marlene had also failed to show up for Cloris's workshop, but given her comment on the phone last week, that was hardly a surprise.

"Why would she do that?" asked Joy.

The woman seated next to her pulled a face and said, "Because she's Marlene. Do you need any other explanation?"

Wanda addressed Cloris again. Her voice bristled with anger as a deep crimson flush traveled from her neck toward the hairline of her over-bleached, slightly frizzy medium length shag haircut. "We've never had a hundred members. I should know. I'm the membership chair. We have thirty members. Five are on a cruise they booked a year ago. There were no extenuating circumstances that caused anyone to drop out at the last minute."

Cloris shot a puzzled look my way before recovering and offering the group a smile. "Well then," she said, "I suppose you're all the beneficiaries of a communications mix-up."

Mix-up? Quite diplomatic of Cloris under the circumstances, but when a few snorts greeted her statement, it became obvious that no one accepted the explanation of a communications mix-up. However, none of the women offered any further comments. So Cloris began the workshop.

The demonstration proceeded without a hitch, and at the end, Cloris also received a standing ovation. She had used the extra twenty-four cupcakes for demonstration purposes, and as the women headed to lunch, she and I remained behind to box them up. "You want to take these home for the boys?" she asked.

"Why not offer them to Tanner?"

"Offer me what?" he asked, entering the room. His eyes widened when he saw the cupcakes. "For me?"

"Help yourself," said Cloris. "Any you don't want, share with the staff."

"Thank you! What about the buttercream? Anything to go back in the refrigerator?"

"There's so little left, you may as well toss it," said Cloris.

"Waste buttercream?" His eyes widened even more. "No way!"

Cloris laughed. "Just pace yourself. I wouldn't want you to get sick."

As Tanner loaded the remaining cupcakes and buttercream onto a luggage cart, Cloris and I headed to lunch. "I think I've made a friend for life," she said.

"You never know when having a butler in your pocket will come in handy. I doubt he's going to want any of the extra needlework kits, though."

"Not unless he can eat them."

"Hmm...edible cross stitch. We'll have to work on that. Maybe start a new trend."

~*~

We arrived at the Chartres Library to find an enormous luncheon buffet spread across tables that lined the far wall. Servers stood behind the tables, dishing out the varied offerings. After we'd made our selections, we scanned the area for a place to sit. The tables nearest the buffet were occupied with groups of women, all deep in muted conversation. No one waved us over, and neither Cloris nor I felt comfortable inserting ourselves into the middle of any group without an invitation. We strolled into the next room and found an unoccupied small table with two upholstered chairs off to one corner.

From our vantage point, we could observe not only the other women in our room, but the wide arched openings between areas also allowed us a sight line into much of the buffet room. Every so often one of the women would surreptitiously glance in our direction, then quickly avert her gaze.

"I wonder what they're plotting," I said.

Cloris looked around. "Insurrection?"

"Maybe. Given what Marlene did to us—"

"What *was* the point of having us do four times more work than necessary? Especially since we were doing her a favor by attending this conference on such short notice."

"Certainly makes you wonder what she's done to piss off the chapter membership." I pulled out my phone, opened a browser window, and pulled up the website for the New Jersey chapter of the Stitch and Bake Society. "Says here the president's term is four years, and the chapter first organized a year ago."

I clicked on the link that brought up the chapter officers. "The plot thickens."

Cloris leaned forward. "What did you find?"

I held my phone out to Cloris. "Our two bribers are the vice-president and secretary. Maybe they were plotting a coup, and Marlene got wind of it."

"And planted the bribes, expecting us to turn them in?"

"That's one way to head off an insurrection. Accuse your rivals of a crime."

She passed the phone back to me. "So much for spending three days with a group of sweet little old ladies."

"At least they're not communists."

~*~

After finishing lunch, we still had half an hour to kill before the first baking competition commenced. Cloris and I decided to explore the parts of the Chateau we still hadn't seen. We checked our laptops with the butler on duty and retrieved our coats, which we'd need when we walked across the compound to the conference center for the baking competition.

The Chateau was a maze of interconnecting hallways that brought us to one spectacular room after another, each exuding an

Old-World charm. Even though the original architect had mixed French, Spanish, and Tudor styles, it all seemed to work. As we strolled from one area to another, I snapped photos of various details, from the intricately carved fireplace surrounds to the hand-painted tiles and various antique furnishings.

Turning a corner, we heard shouting coming from a room up ahead. "You think that's the board meeting?" asked Cloris.

"Only one way to find out."

We inched closer. I ducked down and peered through the large keyhole of the old-fashioned mahogany door. Then I grabbed Cloris and ducked into a nearby alcove that held two chairs and a small console table. Keeping my voice low, I said, "There are seven women inside—Marlene, Rhetta, and five others. I recognized Letitia, Georgina, and Wanda. The remaining two had their backs to me, but they must be the other board members."

Marlene's voice screamed above the others. "I want them out! I don't believe a word of their denials."

"You were outvoted," said another woman.

"Only because you allowed them to vote," said Marlene.

"They deny they sent the bribes, and we have no proof to the contrary."

"That's ridiculous. We have the notes and money."

"Which anyone could have sent. Even you, Marlene."

"Why would I do that?"

"You tell me."

"How dare you accuse me!"

"No one is accusing you."

"You just did! You're all out to get me, aren't you? I know you've been plotting behind my back. Maybe this is all your doing."

"Now you're sounding paranoid."

"So now you're calling me crazy?"

"Marlene," said Rhetta, her voice placating, "No one is calling you crazy. But you have to accede to the board's decision."

"Et tu, Rhetta?" said Marlene. "So be it. You all may be able to keep me from ousting them from the organization, but you can't keep me from kicking them off my property."

Letitia gasped. "You can't do that!"

"Can't I? You and Georgina have ten minutes to pack up and leave," said Marlene. "Refuse and I'll call the police to have you arrested for trespassing."

"We'd better make ourselves scarce," I whispered. Cloris nodded, and we both scurried down the hall and around a corner before the door opened.

FIVE

"Let's wait here," I said when Cloris and I arrived back at the convergence of the main hallway and the one that had led to where the board was meeting.

"Why?"

"Curiosity." I pulled her behind a grouping of oversized potted philodendron, dieffenbachia, and sansevieria that blocked us from sight but allowed us a partial view of the area.

We didn't have long to wait. Seconds later we saw Letitia Cramer and Georgina Malloy storm past our hiding place. As they entered the Chartres Library where many of the attendees still lingered over lunch, Letitia yelled, "She's gone too far this time."

Cloris and I stepped from behind the plants. We lingered close enough to hear but kept ourselves out of view of the women in the Library.

"Marlene?" asked one woman.

"Who else?" asked Georgina. "She's banned us from the premises."

Several women gasped. "Can she do that?" asked another.

"I'm not risking arrest to find out," said Georgina. She nervously raked her fingers through her overpermed salt-and-pepper curls.

"She threatened to have you arrested?" asked another woman. "For what?"

"Trespassing."

"That's ridiculous. You've paid to attend the conference."

"Tell that to Marlene."

"Why is she doing this?" asked another woman.

Letitia folded her tall frame into a nearby club chair and explained how someone had sent bribes to Cloris and me, signing their names. "Does anyone think either of us cares enough about these competitions to bribe the judges?"

"No one but Marlene," said Georgina. "She knows we're her stiffest competition, and we all know she can't stand to lose at anything."

"You're suggesting she's behind this?" asked someone else.

"Wouldn't surprise me in the least."

Another added, "Who else would stoop so low?"

"Agreed," said one of the women. "She's gone too far this time. She needs to be put in her place."

"How?" asked Letitia.

"I have an idea. Gather round, ladies."

At that point their voices no longer carried into the hall, which was probably for the best, especially if their plan included something not quite Kosher. Cloris and I ducked down the nearest branching hallway and exited through a set of French doors onto a patio. At the edge of the patio a sign pointed the way to the various other buildings on the property. Not wanting to arrive for the first round of the baking competition before any of the competitors, we decided to spend a few minutes exploring the grounds.

~*~

The centerpiece of the Rouen Conference Center was a building that resembled a medieval jousting hall. Rough-hewn exposed beams crisscrossed the cathedral ceiling. Floor-to-ceiling windows trimmed in dark wood lined one wall, allowing natural light to flood the interior. The remaining walls were painted a soft cream.

Although under ordinary circumstances the massive room was most likely used as a small exhibition space, today it held twenty-five baking stations spread around the room. Each station included a workspace with a stand mixer, basic dry ingredients, and a combination induction stovetop with convection oven. An industrial refrigerator/freezer and a dozen blast chillers filled one wall. The opposite wall contained freestanding shelving filled with assorted cookie cutters, bakeware, food processors, airbrushes, and other specialty items as well as non-perishables, such as a variety of chocolates, nuts, fondants, extracts, and edible decorations.

Cloris whistled under her breath. "Someone spared no expense."

"It looks like a set from a Food Network baking competition. I wonder what it cost to pull this off."

"Probably more than my daughter's tuition for the semester."

Several of the competitors had already arrived. Others began streaming in behind us and made their way to their stations, each of which held a tall chrome place card holder that displayed an attendee's name.

Rhetta entered the building and after spotting us, made her way over to explain how the competition would work. "For the first round each woman will have two hours to bake half a dozen of two different batches of cookies and a third recipe to create a cookie container to hold the dozen cookies."

"Decorated cookies?" asked Cloris.

"That's entirely up to them."

It would take me more than two hours to bake one batch of cookies, let alone three. I wondered how many women would complete the task in the allotted time. Skeptic that I am, I never believed the contestants on TV baking competitions really had so little time to complete their challenges.

"This evening," continued Rhetta, "you'll eliminate eleven contestants."

"You expect us to sample seventy-five cookies tonight?" I asked. That was an excessive amount of sugar, even for me.

"Sixty-nine," said Rhetta. "Two attendees unexpectedly had to drop out earlier."

Cloris and I played dumb. "Did they become ill?" she asked.

Rhetta hesitated. "I'm afraid there were some extenuating circumstances."

I raised an eyebrow. "*More* extenuating circumstances beyond the *earlier* extenuating circumstances?"

She frowned but refused to elaborate other than to say, "It happens. Anyway, just take a small taste of each cookie to determine which bakers should advance to the next round."

"That's still a lot of nibbling," said Cloris. "Who came up with this schedule?"

Rhetta's features grew tight. "Marlene."

Now why didn't that surprise me? "I hope we don't get pulled over by a state trooper on the way home tonight."

"Whatever for?" asked Rhetta, her eyes widening.

"Sugar intoxication."

"Is that really a thing?"

"Not as far as I know, but how many people have ever had to sample nearly six dozen cookies before getting behind the wheel of a car?"

Rhetta replied with a nervous giggle.

At precisely two o'clock she stepped up to a microphone and announced the dessert of the day. Apparently, quite a few women had a similar reaction to mine concerning the time allotted for three different batches of cookies because an undercurrent of groans erupted throughout the room. I also noticed several women shoot eye-daggers toward Marlene.

A moment later, when Rhetta said, "Your time starts now," twenty-three women raced to the shelves to grab cookie cutters, rolling pins, and baking trays.

Rhetta returned to where Cloris and I had remained. "Marlene requested that you mingle and engage with the contestants as they work," she said.

"Won't they resent the interruption?" asked Cloris.

"I think that's the idea," I whispered.

Rhetta offered up an I-only-work-here shrug, then said, "Enjoy your afternoon."

"You're leaving?" asked Cloris.

"I have paperwork to do. I'll be back in time to close out the competition at four o'clock."

Cloris and I spent the next two hours observing the bakers. We strolled up and down the aisles and made a comment here and there but tried not to get in their way. "They race around faster than my mother at a Lord & Taylor sale," I said.

"How is Flora taking the demise of her favorite haunt?" asked

Cloris.

"Not well. She's in mourning." My mother spent more time with Mr. Lord and Mr. Taylor over the years than she had with some of her many husbands. But department stores were going the way of the dodo bird, and Lord & Taylor had recently become the latest victim.

A loud crash, followed by a string of words normally only uttered by longshoremen, drew our attention across the room. Two women covered in a dozen broken eggs lay sprawled on the floor.

When none of the other bakers ran to assist them, Cloris and I stepped in. "Are you all right?" I asked, offering my hand to one as Cloris helped the other. "Do you need medical attention?"

The women rose to their feet. One said, "I'm fine."

The other brushed eggshell from her apron and nodded in agreement. Leaving egg literally on their faces and many other parts of their bodies, they returned to work, neither bothering to clean up the mess on either themselves or the floor.

Cloris grabbed some dish towels from the shelf and covered the egg residue to prevent anyone from slipping. I walked over to Marlene's station and asked, "Is there someone you can call to clean up the floor?"

"I'm busy," she said, rolling out dough and not even bothering to look at me as she spoke. I felt sorry for the staff member who would later have to contend with the mess of eggshells and dried yolk and albumen glued to several square feet of parquet flooring.

As the competition progressed, the room filled with the aroma of baking cookies, teasing my tastebuds and setting off my salivary glands. However, along with the tantalizing scents, mishaps continued throughout the afternoon. Joy dropped a tray of cookies as she removed them from the oven. Another accidentally flooded all her cookies, along with her baking station, when her bag of royal icing erupted like Mount Etna.

In the end, five women were immediately disqualified for not finishing on time. Another two watched in horror as their cookie containers broke apart after assembly. We'd now be eliminating eight contestants this evening instead of eleven. "Twenty-one less cookies we'll have to sample tonight," Cloris whispered.

"That's the way the cookie crumbles."

~*~

Cloris and I arrived early at the Grenoble Ballroom to allow time for a private viewing of the needlework entries. Painted Japanese rice paper screens had sectioned off half the cavernous area. Tables running the perimeter of the room held the twenty-five numbered entries. Framed pieces perched on easels. Quilts, afghans, and garments were draped over hidden pedestals in a way to best display the handiwork of each.

Unlike the baking competition, the needlework judging was completely blind. However, similar to the earlier contest, expertise differed widely.

After a few minutes, the members of the Stitch and Bake Society began arriving. They had all dressed for dinner, many wearing flowing maxi dresses in various fabrics, colors, and patterns, while others had chosen Audrey Hepburn-inspired little black dresses accessorized with a string of pearls.

Cloris and I took our seats. Instead of the usual round event tables that held eight or ten people, the room had been set up with five smaller tables, each with five place settings. The tables were arranged in the center of the needlework display. Cloris and I were seated at a small rectangular table off to one side of the room between the women and the needlework.

Dinner consisted of a spinach and artichoke hearts salad with shaved Parmesan and champagne vinaigrette dressing. An entrée of New York strip steak with loaded baked potato and roasted vegetables followed.

Knowing the number of cookies yet to come that evening, I exerted Herculean effort not to eat the potato. Although, I will admit to drooling over it. Of course, Cloris cleaned her plate and added insult to injury by including one of the warm dinner rolls from the basket on our table and slathering it with butter. "When I grow up, I want a superhuman metabolism like yours," I told her.

Once dinner was finished and dishes removed, the waitstaff rolled in four carts containing the sixteen entries that had made it to the judging. In front of each cookie basket or box was a business-sized card with a number and a list of the three types of cookies the bakers had chosen.

Before we were served, Cloris and I examined the filled baskets and boxes and made notes on a judging sheet regarding the design and execution of each entry, as well as the difficulty level of the cookies the contestants had chosen to bake. Many of the women had saved time by executing two drop cookies, only baking a more time-consuming cutout icebox or shortbread cookie to construct their edible containers. Others had taken the time to bake cutout cookies for all three recipes, decorating them with intricate designs in a coordinating theme.

Our judging was semi-blind. With sixteen entries and women who were virtual strangers, matching them with their completed offerings was next to impossible. However, some of the entries stood out for either the quality of the craftsmanship or the obvious lack of it. Those had made an impression on us as we'd observed the competition, especially Marlene's entry.

She had constructed a square box covered with navy royal icing and decorated it in a complex white traditional Scandinavian pattern. Her two additional cookies were a star and a heart that repeated the decorative motifs but reversed the colors.

As Cloris and I stood in front of the cart that held Marlene's cookies, I admitted sotto voce, "I'm impressed by Marlene's artistry."

"Certainly the best of the lot," she whispered back.

I glanced across the room and noted the smug expression on Marlene's face. Given her talent, why would she feel compelled to cheat to ensure a win? Even if she wasn't behind the bribes, she certainly had used them as an excuse to ban Letitia and Georgina.

Once we'd finished scoring the aesthetics of each entry, we took our seats. Then one by one the waiters plated two cookies and a piece of the edible container from each baker and included the numbered card. When sixteen plates were set aside for both of us to taste, the waiters divided up the remaining cookies for the attendees.

The women ignored the cookies set in front of them. They sat silently watching us as we sampled a small bite of each cookie, most likely looking for clues in our facial expressions as we ate, then scored, each selection.

Some of the bakers had chosen unique flavor profiles, often combining unexpected sweet and savory ingredients. Others had played it safe with basic sugar cookie recipes that they had doctored by adding liqueurs and nuts or made filled sandwich cookies. One brave woman managed to bake macarons in the short timeframe. Unfortunately, she hadn't let them rest long enough before putting her tray in the oven, and the macarons never developed the essential classic feet as they baked.

Marlene's cookies were on Plate Number Ten. I broke off a small piece of the first cookie and took a nibble, immediately fighting off the urge to spit it out. Grabbing my glass of water, I gulped the entire twelve ounces to wash down the offensive bite and cleanse my tastebuds. Through teary eyes, I turned to Cloris and saw her in the throes of the same struggle.

Gasps and murmurs filled the room. Marlene rose and stormed toward our table. "What do you think you're doing?"

"You baked these?" asked Cloris, pointing to the cookies on her plate.

"You know I did. Why are you acting like there's something wrong with them?"

She held the plate out to Marlene. "You tell me."

"There's nothing wrong with my cookies." Marlene grabbed the remainder of the one Cloris had sampled and popped it into her mouth. As her eyes widened, her jaw dropped, and she spit the mouthful onto the floor. She then turned to the other members of the Stitch and Bake Society and demanded, "Which one of you witches sabotaged me?"

Not surprisingly, no one fessed up.

Marlene wouldn't be advancing to the next round, and she knew it. The woman turned purple with rage. She hurled the plate to the floor and stormed out of the ballroom.

In her wake I wondered, had she inadvertently used salt instead of sugar in her recipe? Or had someone exacted a not-so-sweet revenge?

SIX

When I arrived home, I found Zack, Ralph, Mephisto, and the boys camped out in the den, a hockey game on the TV. No sign of Lucille. "Where's our curmudgeonly commie?" I asked.

"Harriet picked her up earlier," said Zack. "They're either having a sleepover or fomenting revolution."

"Or planning a revolution at a sleepover," added Nick.

Harriet Kleinhample, my mother-in-law's second-in-command, had lost her driver's license months ago, but that didn't stop her from driving. The woman was a terror behind the wheel. Although, that had recently worked in our favor when she broadsided another vehicle, killing an assassin. Life often plays out in mysterious ways.

I ran the fingers of one hand through my hair and expelled a huge sigh. "If it's the latter and she's arrested, the cops can keep her. I've had my fill of elderly drama queens for the day."

"Does that mean I get my room back?" asked Nick.

"Depends on how long she's imprisoned," I said.

Ralph flapped his wings and squawked, "*She does abuse our ears: to prison with her. All's Well That Ends Well*, Act Five, Scene Three."

Zack reached into his shirt pocket and offered Ralph a sunflower seed, then he turned to me. "Getting back to drama queens and your day, anything you'd like to share?"

"Only if you're a glutton for punishment and you first make me a drink."

He quirked an eyebrow. "That good a conference?"

"You have no idea."

"I do have something besides a glass of wine that might cheer you up," he said.

"Watch your innuendos in front of my sons, please."

"Really, Mom?" said Alex.

"Yeah, it's not like we're toddlers," added Nick.

"This is entirely G-rated," Zack assured me. He turned to the boys. "One of you want to get it?"

They raced each other out of the den as I stared at Zack. "What have you done?"

He offered me a sheepish grin. "Something I hope you won't kill me for."

The boys returned before I could respond. They held a long cardboard tube with a red ribbon tied around the center and handed it over to Zack. He then offered it to me. "This is my wedding present to you."

We hadn't even set a date yet, and the man was giving me a wedding present? In a cardboard tube? I stared at the tube in stunned disbelief, then focused on him and the boys. Wide grins covered their faces. "What is it?"

"Open it."

I settled onto the sofa. "A snake isn't going to pop out?"

"Maybe," said Nick.

His brother elbowed him in the ribs. "Way to go giving the surprise away, Doofus."

I shook the tube. It didn't sound like a snake, not that I'd know what a snake in a tube sounds like. Besides, Zack wasn't known for practical jokes.

I pulled off the plastic cap at one end of the tube and peered inside. No snake. Just some rolled up papers which I removed and spread across the coffee table. My jaw dropped at the sight of a series of architectural renderings depicting a kitchen and two bathrooms. My kitchen and bathrooms. But not my current circa ninety-fifties kitchen and bathrooms.

I turned to face Zack, unsure what to say. My throat constricted with emotion. Finally, I forced out some words. "You want to renovate my house?"

"I want to update our home. For you, for me, and for the boys."

"But that will cost a fortune."

"Only half a fortune, and I can afford it. You nixed the idea of moving to a new home. This is my compromise. And it's also a thank you from someone else."

"What do you mean?"

Zack pointed to a box in the corner of one of the drawings. "Jesse?" I asked.

"You nailed the guy who tried to kill him. He and Robyn want to repay you. Jesse will do the work; I'll cover the cost of materials."

Jesse Konopka and his wife lived around the corner. Robyn and I had been in a book club together before Karl died. Jesse worked in construction. A few months ago he'd nearly died in an accident at a job site. Only it hadn't been an accident. "He can't afford to do that."

"He insists. When I first approached him, he wanted to pay for everything. We compromised. I'm also paying for the subcontractors. Jesse's providing the sweat equity."

"That's still huge, considering it takes him away from paying jobs."

Zack shrugged. "You try talking him out of it. He and Robyn insisted. I'll find a way to make it up to him."

"How?"

He shrugged again. "Haven't figured that out yet. Now, about your day?"

"I'm still waiting for that drink."

Zack asked Alex to retrieve a bottle of wine from the apartment above the garage. I no longer kept alcohol in the house, not because I worried my sons would imbibe—I knew they wouldn't—but to hide it from Lucille. As it was, I periodically had to search her room for contraband to keep her from chugging a glass of Merlot to wash down her meds.

When Alex returned, Zack and I left the boys and Mephisto to the hockey game. Ralph accompanied us to the living room where I told Zack about my day at Beckwith Chateau.

"Marlene Beckwith's sense of entitlement is off the charts," I said. "She went ballistic when she realized she'd been eliminated from the competition. I don't understand why a woman who has everything would care about something so unimportant."

"Some people have to win at any cost."

"That's what I told Cloris. I'm aware of that in the abstract, but I've never come across a living, breathing embodiment of such an attitude."

"You think she's behind the attempted bribery?"

"After what happened this evening? Makes sense."

"And the salt? Accidental or intentional?"

"Definitely intentional. Each station contained labeled cannisters of the dry baking ingredients. I remember that the salt, baking soda, and baking powder were in small cannisters, the flour and sugar in large ones. Marlene couldn't have accidentally grabbed the wrong cannister."

"So now what, Nancy Drew?"

"I think Marlene will retaliate. She owns the Chateau. What's to prevent her from sneaking into the conference center tonight and sabotaging whoever she suspects of having sabotaged her?"

"From what you've told me, that could be the remaining eight contestants."

I nodded. "Tomorrow should be fun. Along with the next baking round, I still have to judge the needlework competition—assuming Marlene doesn't destroy all the entries but hers tonight."

~*~

Since we didn't need to haul cartons and cupcakes Wednesday morning, I offered to drive. After picking up Cloris, we stopped at a Starbucks drive-thru for coffee and a couple of bagels with schmear, once again eating as we sat in the ever-present rush hour backup on the Garden State Parkway. Even so, we arrived at Beckwith Chateau in plenty of time to mingle with the attendees before the start of my workshop. We checked our coats and computer cases, but I held onto the canvas conference tote, having stashed the remains of my bagel within it. Then we wandered into the Chartres Library.

As we had expected, the women were abuzz over last night's baking competition, gleefully speculating on who had sabotaged Marlene. A quick head count revealed twenty-two of the remaining twenty-three attendees, all but Marlene. Unless either Georgina or Letitia had dumped the salt into Marlene's sugar cannister before leaving the Chateau grounds, the saboteur was currently in this room.

Too bad I was unable to get a look at the woman who claimed to have a revenge plan yesterday. However, at least some of these women knew very well who'd salted the sugar. The woman had divulged her plan to them.

When one of the women noticed Cloris and me standing off to the side, she practically pounced on us. "We're all dying to know what was in Marlene's cookies."

"Salt instead of sugar," said Cloris as some of the other women gathered around us.

"A salt mine worth of salt," I added. Just thinking about that cookie brought the nasty taste back to my mouth. "Someone had it in for Marlene."

"I guess so," said a woman wearing a vertigo-inducing black and white op art print maxi-dress.

I glanced at her nametag. "Tell me, Jacqueline. We've been curious about something."

"What's that, dear?"

"No one seems to like Marlene. How did she wind up president of your chapter?"

Jacqueline turned her hands palms up as she raised her shoulders. "No one ran against her."

"We won't make that mistake twice," said one of the others. I recognized her from my keyhole peeping yesterday as a board member. Her nametag read Hildy. A petite woman with a heart-shaped face and a head of short silver waves, she wore a neon orange crocheted vest over a neon green velvet baby doll dress with trumpet sleeves. Taking a quick glance downward, I noted she'd accessorized with neon orange go-go boots. "Maureen is a narcissistic megalomaniac," she added.

"And although Hildy is a retired corporate psychologist," said Jacqueline, nodding in Hildy's direction, "she didn't need an advanced degree to figure that out. Right from the start, we all pegged Marlene."

"Although too late," chimed in another member of the group.

Around us, an assortment of mostly stylishly coifed silver, white, and perfectly dyed heads bobbed in agreement.

"She's in for a rude awakening, though," said Wanda, who had swapped out yesterday's floral bellbottoms for a retro pink, purple, and magenta abstract Pucci print pantsuit. She lowered her voice. "Can the two of you keep a secret?"

Hildy placed a hand on Wanda's arm. "Do you really think that's a good idea?" she asked.

Wanda directed her piercing blue gaze at Cloris and me. "These two have already been manipulated by our not-so-illustrious president. They're certainly not on Team Marlene."

"I get the feeling Team Marlene is a team of one," I said.

"Truer words were never spoken," said Jacqueline, bobbing her head with enough force that her silver-streaked bangs bounced against her forehead. "Even her husband can't stand her. They live in separate cottages and rarely cross paths."

"So you'll keep quiet?" asked Wanda.

When we both agreed, she said, "The board met in an emergency session last night and voted to oust her."

"We've already contacted the national director to have her membership revoked," added Hildy.

"Does she know?" I asked.

Wanda shook her head. "Not yet. She'd kick us all out of the Chateau like she did Georgina and Letitia. Marlene will receive a very unpleasant surprise tomorrow night after the awards ceremony."

"Remember," said Hildy, placing a finger to her lips. "Mum's the word."

"She won't hear anything from us," I said. "But now, if you ladies will excuse me, I need to prepare for your class."

"Wow," said Cloris as we made our way to the Bordeaux Room.

"I'll say! Intrigue, conspiracies, and scheming galore." Ralph would be in his glory around this crowd. They put Lady Macbeth to shame.

We'd made our way to the rotunda when we saw Rhetta, wide-eyed and pale as a ghost, running toward us.

"She's dead!"

"Who?" we both asked.

"Marlene!"

SEVEN

"I don't know what to do," cried Rhetta.

I grabbed her by the shoulders. "Take a deep breath."

She tried but without success, producing only shuddering sobs while her body trembled under my grip.

I led her to one of the nearby loveseats placed strategically around the circumference of the rotunda. After I'd forced her to sit, I said, "Rhetta, this is important. Are you absolutely certain Marlene is dead?"

She stared at her hands, clutched tightly in her lap. Then she raised her head. Her eyes widened, fear and uncertainty written across her face. "I...I...I...couldn't wake her."

"Was she breathing?" asked Cloris, hovering over us.

Rhetta stared at her, then at me. "I don't think so, but now...now...I was so freaked...I don't think so, but I can't remember checking." She jumped to her feet. "Maybe she isn't dead."

She raced toward the nearest door leading outside, Cloris and

I following on her heels. As Rhetta ran down a brick path that bisected the English garden and made a sharp turn to the left, I thought I heard the slamming of a door echoing behind us.

After several more turns within the garden, we emerged onto a path that led to a plantation-style two-story white brick house, complete with fluted columns and a sweeping front porch.

Rhetta sprinted up the steps and through the front door she'd apparently left open in her haste to find help. I paused to catch my breath before tackling the dozen steps leading to the porch.

"*Cottage?*" I said to Cloris between gulps of air. "Not by any stretch of anyone's imagination."

"The rich have their own proprietary concept of size," she said as we hauled ourselves toward the entrance.

We entered into a massive marble foyer with a split staircase leading left and right. With no sign of Rhetta, I called out to her. "Where are you?"

"Up here!" came her reply.

Cloris and I climbed the six steps that led to the branched landing. "Left or right?" I called again.

"Left! Hurry!"

We scurried up the remaining stairs and found Rhetta in the first room. "She hasn't moved. This is the way I found her. I thought she was sleeping, but she never sleeps this late."

Marlene lay on her back, her eyes closed, a quilt pulled up to her chin. At first glance she appeared to be sleeping peacefully. However, I'd had enough experience with dead bodies at this point that one look at the pallor of her skin and I knew she was dead. Still, Rhetta was so terror-stricken that I searched for a pulse. Not only didn't I find one, but Marlene's body was ice cold. I turned to Rhetta and shook my head. "I'm sorry."

Rhetta faltered. Cloris reached for one arm; I grabbed hold of the other, and we led her to an antique mauve velvet fainting couch flanking the fireplace. While Rhetta struggled to regain her composure, I walked over to the bedside table, which held a silver tea service along with a nearly empty cup and saucer.

I glanced over at Marlene. Although her death appeared natural on the surface, with no outward signs of trauma to her head and a calm expression on her face, my sleuthing talents only extended so far. I had no medical skills beyond dealing with skinned knees and caring for the standard childhood ailments.

What if someone had smothered Marlene while she slept? Or poisoned her? Had her seemingly peaceful death been staged?

I scanned the room for signs of anything out of the ordinary, but nothing raised any red flags. No furniture overturned, no drawers open and ransacked, no broken glass or lamps, no blood spatters. Still, given my track record, could I really be so lucky to have encountered a death by natural causes and not a victim of murder?

I stepped into the master bathroom where I found a clean glass sealed in Chateau wrapping in the medicine cabinet. I also noted a myriad of prescription drugs lining one of the shelves, including one container devoid of any labeling.

Had Marlene accidentally overdosed on her meds?

Before reaching for the glass, though, I experienced a moment of doubt. If Marlene had died by someone else's hand, her bedroom was a crime scene. But with no evidence of a crime having taken place, what were the odds that the killer had left his fingerprints on the paper wrapping of a sealed glass? I was letting my imagination run amuck. Besides, his fingerprints would also be on the medicine cabinet door and elsewhere in the room.

Logically, the only fingerprints on the glass wrapper were those of the housekeeping staff member who had placed the glass in the cabinet.

I lifted the glass off the shelf, removed the wrapping, and filled the glass with tap water. Then I returned to the bedroom and handed the glass to Rhetta. Both her hand and her lips trembled as she took a few tentative sips.

Once Rhetta's breath calmed, she said, "Thank you for coming. I know I shouldn't have fallen apart, but I've never seen a dead body before. I'm not sure what to do now. Who do I call?"

"First call 911, then call Marlene's husband," I said.

Rhetta chewed her lower lip. "I don't know that Marlene would want Mr. Beckwith to see her like this."

"He's her next of kin, isn't he?" asked Cloris.

"Yes, but they don't...didn't exactly get along, especially since the investigation began into Beckwith Pharmaceuticals. All they ever do...did..." She gave her head a sharp shake. "Sorry, I still can't believe she's dead. He lives in one of the other cottages."

"That doesn't matter now," I said.

"I suppose not." She pulled out her phone.

Before she placed the call, I said, "We'll give you some privacy."

Panic again took hold of Rhetta. "Please don't leave!"

"We're not leaving, just stepping into the hall."

Before Cloris and I exited the room, I took one final visual sweep. Still not seeing anything amiss, other than Marlene's dead body, I pulled the bedroom door closed behind us.

"Should we have left her alone in there?" asked Cloris.

"Why not?"

"I'm worried that your Sleuth-meter is on the fritz. What's to say Rhetta didn't kill Marlene and is putting on an Oscar-worthy performance?"

I shook my head. "I'm sure the police will question her as a suspect. They'll question everyone at the Chateau, including us. I don't think she harmed Marlene. She's the only person we've come across so far who has shown any loyalty to her."

"Again, that could be an act."

"True, but if so, she's had plenty of time to do whatever she wanted or needed to do in that room before running to the Chateau." I stepped closer to the door and placed my ear against one of the wooden panels. "She's speaking on the phone, not making noises to indicate anything beyond placing a call."

A moment later we heard the front door open. Voices filled the foyer and grew louder, coupled with the sound of footsteps ascending the staircase.

The Stitch and Bake Society headed toward us, the remaining board members in the lead. When they spotted us standing at the top of the stairs, they paused. "Is Marlene dead?" asked Hildy.

My reluctant amateur sleuthing senses immediately went on high alert. "Why would you think that?" I asked.

"We heard Rhetta yelling and followed you."

I nodded.

"How?" asked Wanda.

"It appears she died in her sleep."

"Seems too peaceful a way for her to go," said a woman toward the back of the crowd. She sported a shoulder-length silver pageboy with a playful streak of pink running down the left side of her head. I squinted to read her name tag. Celeste.

Cloris gasped. "That's extremely harsh."

"Agreed," said another woman in the middle of the group. She turned to address the others. "Marlene had her faults, but so do we all. You don't get to where we've gotten by being Mary Sunshine."

"I suppose," said Jacqueline.

"You should all leave," I said. I had no idea what else Marlene had done to these women, but their callousness rubbed me the wrong way.

"What about our workshop?" asked another woman.

A woman is dead, and she's worried about a cross stitch class?

I'd try to reserve judgment. After all, I could hardly apply twenty-first century attitudes to women who'd entered the workforce prior to the dawn of the sexual revolution.

I knew that professional women of their generation often had had to develop killer instincts—no pun intended—to make it in male-dominated professions. They'd fought beyond tooth and nail to climb each rung of the corporate ladder, and those battles had to have taken their toll. Their sacrifices had paved the way for my generation.

Given what I'd witnessed since yesterday, though, I had to wonder if those killer instincts had also killed their compassion and empathy. With few exceptions, both qualities seemed completely lacking in the Stitch and Bake Society membership.

I reached into my blazer pocket to retrieve my phone and checked the time. We still had twenty minutes before the start of my workshop. "I'll be there shortly. Rhetta is extremely upset. I'm going to wait with her until the EMTs and Marlene's husband arrive."

"He's not coming."

I turned around to find Rhetta standing near the entrance to Marlene's bedroom. She walked toward us. "After thinking about it, I decided I should call Mr. Beckwith first. His secretary said he can't get away right now. He's in depositions."

"Does he know his wife is dead?" I asked.

"His secretary said she told him."

I clamped down on my tongue to avoid spewing the words fighting to force their way out. No matter how badly Marlene and Vernon Beckwith's relationship had deteriorated, how could he not ask to reschedule the deposition? Under the circumstances, I couldn't imagine any district attorney denying such a request. Even Karl, with all his faults, would have dropped his dice and rushed home to be with his sons if I had suddenly died.

After I'd managed to control my temper, I asked, "Did you call 911?"

Rhetta shook her head. "She told me Mr. Beckwith said to call the concierge physician. He'll know what to do."

"The Chateau has its own physician on staff?" I asked.

"No," said Rhetta. "Dr. Hargrove is...was...Marlene's private physician. She keeps...kept him on retainer. I've already spoken with him. He resides on the property and should arrive momentarily."

Cloris and I exchanged a quick glance. The one percent really did live differently from the rest of us. Still, I'd never trade my life for Marlene's wealth. Some things are far more important than money. Karl may have depleted our bank accounts and left me with staggering debt, but he gave me two fantastic boys. My life is rich with love, even more so now with Zack as part of our family.

After again urging the stitchers and bakers to return to the Chateau, we waited upstairs for the doctor. He arrived within minutes.

"Up here," I said after hearing him enter the house.

"I'm well aware of the way," he answered with a note of arrogance in his voice.

He was much younger than I expected, possibly not long out of med school, yet he wore a Burberry cashmere overcoat. Either Dr. Hargrove came from money or Marlene was paying him far more than most freshly minted doctors earned—especially ones who ministered to a single patient.

After making his way upstairs and into Marlene's bedroom, he took one look at Marlene, pulled the quilt over her head, and pronounced her dead.

"You're not going to examine the body?" I asked.

"No need. It's obvious she's expired."

"I'm aware of that, but what about cause of death?"

"I'm a personal physician, not a medical examiner."

"Still," I insisted, "wouldn't a cursory examination of the body rule out any obvious signs of foul play?"

The man hadn't even bothered to check for bruising or lifted Marlene's eyelids to determine petechial hemorrhaging, which might have indicated asphyxiation or strangulation. I'd learned about that during my mother-in-law's brief stay at a rehab center after she'd suffered a minor stroke. Someone had strangled her roommate one night.

The doctor eyed me with contempt. "Are you a medical professional?"

"No."

"Then I can only assume you've watched too many television crime dramas and consider yourself a couch detective."

"I'm only saying—"

"You should do whatever it is you're trained to do and leave medicine to those of us with medical degrees. Not that it's any of your business, but Marlene suffered from several underlying medical conditions, including heart disease, hypertension, and high cholesterol. Couple that with a lack of exercise and a diet high in sweets, fats, and alcohol, and..."

He paused and twisted his mouth into a condescending smirk as he narrowed his eyes at me before continuing, "Even a layman such as yourself can see she was slowly killing herself. I saw this coming and told her so. She wouldn't listen. In my professional opinion as her personal physician, Marlene Beckwith died in her sleep from either a massive heart attack or stroke."

He strode across the room and reached for the doorknob. With a sweeping gesture of dismissal, he said, "Now if you ladies will leave, I'll execute my final duties for my patient."

Once Cloris, Rhetta, and I had exited into the hallway, the self-important doctor slammed the bedroom door behind us and clicked the lock.

"I wonder if he speaks to men in that dismissive manner," said Cloris.

"Highly unlikely," I said. "But I do find his behavior strange."

"What do you mean?" asked Rhetta as we made our way downstairs.

"For starters, let's just say I find it odd that under the circumstances any doctor would arrive on the scene without his medical bag."

"Exactly," said Cloris. "What if Marlene wasn't dead? He wouldn't take Rhetta's word for it. If nothing else, he'd bring his stethoscope, right?"

"It's what I'd do if I were a doctor," I said. "And what final duties could he possibly be doing? It's not like he's a priest administering last rites."

Rhetta's brows knit together. "He really didn't bring his medical bag? I hadn't noticed. I'm so used to seeing him with it.

What do you think he's doing in there? And why did he lock the door?"

My inner skeptic answered for me. "Helping himself to some of her jewelry?"

Rhetta stopped short and turned, about to race back upstairs. I stopped her. "You can't search him."

"Then how do we make sure he doesn't take whatever he wants?"

"The police would need probable cause for a judge to sign off on a search warrant."

"How do we get them to do that?"

"Not with speculation. You'd need to prove some of Marlene's jewelry is missing, and even then, he could claim she'd previously gifted the pieces to him."

"Besides," said Cloris, "for all we know, he's gathering her meds for the medical examiner. Just because the guy needs an attitude adjustment, doesn't mean he's a thief."

"What if he's removing pills she shouldn't have?" asked Rhetta.

"Has he prescribed meds she shouldn't have taken?" I asked.

"I...I...think so."

"What kind of pills?" asked Cloris.

"Opioids."

That would explain the unmarked pill bottle in the medicine cabinet. "If that's the case," I said, "they'll show up in an autopsy. If opioids contributed to her death, the medical examiner will turn his findings over to the police."

"Assuming there is an autopsy," said Cloris.

I nodded in agreement. "True, if no foul play is suspected, there likely won't be reason for an autopsy, especially with her underlying conditions and her doctor verifying her death from natural causes."

Another thought occurred to me, though. "Beckwith Pharmaceuticals manufactures opioids. It's possible Hargrove didn't prescribe them but intends to protect her supplier."

"My head is spinning," said Rhetta. "For a crafts editor, you certainly know a lot about these things."

"Not by choice," I said.

Rhetta knit her brows together but didn't ask for an explanation. Instead, she paused at the front door. "Hold on a second. I need to get something. Follow me."

She led us through a formal living room, dining room, and kitchen, eventually arriving at a door at the back of the house. After retrieving a large set of keys from her coat pocket, she rifled through them until she found the one she wanted, and unlocked the door. It swung open, revealing a large office with floor-to-ceiling built-in bookcases along the two side walls. Opposite the door, a massive Louis Quatorze antique writing desk—an original, no doubt—sat in front of a wall of windows with patio doors leading out onto what was most likely a spectacular rose garden when in bloom.

Rhetta locked the door behind us, crossed the room, unlocked the desk, and removed a laptop. "This way," she said, unlocking the patio doors and stepping outside.

I stopped her. "Rhetta, everything we've just discussed is conjecture. We don't know how Marlene died. If it was under suspicious conditions, that laptop might be evidence. You can't just take it. Put it back."

"And let Doctor Hargrove, Vernon, or someone else walk off with it? No way. Someone has to protect what's on this." She slipped the laptop under her coat and stepped outside. We had no choice but to follow. Rhetta relocked the doors behind us.

The temperature had plummeted since we first entered the house, and dark clouds had rolled in. Cloris and I had raced to Marlene's "cottage" without first grabbing our winter coats.

"I understand your motives," I said, rubbing my arms to keep warm as the first icy pellets began to hit us, "but what you're doing is a crime."

"No," said Rhetta, hurrying us along a circuitous path through various gardens toward the Chateau. "I worked on Marlene's laptop all the time. You have to trust me on this. It's best that it doesn't fall into the wrong hands."

"Meaning?"

Before answering, she glanced furtively left and right, as if expecting to discover someone lurking behind one of the boxwood hedges. Finally, she asked, "Aren't you suggesting someone killed Marlene?"

"Not necessarily, but I've witnessed enough crime scenes to wonder about a doctor who jumps to conclusions without any evidence."

She stopped short and spun around to confront me. "Actual murder scenes? Not on TV or in the movies?"

"Real-life dead people," I said, aware of the oxymoron.

Rhetta shuddered. Then, as we continued toward the Chateau, she asked, "What should the doctor have done?"

"For one thing, he didn't pull down the quilt to examine her body for signs of trauma."

"Neither did you."

"I knew not to disturb anything in case a crime had been committed, but Marlene was his patient. He should have performed a cursory sight examination."

"I see." She hugged the laptop tighter against her chest. "All the more reason to remove the laptop."

"Why?" asked Cloris.

"Because Marlene was involved in some questionable activities."

"Activities that might have led to murder?" I asked.

"I don't know." She grimaced. "Do you think she was murdered?"

"Hard to say. We'll know more after an autopsy."

"Those questionable activities you mentioned," said Cloris. Do they have anything to do with the lawsuits against Beckwith Pharmaceuticals?"

"Some," said Rhetta, "but there are other things involving people not connected to the business."

"And the laptop contains evidence?" I asked.

"Quite a bit. Reports, correspondence, emails, texts."

"How do you know all this?" I asked.

Rhetta hesitated. I reached for her arm to break her stride. Crimson embarrassment suffused her face. "What aren't you telling us?"

She hung her head. "You have a workshop to teach. I can't explain all of this in a minute or two. It's overwhelming." She raised her head and met my eyes. "If you'll both come to my office after your workshops, I promise I'll fill you in on everything I know."

"What do you plan to do with the laptop?" I asked.

"Hide it for now. If it turns out Marlene was murdered, I'll turn it over to the police."

"Do you think it's safe to hide it here?" I asked.

"No." she removed the laptop from under her coat and forced

it on me. "That's why I'm giving it to you. For safe-keeping."

EIGHT

After my initial shock, I stammered, "I...no...I can't." But Rhetta had already spun on her heels and was rushing toward the Chateau.

"Now what?" asked Cloris.

I shoved the laptop into the canvas conference tote to protect it from the sleet. "We get inside before we both wind up with pneumonia. I'll figure this out later."

"Sensible plan," said Cloris as we picked up our pace.

Once inside the Chateau, we first hit the ladies' room to dry off as best we could. Luckily, along with the wall-mounted hand dryers, there was a basket of assorted toiletries and sundries, a stack of real terrycloth towels, and a hair dryer. Cloris finished first, her blonde pixie cut showing no evidence of a weather assault after a quick toweling and brushing. My bedraggled locks took longer, but eventually I'd returned myself to semi-okay, assuming the frizzy perm look of the eighties was back in style.

Cloris headed to the Avignon Room to set up for her

workshop. "I'll join you shortly," she said.

I entered the Bordeaux Room to find all the attendees mingling about and Tanner standing guard over my cartons of kits. "They wanted to help themselves," he said when I joined him at the front of the room. "I didn't think you'd want that."

"I definitely do not. Thank you, Tanner." I then handed him my numbered plastic check stub and asked him to retrieve my computer case from the coat check room.

As the women took their seats, I was stunned to see Letitia Cramer and Georgina Malloy in the group. They both smiled when they noticed me staring.

"Surprised to see us?" asked Letitia.

"I heard Marlene kicked you out."

"We spent the night, anyway," said Georgina. "Rooming with friends. She had no idea."

"And now that she can't do anything about it," said Letitia, "we're free to resume the conference."

I thought back to the conversation Cloris and I had overheard. Someone had hatched a plot to get even with Marlene. Originally, I'd thought that involved the salt incident. But maybe substituting the sugar for salt was only a precursor to murder. While we were all at dinner last night, had that person also tampered with Marlene's medications? If the evidence wasn't preserved, the killer would get away with murder.

I could think of only one way to prevent that from happening, and it was a longshot. "Ladies," I said, gaining their attention, "forgive me, but I'm in sudden need of the restroom. I'll be right back."

I dashed out of the room and made a beeline down the corridor to an empty room at the end of the hallway. Once inside, I locked the door and placed a call to Detective Spader.

"Mrs. Pollack," he said, answering on the first ring. "I hope you're not calling about another murder."

Detective Sam Spader and I first crossed paths last summer when he investigated the strangulation murder of my mother-in-law's roommate at the Sunnyside of Westfield Assisted Living and Rehabilitation Center. We've been crossing paths over dead bodies ever since, and throughout that time, our relationship has morphed from antagonistic to one of growing respect—on both sides.

"I'm not sure," I said.

Spader groaned.

Before he responded further, I asked, "You used to work homicide in Essex County, right?"

"I did."

"I think someone may have killed Marlene Beckwith."

"She's dead? When did this happen?"

"I don't know. Sometime between after dinner last night and earlier this morning."

Spader grunted. "That woman has been a thorn in law enforcement's side for years."

"In what way?"

"Never mind. What makes you think she was murdered?"

I quickly explained the situation to him. "Of course, it's quite possible she died of natural causes."

"With you involved?" Spader spit out an ironic laugh. "I should be so lucky."

I decided to ignore the jab. "Something isn't adding up. If nothing else, shouldn't the police check her teacup and pills?"

He didn't answer right away. At first, I thought my phone had dropped the call. "Detective?"

Finally, he said, "If you were anyone else, Mrs. Pollack, I'd consider this a crank call, but I've learned to trust your instincts. It may already be too late, especially if your suspicions are correct, but I'll place a call to Essex County P.D."

I thanked him and headed back to my class. Tanner had returned with my computer case. I pointed out the cartons I wouldn't need until tomorrow, and he returned them to storage. Meanwhile, I plugged my laptop into the projection equipment.

While my laptop booted up, I passed out the kits, explaining that today's workshop would feature a beginner's cross stitch sampler. "I'll also show you how to personalize your samplers," I said. "Each kit contains a sheet of graph paper and an alphabet to chart your name and the date."

Cloris had finished her setup and entered the room. While she took over handing out the kits, each of which also contained a pair of embroidery scissors, thanks to a generous manufacturer, I returned to the front of the room and brought up the first slide. "This is what your finished project will look like."

The framed sampler, although a beginner project consisting of only full stitches and no shading or backstitching, was designed in the style of early American samplers with traditional motifs. The tea-dyed fabric with which I had paired the design added to the eighteenth-century vibe.

"It's a very easy project," said one of the women, scowling at the screen.

"But a lovely one," said Hildy. "I know exactly where I'll hang mine."

This was followed by an enthusiastic chorus of, "Me, too."

"Do many of you already know how to do counted cross

stitch?" I asked.

When about half the women bobbed their heads up and down, I explained, "I was told to come up with one easy project for today and something more complex for tomorrow. It was agreed that counted cross stitch would tie in nicely with yesterday's talk."

"By Marlene?" asked Letitia.

"As a matter of fact, yes."

"Figures," said Wanda.

I quickly changed the subject, not wanting to set off another round of Marlene-bashing. After all, no matter the animosity toward her, the woman was now dead. "In your kit you'll find two pieces of Aida cloth. For those of you unfamiliar with this form of needlework, Aida cloth is the most common cross stitch fabric. Use the smaller piece to practice, stitching the small heart design first."

I then proceeded to instruct the women on basic cross stitch technique, illustrating each step with more slides, although I noticed the experienced cross stitchers had set right to work on their samplers. Once the inexperienced women got the hang of the stitching technique, everyone settled into chatting as they worked on their samplers.

"Are we supposed to be able to finish this in an hour?" asked Georgina.

"No, but depending on how much of your spare time you devote to stitching, you might finish before the conference ends tomorrow."

Aside from a few other questions, conversation eventually segued to the late Marlene Beckwith. Most of the comments involved Karma finally catching up with her, but a few women defended her.

The most vocal was a woman whose rosy cheeks and white curls reminded me of Mrs. Claus. Her red polyester pants and white blouse with lace collar and bishop's sleeves added to the elfin image. She was the woman who had berated the others at Marlene's home. "I've known Marlene most of my life," she said. Her nametag identified her as Arla. "She had her flaws, but she could also be a good friend."

"I find that impossible to believe," said Celeste. "Marlene never cared about anyone but herself."

"Then you never really knew her," said Arla.

"I knew her well enough," said Celeste.

Wanda turned to Arla. "Why should we believe you?"

Arla stood to address the other women. "Several years ago, when I was diagnosed with cancer, Marlene pulled strings to get me into a Beckwith Pharmaceuticals immunotherapy drug trial. It saved my life."

That silenced Marlene's detractors for a few seconds, and Arla returned to her seat. However, I decided not to let the topic die. "Why do so many of you harbor such animosity toward Marlene?"

"She's ruthless," said Letitia. "The woman always has to win, and she'll stop at nothing to make sure she does."

"You saw firsthand what she did to Letitia and me," said Georgina.

Except the jury was still out on that unpleasant episode. On the one hand, Marlene might have orchestrated the attempted bribery to rid herself of competition. Or Letitia and Georgina could have concocted the entire plot, hoping to beat Marlene at her own game, which might have worked if Cloris and I had no scruples.

"Don't take our word for it," said Wanda. "Just ask Vernon

Beckwith's adult sons from his first marriage."

"Assuming anyone could find them," said Celeste.

"What do you mean?" I asked.

"Their mother moved out of state with them years ago," she said.

"After Marlene manipulated Vernon into cutting them out of his will," added Wanda.

"How do you know that?" asked Cloris.

"She bragged about it," said Jacqueline. "Gleefully."

"Did she and Vernon have any children?" I asked.

Wanda laughed. "You don't want to know what Marlene thought of children."

Conversation eventually veered away from Marlene, and unlike an old Perry Mason episode, the remainder of the hour passed without anyone standing up and admitting to having committed murder. Before they departed, I reminded them to bring their embroidery scissors to tomorrow's class. They then packed up and raced to the restroom before the start of Cloris's workshop.

"What will you do with all these unused kits?" asked Cloris as she helped me pack up. "I don't think Tanner will be interested in them."

I laughed. "Not unless he can eat them. I'll talk to Naomi. She may want to use them as part of a promotion in the magazine or hold them for our next consumer show."

A moment later, as if on cue, Tanner stepped into the conference room to retrieve the cartons. "Anything else you need?" he asked after loading the luggage cart.

"A winning lottery ticket?" I quipped.

"Sorry, if I had one of those, I'd keep it for myself."

"And here I thought we'd developed such a deep connection, Tanner."

He blushed. "Well, maybe if I won a cool billion."

"Careful," I said. "I may hold you to that. I've got a witness."

His blush deepened, and his eyes widened. He turned to Cloris. "Can she really do that?"

Cloris shrugged. "I'm not a lawyer, and I don't even play one on TV, but I think you're safe, Tanner."

His gaze flicked between Cloris and me. Then his eyes lit with comprehension, and he exhaled a huge rush of air. "You're pulling my leg, right?"

"In good fun," I said. "Your potential windfall is safe from my greedy grasp."

"Much appreciated," he said. "I don't think my girlfriend would be thrilled to learn I had to share my lottery winnings with another woman." He then tipped his cap toward us before pushing the luggage cart from the room.

Once Tanner had gone, Cloris and I headed to the Chartres Library for our mid-morning caffeine fix before the start of her workshop. I decided to forego the remains of the bagel in my tote for the more tempting pastries set out for us. Coffees and croissants in hand, we walked back to the Avignon Room. While we waited for her class to arrive, I filled Cloris in on my brief phone conversation with Detective Spader.

"What are the chances Marlene's meds and teacup are still in the house?"

I shrugged. "Depends on whether or not she was murdered. Probably slim to none if she was, but stranger things have happened."

"And if they're gone?"

"If the doctor signed the death certificate, listing cause of death as cardiac arrest due to an underlying medical condition and advanced age, someone will get away with murder—assuming it was murder."

"Which we don't know. What about an autopsy?"

"The police would have to suspect foul play. Unless they noticed something suspicious after they arrived—something we missed—they'd have no reason not to believe the doctor."

"What about her husband? Couldn't he request an autopsy?"

"Sure," I said. "But why would he? If it's discovered Marlene was murdered, he becomes a suspect."

"But if he suspected she was murdered, wouldn't he want the killer caught?"

I shrugged. "Maybe. Maybe not. They didn't get along and lived separately. He may have paid someone to kill her."

"Someone like the doctor?"

"Given the way he acted, he's at the top of my suspects list."

"So what do we do, Sherlock?"

"As soon as your class ends, we have Rhetta go back to the house with us and secure the pills and teacup, assuming they're still there."

"How likely is that?"

"Unfortunately, I'm guessing highly unlikely, but we have to give it a shot."

At this point, some of the Stitch and Bake ladies began filing into the room, forcing Cloris and me to table any further discussion.

~*~

Cloris scored a huge hit with her geode cake presentation, especially after revealing the actual cake. The bakery had created a super moist dark chocolate three-tier cake with a raspberry mousse filling. The sugar geode in various shades of pink, looked exactly like a real crystal geode.

After setting a slice aside for Tanner, Cloris divided up the remaining cake for the conference attendees. One of the women suggested they retire to the Chartres Library so they could pair their cake with coffee or tea, and the room soon emptied. Tanner arrived a few seconds later.

Five minutes after Tanner left, Cloris and I were seated in Rhetta's office. As eager as I was to hear what she had to say about the contents of the laptop, we first had to get back to the house.

"Grab your coats," said Rhetta. "It's nasty outside. I'll meet you at the door we left from this morning."

Nasty was an understatement. When we stepped outside, it became obvious we were in the throes of a full-fledged ice storm. I worried about driving home later that evening, but at that moment all three of our phones dinged an alert. The State Police had closed down all major roadways throughout the northern half of New Jersey. Cloris and I wouldn't be going anywhere anytime soon.

A moment later I received a text from Zack: All roads shut down. Make arrangements to spend the night.

I sent him a thumbs-up emoji and added that I'd call him later. Then I asked Rhetta, "Do you have any extra rooms for the night?"

"Don't worry," she said, leading us down a different path from the one we'd taken that morning. "Not all the rooms in the Chateau were filled for the conference."

Conditions necessitated that we step gingerly and take our time, even though the stinging ice pelted us. Luckily, the grounds crew had salted the walkways, which kept them from turning into an ice rink.

The path led to an outbuilding that housed several golf carts. We climbed into one, and Rhetta drove us the remainder of the way to Marlene's house, parking under an overhang at the back door.

We entered into chaos.

NINE

Someone had ransacked the kitchen. Cabinets lay bare, their contents scattered across the floor in a haphazard array of pots, pans, and broken glassware and dishes. Drawers had been yanked out and tossed aside, appliances swept from the counters. Not a single package of food remained on the pantry shelves or in the refrigerator. Whoever had trashed Marlene's kitchen had taken the time to open boxes, bags, and canisters and dump all the food. Everything from raisin bran to frozen broccoli florets to dried pasta peppered the room. A dusting of flour and sugar lay over everything like newly fallen snow.

"Why would someone do this?" asked Rhetta, her voice trembling.

"He was definitely desperate to find something," said Cloris.

"Or not," I said. With a sweep of my arm, I indicated the damage confronting us. "You can search a house without leaving it looking like the aftermath of a tornado. This is a sign of rage. Let's check the rest of the rooms."

"What if he's still here?" asked Rhetta.

I pointed to a carton of ice cream, the lid missing and the contents pooled in a pink puddle. "This mess was made at least an hour ago. I think it's safe to say he's long gone, with or without whatever he was searching for."

Rhetta stooped to pick up a carving knife. "Just in case," she said.

"Good idea," said Cloris, arming herself with a boning knife. Not worrying about leaving fingerprints, I followed suit and grabbed a meat cleaver.

We gingerly picked our way around the broken glass toward the office. The door had been kicked in, the wood molding splintered around the lock. As with the kitchen, everything that had once lined the shelves and filled the drawers—books, papers, and files—now covered the floor, the mountain of wreckage topped off with the toppled Louis Quatorze desk and chair.

"I'm glad the computer is safe," said Rhetta.

I certainly hoped so. I'd slipped Marlene's laptop into my computer case and left the case at the coat check when I retrieved my coat. "You think that's what he was after?" I asked.

She shrugged. "I guess it depends on who did this."

"What's on that computer?" asked Cloris.

"Later," said Rhetta. "I want to get out of here as quickly as possible just in case he comes back."

We decided to head to Marlene's bedroom since our initial objective was to secure her pills and teacup. We arrived to find her bed empty. "When did the medical examiner arrive?" I asked Rhetta.

"He didn't."

"Then where's Marlene?" asked Cloris.

"A hearse showed up from the funeral home about two hours ago," she said.

Which meant unless the funeral director noticed suspicious wounds on Marlene's body, she'd be embalmed or cremated without anyone ever officially determining cause of death. Someone—most likely the doctor—was doing an excellent job of covering his tracks.

My expectations of finding the tea service, cup and saucer, and pill bottles had plummeted into the don't-hold-your-breath zone, especially considering Marlene's bedroom had also been ransacked. After a thorough visual search, we found neither the silver tea service nor the teacup and saucer.

"I don't see Marlene's jewelry box anywhere," said Rhetta, hands on hips as she surveyed the room.

I made a beeline for the bathroom. The medicine cabinet door stood open, the shelves empty. With no sign of a single pill bottle amid the cosmetics and toiletries littering the Carrera marble floor, I was now convinced Marlene Beckwith had not succumbed to any underlying medical condition, no matter how advanced her age.

When we exited the house, I glanced around at the exterior. "What are you looking for?" asked Rhetta.

"I don't see any security cameras."

"There are none within the grounds," she said. "Only around the perimeter."

"Why is that?" asked Cloris.

"Privacy is a huge selling feature of membership."

Cloris raised an eyebrow. "Really? So no one is concerned about staff members or outside vendors with sticky fingers?"

Rhetta shrugged. "I suppose it's a trade-off. The staff is

thoroughly vetted and paid quite well."

"No crimes at all?" I asked.

"Not in the ten years I've worked here."

"Well," I said, nodding toward the house, "you have one now. Security tapes would have revealed who entered Marlene's house last night and after we left earlier."

"Telling us who killed her and who ransacked the house," added Cloris.

Rhetta's eyes widened. "I never thought about it before, but I guess some things are more important than privacy. Security cameras might have prevented a murder."

"Or at least made it easier to solve," I said.

We headed back to the Chateau, and while Cloris and I dropped off our coats and retrieved my computer case, Rhetta placed a call to the police. When I knocked on her office door moments later, she swung the door open and waved us in as she spoke on the phone. "I see. Thank you." She then disconnected the call, shook her head, and frowned.

"What's wrong?" I asked as she walked toward her desk and settled into her chair.

"The police won't be coming anytime soon."

Cloris and I both let out a simultaneous gasp along with a "What?" and a "Why?" in rapid succession.

"They're busy dealing with a huge pileup with multiple casualties on the Parkway. A burglary at the Chateau is at the bottom of their priorities right now."

I'd never thought about it before, but a sleet and ice storm would create a field day for enterprising criminals able to navigate harsh weather conditions. "I'll place another call to Detective Spader." Under the circumstances, I had little hope he could pull enough strings to muster the cavalry, but I wanted him to know what we'd discovered.

I also needed to call Zack, which would involve a longer, more involved conversation. Especially after he learned there was a murderer on the loose. I had no doubt closed roads wouldn't stop him. He'd strap on a pair of skis and trek the nearly fifteen miles from Westfield to the Chateau, no matter how much I downplayed the situation. For that reason, a part of me toyed with not telling him about Marlene's death. At least not right away. But then I'd have to come up with some excuse later, and that would unleash the proverbial can of creepy crawlies.

Meanwhile, my call to Detective Spader went directly to voicemail. I left a short message asking his advice regarding what we'd discovered. When I ended the call, I said, "I don't expect a return call anytime soon, given the weather and road conditions. I'm sure there are accidents up and down the Parkway, and he's been drafted into helping out."

"We should get you set up in guest rooms," said Rhetta. "And I'll make arrangements for you to pick out whatever toiletries and clothing you'll need from the spa's gift shop."

She started to rise from her chair, but I held out my hand. "Before we do that, tell us what's on Marlene's computer."

Rhetta lowered herself back into her seat and picked up her phone. "I'll have some lunch brought over for us."

Was she stalling for a reason or simply unnerved by Marlene's death?

We didn't have long to wait, though. Within minutes a waiter arrived with a rolling cart and set up a luncheon service consisting of finger sandwiches and crudités on a small conference table at the far end of Rhetta's office. Once he poured coffee for us and departed, Rhetta said, "As I told you yesterday, along with my position as head concierge, I also worked as Marlene's personal assistant."

"What were your duties?" I asked, filling my plate with a sampling of food.

"Basically, whatever Marlene wanted me to do. I was working on the conference when I noticed a file folder I didn't recognize buried within a sub-sub-folder. When I clicked on it, I discovered it contained records and correspondence."

"About?" asked Cloris.

Rhetta hesitated, taking a sip of coffee before speaking. "From what I could gather, it appears for some time now Vernon Beckwith has been using free memberships to the Chateau as bribes to doctors and pharmacists."

"Are you talking Medicare fraud?" asked Cloris.

Rhetta shook her head. "No, for writing and filling fraudulent prescriptions."

"Opioids?" I asked.

When Rhetta nodded, red flags began popping up throughout my cerebral cortex. Last year the attorneys general of several states had charged a group of pharmaceutical companies with pushing the highly addictive painkillers, resulting in the massive opioid epidemic that has ravaged so many communities across the country the last few years. Several other states had opened criminal investigations.

However, when Zack told me of Beckwith's financial problems, he hadn't mentioned anything about an opioid investigation. "Is Beckwith under investigation?"

"I haven't heard anything one way or the other."

Of course, that could mean New Jersey's attorney general had opened a probe but hadn't yet gone public with it. Under the circumstances, it's not like Beckwith would alert the press. Whoever said all publicity was good publicity hadn't considered the purveyors of criminal activity.

What had I gotten myself into this time? It's not like I'm some nosy neighbor who snoops around looking for trouble. Yet once again, I'd found myself smack in the middle of something best left to the authorities. Worse yet, thanks to Mother Nature, this time it didn't look like the guys in the white hats would be riding to my rescue anytime soon.

"Opioids are big moneymakers," said Rhetta. "Beckwith Pharmaceuticals is teetering on the brink of bankruptcy."

Cloris placed her hands on the table and leaned forward. "Are you making excuses for them?"

Rhetta's jaw dropped. "Of course not! Why would you suggest such a thing? I'm horrified by what I discovered."

Cloris pressed further. "Then why didn't you report it to the police?"

I reached out and placed a hand on Cloris's shoulder. "Deep breath time."

She leaned back against her chair. "I'm sorry, but it's a valid question."

Rhetta was the one who took a deep but shaky breath. "I was afraid I'd lose my job. I didn't know if Marlene was involved or not. I needed time to do a further search of her computer, to see what else she'd hidden, then figure out what to do. But now it's too late. Marlene is dead, and maybe if I had said something, she'd still be alive."

"Whether she was involved or not," I said, "it sounds like someone figured out a way to shore up the Beckwith bottom line.

But Marlene didn't strike me as a woman who would enjoy going broke. So wondering about her involvement makes perfect sense."

Rhetta pushed her plate away, worry clouding her features. "The thing is, though, Marlene never worked at Beckwith Pharmaceuticals. She had no involvement in the company. How would she know what Vernon was doing?"

"What did she do before she retired?" asked Cloris.

"She inherited a small medical supply company from her father," said Rhetta. "Over the years she built it into an international corporation before selling it a few years ago. Rumor has it, she was worth close to a billion dollars."

"That would go a long way toward digging Beckwith out of his financial troubles," said Cloris.

"Do you know how their finances were handled?" I asked. "Did they keep separate or joint accounts?"

"Separate," said Rhetta. "They may have shared everything at one time, but not in the ten years I've worked for her. Marlene was too savvy a businesswoman."

"Maybe Vernon tried to pressure Marlene into bailing him out, and she refused," said Cloris.

"There's another possibility," said Rhetta. "What if Vernon killed Marlene because she was blackmailing him?"

"Is that what you think?" I asked.

Rhetta nodded. "I overheard conversations when she didn't realize I was within earshot. At first, I thought she'd hired a private investigator, looking for evidence that Vernon was having an affair. But that made no sense."

"Why?" asked Cloris.

Rhetta shrugged. "It was no secret that Vernon cheated on Marlene. But Marlene also cheated on Vernon."

Cloris's eyebrows shot up under her pixie bangs. "At her age? The woman was in her seventies, wasn't she?"

I knew from the murder that had occurred last summer at the Sunnyside of Westfield Assisted Living and Rehabilitation Center that some elderly women continue to enjoy robust sex lives. So it didn't surprise me that even at her age, Marlene might have been having an affair.

"I never understood why Marlene and Vernon stayed married," said Rhetta, "given how much they seemed to hate each other. But once I saw what was in those files, I realized she probably hired someone to hack into Vernon's personal computer."

"If she had nothing to do with the company, and she and Vernon rarely spoke," I asked, "how would Marlene even suspect Vernon was involved in criminal activity?"

"I can't answer that," said Rhetta. "Possibly a whistleblower? Or a disgruntled employee?"

"A whistleblower would have gone to the police," I said.

"And a disgruntled employee wouldn't know if Marlene could be trusted," said Cloris.

"Unless," I said, "the disgruntled employee had a relationship with Marlene. Or was working for her."

Rhetta's eyes grew wide. "You think Marlene had someone on the inside spying on Vernon?"

"She was a total control freak, wasn't she?"

"Absolutely," said Rhetta.

"Then it stands to reason she'd want to know what Vernon was doing," I said. "Especially if she didn't trust him. What better way than to pay off someone on the inside? Someone who learned what Vernon was up to and told Marlene. She then paid someone to hack into his computer to gain evidence."

"And once Marlene had proof of the fraud," said Cloris, "she blackmailed Vernon? Even though she was a millionaire many times over in her own right?"

"She wouldn't have done it for the money," said Rhetta.

"Then what?" asked Cloris.

"Revenge."

"If Marlene planned to expose Vernon," I said, "and he found out, he'd have everything to gain by eliminating her. Both her money and her silence."

"So you think Vernon killed Marlene?" asked Rhetta.

"No," I said. "Men like that pay others to do their dirty work for them."

"Like Marlene's full-of-himself personal physician?" asked Cloris.

I nodded. "The doctor certainly had both the means and opportunity. Given the missing tea service and pills, he easily could have tampered with either her tea or meds. Maybe both, just to be on the safe side."

"You think Vernon made Dr. Hargrove an offer he couldn't refuse?" asked Rhetta.

"I certainly think it's a possibility. Dr. Hargrove strikes me as a man who enjoys the finer things in life, whether he can afford them or not."

"How would you know that?" asked Rhetta.

"His Burberry cashmere overcoat sells for several thousand dollars, and it didn't look like a hand-me-down from some rich uncle."

"Time out," said Cloris. She turned to face me as she executed the traditional T-sign with her hands. "Not to change the subject, but how in the world do you know the cost of Burberry cashmere overcoats?"

"Ricardo," I said, wrinkling my nose at the unpleasant memory of Karl's loan shark.

Cloris nodded. "I forgot about him."

"I wish I could." A year ago, I got caught up in a failed police sting that required me to make a purchase at Burberry, luckily with law enforcement funds. It was my one and only foray into the designer boutique at the Mall at Short Hills. I quickly learned that crafts editors at third-rate women's magazines don't make enough money to support a Burberry habit. Even the cost of their signature plaid scarves blew my mind.

"Who's Ricardo?" asked Rhetta.

"That's a story for another time and place," I said. "Bottom line, money is often a huge motivator, especially when dealing with the greedy and unscrupulous."

"That certainly fits Dr. Hargrove," said Rhetta.

I popped a grape into my mouth. "What can you tell us about him?"

"He arrived about six months ago."

"Do you know who hired him?" I asked.

Rhetta shook her head. "Not the Chateau. I'm guessing either Vernon or Marlene."

"Any chance you can find out?"

"I'll try. There may be something on Marlene's computer. Feel free to check. Her password is HEARMEROAR. All caps."

"From *I am Woman*?" I asked.

Puzzlement settled over Rhetta's features. "What's that?"

Cloris and I rolled our eyes. "A song from the early seventies," I said.

Rhetta shrugged. "Way before my time."

"Ours, too," said Cloris, "but the song is a classic."

"If you say so." Rhetta shrugged again. "I figured the password was because she liked to throw her weight around. Anyway, what I can tell you is that right from the start Dr. Hargrove constantly fawned over Marlene."

"In what way?" I asked.

"In a creepy old geezer sort of way, except he's young enough to be her grandson."

Cloris shuddered. "You think they were sleeping together? Ick!"

Rhetta nodded in agreement. "I know, right?"

"Do you have any proof of an affair between them?" I asked.

"No, but it wouldn't surprise me. Marlene loved the attention he showered on her."

"I wonder when Marlene last updated her will," I said.

Rhetta's eyes grew wide. "You think he was after her money?"

"Sounds like he was definitely after something," I said.

~*~

Rhetta arranged for us to have two connecting rooms for the night and carte blanche at the well-stocked boutique within Spa de la Mer Violette. We were gifted with an array of toiletries and cosmetics, along with pajamas, fuzzy socks, and a change of clothes for the next day. Our rooms included a complimentary plush robe and slippers.

"I could get used to this," said Cloris, executing a jeté across the exposed polished hardwood floor not covered by a thick Persian rug, before leaping onto her four-poster bed.

"Good thing Rhetta arranged to comp us," I said. "Can you imagine submitting the cost of a night at Beckwith Chateau on our expense reports?"

Cloris laughed. "The pencil pushers would bust a gut. This certainly isn't our usual Holiday Inn accommodations."

"And we don't have to share a room as if we were back in a college dorm."

Cloris needed to call her husband, and I needed to call Zack. We closed the connecting door, arranging to meet in a few minutes to begin judging the needlework competition in the Grenoble Ballroom.

I climbed onto the bed, leaned back against an array of pillows that covered the lower half of a massive carved headboard, and placed my call. I could hear the relief in Zack's voice the moment he answered. "I'm fine," I assured him. "Cloris and I are being treated like royalty. Everything okay on your end?"

"As long as we don't lose power. Right now our biggest problem is coaxing Mephisto outside to do his business. That dog is a wuss."

"And his owner?"

"Still not back from wherever she headed with Harriet."

"I hope wherever they are, they have enough common sense to stay hunkered down."

"Those two are on law enforcement's radar twenty-four/seven. Both the Westfield and Union County PD have you on speed dial," he assured me. "You'd hear immediately if something had happened."

"You're right. They're probably binge-watching *Ninety Day Fiancé* or *The Real Housewives of Atlanta*." My mother-in-law, for all her communist commentary about American television, had been outed months ago as a reality TV junkie.

"You're lucky," I added. "I know what it's like to deal with

Lucille during a power outage. It's not pretty."

"I am lucky," he agreed, "but I miss you."

"You have Ralph."

"Not quite the same. He doesn't put his cold feet on me at night."

"And that's a bad thing?"

"I've grown accustomed to your cold feet. Listen," he said, changing the subject. "The storm is supposed to continue into tomorrow. You may have to stay a second night before the roads open up again."

"Really? I haven't had a chance to catch any weather reports."

"They're keeping you that busy?"

"Well...there have been some extenuating circumstances."

"What sort of extenuating circumstances?" he asked, dread filling his voice.

"I'm about ninety-nine percent certain someone killed Marlene Beckwith."

TEN

Before Zack could respond, I rattled off the events of the day.

On the other end of the line, I heard him heave a huge sigh, then mutter something unintelligible. Another few seconds ticked by before he said, "So what you're telling me is that you and Cloris are trapped at Beckwith Chateau with a killer on the loose."

"Not necessarily."

"Really? Explain *not necessarily*."

"I think Marlene's husband is behind her death, and he's not here."

"How do you know that?"

"When Rhetta—"

"Hold up a minute. Who's Rhetta?"

"The head concierge and Marlene's personal assistant. When she called Vernon Beckwith after we discovered Marlene's body, he told her he was stuck in depositions and to call Marlene's personal physician."

"But you have no idea whether Beckwith made it back before

the roads shut down. For that matter, you have no proof he ever left the Chateau compound."

"But Rhetta—" I cut myself short. Zack was right. "If he had killed Marlene, he established his alibi by lying to his secretary."

"Or tried to," said Zack. "If so, the guy's a few drams short a dose."

"Because his alibi is easy to check out," I said.

"Along with the timeframe if the murder occurred last night. But how do you know Rhetta was telling the truth about her call to Beckwith?"

"I suppose I don't." My gut told me Rhetta wasn't involved in Marlene's death, but guts have one huge shortcoming. They never supply evidence to back up their instincts. Rhetta may have orchestrated everything and was playing me. She certainly had the opportunity, but what about a motive?

"Nor do you know," continued Zack, "that the doctor ever left the grounds."

"Actually, he lives here."

More muttering ensued before Zack added, "Or that this Rhetta person or someone else isn't your killer."

"I suppose when you put it that way—"

"I *am* putting it that way."

It was my turn to heave a huge sigh.

"You want my advice?" asked Zack.

"Of course."

"Lay low and get out of there the moment the roads open up. I won't get any sleep until you're safely home with me and the boys."

At least he hadn't said he was strapping on his skis, but part of me wished he had. Sometimes a girl could use a white knight riding—or skiing—to her rescue. However, it would do no good if he arrived half frozen to death and having turned blue from frostbite.

~*~

When Cloris and I met up after our calls, she took one look at me and said, "You told Zack, didn't you?"

I nodded. "And you?"

"I took the coward's way out and didn't mention Marlene's death one way or the other."

"I thought about not saying anything, but you're not the one constantly tripping over dead bodies. I had to tell Zack."

"Of course you did."

I studied her features but couldn't tell if she was being sarcastic or not. Instead, I changed the subject. "Let's go judge those needlework projects before we have to head to the baking competition."

Cloris swept her arm in front of her. "Lead on, Macduff."

I grabbed my computer case off the desk. Not that I wanted to lug two laptops around with me the remainder of the day but given those files and what else might be stored on Marlene's laptop, I worried about letting it out of my sight.

We made our way down the sweeping staircase to the rotunda and entered the Grenoble Ballroom. "What's our criteria for judging?" asked Cloris.

I pulled two clipboards from my tote. Each contained twenty-five scoresheets. I'd discarded the remainder once I learned how few stitchers and bakers were actually attending the conference. "With such a wide variety of needlecrafts," I said, "we're basically judging apples and oranges. Not to mention strawberries, plums, bananas, and watermelons."

"Don't forget the lemons," said Cloris, her chin indicating the worst entry of the lot. "She didn't even center her design on the fabric."

I stepped closer to the crewel embroidered floral pillow and frowned at the uneven stitches, non-uniform tension, loose threads, and knots showing through from the back of the fabric. "Truthfully, I'd be hard-pressed to find anything positive to say about this one. Which is why we're only awarding first, second, and third place. We won't return scoresheets or offer any feedback. I really don't want to bring any of these women to tears."

"Or to a tirade," added Cloris.

"That, too." I handed her one of the clipboards. "I've broken down the criteria into three basic categories—design, complexity, and workmanship. Choose the five best entries, then we'll compare notes and whittle the two lists down to pick our winners."

"Any tips?"

I suggested she circle the exhibits clockwise while I headed around the room counter-clockwise. "Do a broad sweep first to pinpoint the crafts that stand any chance of winning. Once you've narrowed down your selections, circle around again, this time jotting down comments and snapping photos on your phone. We can use them as reference later when we compare notes."

In less than ten minutes both Cloris and I had pared down the twenty-five entries to five each. I pulled out my phone to check the time. "We still have nearly half an hour before the start of the baking competition. Let's grab coffee and find a quiet place to discuss our selections."

We were about to step out of the ballroom when a barrel-chested man stormed through the entryway. Cloris leapt to her left, I to my right, both of us narrowly avoiding a collision. "Where is she?" he roared. Fists planted on his hips, he scanned the ballroom.

He wore a pair of plaid golf pants in shades of greens, yellows, and oranges. His knit tangerine golf shirt clashed with the deep crimson anger covering his neck and face.

"Where is who?" I asked, craning my neck to make eye contact. The guy had to be at least six-six with deeply wrinkled and weathered skin and an even deeper scowl. "And by the way," I added, "an apology would be nice."

He squinted piercing glacier blue eyes at me. "Who the hell are you?"

"One of the two women you nearly flattened just now."

"Where's Rhetta?" he demanded, completely ignoring my request.

"How should I know?" I turned to Cloris. "Looks like the *gentleman* is anything but a gentleman."

Cloris eyed him up and down. "Maybe his mama never taught him any manners."

"Maybe he was raised by wolves," I suggested. "Let's go." We turned our backs on him and stepped from the ballroom into the rotunda.

Behind us, he bellowed, "Get back here. I haven't dismissed you."

I glanced back at him. "Not a problem. We've dismissed you."

A cluster of women had gathered near the ballroom entrance. Several of them began clapping as we approached.

"Brava!" said Letitia. "You certainly have chutzpah, my dear."

"For what?" I asked. "Putting an oaf in his place?"

"Do you know who that oaf is?" asked Celeste.

"Haven't a clue and couldn't care less."

"That's Vernon Beckwith," said Georgina.

Cloris and I exchanged a knowing look. Good thing Beckwith had no idea who we were and more importantly, that I had his wife's laptop. I hugged the computer case closer to my body, certain that I knew why he was in search of Rhetta.

Two minutes later, with the case hitched on one shoulder and my purse and tote on the other, I juggled a cup of coffee and plate of miniature French pastries as Cloris and I searched for a quiet corner away from prying stitcher and baker eyes and ears. Not an easy task. Many of the women had realized why we were in the Grenoble Ballroom. They hovered nearby like gnats on a muggy summer evening.

Finally, we had no recourse other than to return to my room. The bedroom included a small seating area with two comfortable reading chairs and a small coffee table where we spread out our scoresheets. "Great minds think alike," said Cloris, comparing her sheets to mine.

We had each chosen the same five needlework designs: a velvet crazy quilt, a silk embroidered bolero jacket with a peony motif, a Scandinavian knitted lap blanket consisting of blocks of individual intricate patterns, a counted cross stitched wedding sampler stitched on linen and incorporating seed beads and brass charms, and a smocked baptismal gown edged in delicate handmade lace.

"That was the easy part," said Cloris. "How do we pick a winner? They're each exceptional in their own way."

I transferred the photos from my phone onto my laptop and placed them side by side. "The crazy quilt, although beautiful, is the easiest craft to master. I'd eliminate that one."

Cloris nodded. "I've made Scandinavian sweaters. They're not that hard as long as you take your time and follow the pattern precisely."

"Agreed." I moved the quilt and lap blanket to my trashcan.

"That leaves us with the jacket, baptismal gown, and wedding sampler," she said. "Never having attempted any of those crafts, I'll bow to your expertise in ranking them."

I enlarged the three remaining designs and studied them for a minute. Finally, I said, "I'm tempted to use the eeny-meeny-miny-moe method, but I suppose that wouldn't be quite fair."

"So how do we choose?"

"The sampler and baptismal gown both incorporate more than one craft," I said, "but it's not that difficult to add beadwork and charms to a cross stitched piece. I'd award third place to the wedding sampler."

"But the jacket only features embroidery," said Cloris.

"True, but that silk embroidery is museum quality craftsmanship. Let's give second place to the jacket and first place to the baptismal gown. Of all the crafts, the lace and smocking are the most difficult, and in this case, the workmanship is flawless."

"Sounds good to me," said Cloris.

Our task completed, I pulled out a sheet of Chateau stationery from the desk that sat in a corner of the room and listed the winners to give to Rhetta. Then we headed downstairs to retrieve our coats for our trek across the compound to the Rouen Conference Center.

Once downstairs we discovered the Chateau's shuttlebus parked in the port cochere, waiting to ferry us and the others to the conference center. We squeezed onto the bus and grabbed two of the remaining seats. "This definitely beats traipsing through icy rain," said Cloris.

Someone seated behind us tapped me on the shoulder. When I turned around, Arla asked, "Did you pick the winners?"

I offered her a friendly smile. "Sorry, that information is on a need-to-know basis."

"Well, I hope Marlene wins. It's the least you can do, given her untimely death."

The least I could do? She made it sound like I had a hand in Marlene's death. I bit down on my tongue for a count of ten, then pasted a not-so-friendly smile on my face. "The judging is blind. I have no idea who created each of the needlework designs and won't learn the names of the winners until they're announced at tomorrow's banquet."

"There are ways to find out," she said, offering me a wink.

"But that would spoil the surprise." I shifted in my seat to face forward, putting an end to the conversation.

"You'd think we were choosing the winner of *Time* Magazine's Person of the Year," muttered Cloris.

I suppose I shouldn't have been surprised by the cutthroat attitudes of these women. After all, they had clawed their way up the corporate ladder at a time when most of their peers were relegated to secretarial positions. "They certainly take competition to new heights," I whispered back.

Cloris shot Arla a quick look over her shoulder before adding, "Or new lows."

Shortly thereafter the bus arrived at the entrance to the conference center. Everyone filed off and entered the building. After we shed our coats, the eight women who had made it through the first round of elimination, plus Letitia and Georgina, took up positions at their stations.

No one offered any objection to the participation of the two women previously banned from the premises, even though neither had taken part in the first round. With Marlene no longer able to object, perhaps the board had made an executive decision to allow them to participate.

The other women gathered in seats around the perimeter of the room to watch the competition. The minutes ticked by as we waited for Rhetta to arrive. Five minutes turned into ten and ten into fifteen. "The natives are growing restless," observed Cloris as the room swelled with mutters of annoyance.

Finally, Rhetta entered the room. Her entire body radiated anger. And something more, evident as her gaze darted around the room liked trapped prey—fear.

After completing her scan of the room, she inhaled a deep breath and stepped to the mic. "Good afternoon," she said, her voice slightly shaky. "Sorry I'm late. We'll extend the competition time to make up for the delay."

She then gave the remaining contestants their challenge for the afternoon, a croquembouche. "And your dessert must incorporate spring flavors," she added. "You have three hours. Your time starts now."

"What's a croquembouche?" I asked Cloris as the contestants uttered a collective groan. Thinking back to high school French, I remembered that *bouche* translated to *mouth* and *croque* meant *bite*. But *croquem* rang no vocabulary bells for me.

Cloris pulled out her phone and brought up a picture to show me. "It's a tower of cream puffs held together with caramel."

Once I saw the photo, I realized I'd not only previously seen the confection, but sampled the delicate dessert when Cloris baked one for Christmas a few years ago. "And the name?"

"It means *a crunchy bite*."

"Definitely not a literal translation." I failed to see where the crunchy came from. When she shrugged, I changed the subject. "Are the cream puffs attached to a support armature?"

"Not traditionally, and I don't see anything that our bakers might use to form one. It's a difficult challenge. Lots can go wrong from the pâte à choux not rising to the tower collapsing. There's no room for error in such a limited timeframe."

"I'll stick to crafts," I said as Rhetta made her way over to us.

"We need to talk," she whispered upon arriving. "In private."

She led us from the cavernous room out to the lobby. Even though we were alone, she took a moment to scope out our surroundings before she said, "My apartment was ransacked."

"You drove home in this weather?" I asked.

Rhetta shook her head. "I live on the grounds above the old carriage house. It's a perk of the job."

"Was anything taken?" asked Cloris.

"Not that I could tell. I'm sure I know what he was looking for, though."

"He meaning Vernon?" I asked. "We had a run-in with him earlier."

Rhetta's eyes grew wide. "When?"

"A little while ago in the ballroom. He stormed in demanding to know where you were."

"Why would he ask *you*?"

"I think he thought we were staff."

"Charming man, by the way," said Cloris. "Not."

Rhetta scowled. "Yeah, he made Marlene look like the female version of Mr. Rogers." She glanced down at my computer case. "I'm so glad you have that. He wouldn't suspect you."

"Let's hope not." I patted the case. "This baby doesn't leave my sight, but just in case, I plan to transfer any pertinent files I find onto a jump drive."

"You haven't looked at anything yet?"

"Haven't had time. I'll start as soon as the competition is over. If I don't finish before dinner, it will have to wait until later this evening."

"What do you plan to do when Vernon catches up with you?" asked Cloris.

Rhetta shrugged. "Depends what he wants. If he's looking for Marlene's computer, I can honestly say I don't have it." She paused and offered us a wicked grin. "Then I'll mention the missing jewelry box and suggest he speak with both the good doctor and the funeral personnel who removed Marlene's body."

She nodded toward the door that led into the competition area. "For now, the two of you had better get back inside. I'll return right before the end of the competition."

~*~

Rhetta arrived back at the conference center three hours later to call time's up on the second round of the baking competition, the results of which were more croquem*bust* than croquembouche. Afterwards, she quickly departed the conference center without saying anything further to either the competitors or to Cloris and me.

Of the ten semi-finalists, two had failed to complete the challenge. The remaining eight bakers squeaked over the finish line with mere seconds to spare, only to have two of the towers immediately collapse. None of the desserts looked anything like the mouth-watering photo Cloris had shown me.

ELEVEN

By the time the competition ended, so had the icy rain and sleet, hopefully for good. Everyone carefully filed into the shuttlebus for the quick trip back to the Chateau. A gloom had descended over the semi-finalists who had taken part in the croquembouche challenge.

Several rows behind me, I heard Wanda say, "I wonder how many croquembouche Marlene made over the last few weeks to perfect her skills so she could tip the scales in her favor."

Across the aisle from where Cloris and I sat, Georgina twisted in her seat to face toward the back of the bus and responded, "Karma's a royal B, ladies."

"It certainly didn't seem right that she chose the challenges," said Jacqueline.

"Maybe she didn't," said Arla, once again defending her longtime friend. "Do any of you know for a fact that Marlene tried to rig the competition? That she chose the challenges? Or that she sent the bribes that were made to look like they came from Letitia and Georgina?"

When no one offered any proof, she issued a snort and added, "I didn't think so." Her comment silenced any further conversation on the topic for the remainder of the short drive.

After the shuttlebus parked in front of the main entrance to the Chateau, Cloris and I waited in our seats until the others had queued up in the aisle and began exiting. By the time we entered the building, the lobby was empty except for Tanner and Justin. The two young men lurked outside Rhetta's office, their ears plastered to her door as they eavesdropped on a shouting match going on within. Cloris and I crept closer, using one of the massive potted plants as cover.

"I know you have it," shouted a male voice.

"Looks like Vernon Beckwith finally caught up with Rhetta," I whispered to Cloris.

"And what makes you think that?" asked Rhetta. "Could it be because you trashed both Marlene's house and my apartment looking for it?"

"How dare you!"

"Oh, I dare! Instead of accusing me, maybe you should talk to that pompous ass of a doctor you hired to keep an eye on your wife."

Beckwith sputtered. "What the—? How...how did you—?"

"How did I find out? I didn't. It was a wild guess. Which you've just confirmed. By the way, her jewelry is also missing."

Cloris whispered in my ear. "Way to go, Rhetta."

I had wondered how Rhetta planned to find out if Beckwith had hired the doctor. Now I began to speculate on what other connections might tie the two men together.

Beckwith continued with his accusations, "How do I know

you didn't take her jewelry along with her laptop?"

"Because I'm the one telling you about it, and I'm not a thief."

"Really? And I'm supposed to take your word?"

"Fine. You don't trust me? Then why don't you call the cops? I'm sure they'd be interested in hearing from you concerning the possible murder of your wife."

"What the hell are you talking about? Marlene died from natural causes."

"Did she?"

"Of course, she did. And since when do you have a medical degree?"

"It doesn't take a doctor to realize your wife's death is extremely suspicious."

"There was nothing suspicious about Marlene's death. She had severe health problems."

"Prove it. Request an autopsy."

"There will be no autopsy."

"Why not? What are you afraid of?"

"I'm not afraid of anything. I haven't done anything wrong."

"That's debatable."

"Are you accusing me of killing my wife?"

"Did you?"

"Of course not!"

"Then why no autopsy?"

"Because she's already been cremated."

Rhetta's voice hit a glass-shattering octave as she screamed, "What?!"

Cloris and I exchanged jaw-dropping looks. With the main body of evidence destroyed—no pun intended—case closed. Vernon Beckwith and/or Marlene's personal physician would get away with murder.

"At her request," continued Beckwith.

"How convenient," said Rhetta, her voice dripping with sarcasm. "I suppose you have some proof of that?"

"I don't need to provide you with proof."

"No, but maybe you'll need to provide it to the police."

"So now you're also a detective?"

"No, but I'll bet the cops will be curious about the timing. Seems awfully convenient, especially in the middle of a storm that shut down all the roads."

"The hearse arrived before the shutdown."

"How lucky for you," she sneered. "Maybe you'd also like to explain why, along with her laptop and jewelry, Marlene's medication is missing."

"Don't be stupid. Pills are worth money. Someone took advantage of the storm to break into a few of the residences on the estate."

"Targeting only Marlene's house and my apartment?"

"You're closest to the service road. Finding nothing, he went on to Marlene's house where he hit the motherlode and decided not to press his luck."

"What about the surveillance cameras around the perimeter? They picked up nothing last night. I checked."

"Maybe the thief was a delivery person who had scoped out the camera locations on a previous visit."

"Since you seem to have so many answers, what about the china teacup that held the remains of Marlene's evening chamomile? Why is that missing? Are you going to tell me the thief mistook it for a priceless antique?"

When Beckwith blustered something unintelligible, Rhetta

said, "I'm willing to take a lie detector test, are you?"

"I don't have to put up with this insolence. I should fire you right now."

"Go ahead."

Several seconds of silence ensued during which I envisioned Rhetta and Beckwith, both with arms crossed over their chests, staring down each other. Finally, he roared, "This isn't over."

Suddenly Tanner and Justin darted away from the door. Cloris and I took our cue and rushed down the hall to avoid being discovered. We ducked into the Chartres Library just as Vernon Beckwith stormed down the hall.

After a few minutes we made our way back to Rhetta's office. When I rapped lightly on her door, she shouted, "Go away!"

"It's Anastasia and Cloris." A moment later the door swung open and a puffy-eyed Rhetta ushered us inside.

"Vernon just left," she said.

"We know," said Cloris.

"He already had Marlene's body cremated."

"We heard," I said. When her eyes widened, I explained. "Tanner and Justin also heard."

"Great!" Rhetta collapsed into her desk chair, grabbed a tissue, and blew her nose. Now what?"

"Now," I said, "I go upstairs and search through Marlene's computer."

~*~

With limited time prior to dinner, I first decided to download all of Marlene's files to my Trimedia cloud storage for safekeeping. Once I began opening individual folders and files to check the contents, I'd also transfer anything pertinent to a jump drive. Given we had no proof of a murder—and now never would—and a desperate killer was in search of whatever was stored on the laptop, redundancy seemed an appropriate precaution.

Once I finished the transfer to the cloud, I opened the folder Rhetta had indicated she'd found. "Holy guacamole!"

"Success?" asked Cloris from her adjoining room.

"I'll say. If this stuff is legit, it's explosive. It appears that Marlene hired a private investigator who somehow gained access to Vernon's personal computer. I'm guessing either he hacked into it or hired someone to do it for him."

"Anyone you know?" she asked, entering my room.

I knew she referred to Tino Martinez, former Special Forces and my own personal hacker extraodinaire who had saved my life on more than one occasion. "No name mentioned. I suppose it's possible, but that would be some coincidence." Still, I made a mental note to shoot Tino a text later.

I continued reading. "I think Rhetta stopped looking when she found the quid pro quo between Vernon and the doctors and pharmacists. It gets worse."

"How much worse?"

"Life imprisonment worse. According to one of the investigator's reports, not only was Vernon trading Chateau memberships in exchange for doctors and pharmacists pushing his opioids, but the investigator found evidence of someone running a fentanyl ring within Beckwith Pharmaceuticals."

Cloris whistled under her breath. "Given his current financial troubles, if that got out, Vernon Beckwith can kiss his company goodbye."

"Not to mention his freedom," I added. "Depending on his involvement, he might be trading his fancy golf duds for an orange jumpsuit. And we already know he doesn't look good in orange, especially when he's angry."

Cloris chuckled, then quickly sobered. "No wonder he's so eager to get his hands on Marlene's laptop."

"If she was threatening to expose him, it's also a darned good motive for murder."

"Too bad we can't skip dinner and order room service," she said. "I have a feeling finding out what else is hidden on that laptop will be more interesting than sitting through another Stitch and Bake dinner and judging round."

I raised an eyebrow. "Really? After last night I'm wondering what bombshell might drop tonight."

"Please, don't even think it! With Marlene gone, I'm hoping for no drama this evening other than some disappointment from the bakers who don't make it to the final round of the competition."

I laughed as I powered down Marlene's laptop. "With those women? Good luck with that. I'm expecting nothing but drama until Beckwith Chateau is in our rearview mirror."

"Let's just hope it doesn't involve another murder."

~*~

Our second dinner at the Chateau featured a salad of spring greens with sliced pear and blue cheese dressing, followed by duck l'orange with mashed potatoes, and grilled asparagus. At least Beckwith Chateau fed us well, unlike the standard conference chicken, always tough and dry, which both Cloris and I had suffered through at countless other business events.

The Stitch and Bake ladies had once again dressed for dinner in a variety of styles that harkened back to the fashions of the nineteen-sixties. So far over the past two days, not a single conference attendee had worn anything but retro sixties outfits. I wondered if they had unanimously chosen the decade as a theme for the conference or since retiring, routinely wore clothing they never would have dared to wear to the office when the styles were popular.

Once again, after the staff cleared away the dinner dishes, they rolled in carts with the eight entries for the second round of judging. "Why are the two with collapsed towers included?" I asked Cloris. "They failed the challenge."

She shrugged. "I'm not sure, but since we're judging on both taste and presentation, we might find the quality of the bake outweighs the failure of the structure."

"I'm just hoping we don't have another salt incident. Just in case, though, I plan to take extremely small nibbles."

"Smart woman," said Cloris. "You learn fast."

In the end, picking the four finalists proved far more difficult than the first challenge. Every croquembouche had major flaws. One had deflated cream puffs. Another consisted entirely of outer crust. One was slightly overbaked, another not baked enough, resulting in centers of raw dough. One baker had added too much lemon extract to her filling, leaving a powerful chemical aftertaste in our mouths. Another had burnt the caramel used to assemble her tower.

Rather than choosing the four best croquembouche, we wound up with our finalists by eliminating the four worst. For that reason, the two toppled towers moved on to tomorrow's deciding round of competition, along with a slightly overbaked entry and the one with burnt caramel.

Cloris rose to announce the numbers corresponding to the croquembouche whose bakers would move on to the final round. These turned out to be Letitia, Georgina, Arla, and Jacqueline.

Arla and Georgina had baked the two croquembouche that failed the presentation part of the challenge.

Needless to say, vociferous complaints arose from the four eliminated bakers. "My croquembouche is perfectly symmetrical," whined Wanda. She stabbed a finger toward the two toppled croquembouche. "How can you eliminate me over either of those?"

"What's wrong with mine?" asked a woman seated to the side of the room.

"Maybe the judges were paid off," accused Joy. "Not by Marlene, obviously, but by whoever baked the ones that collapsed."

A crescendo of accusations arose throughout the room. "Talk about sore losers," whispered Cloris.

"I know you didn't want to offer critiques," I said, "but I think we need to justify our choices."

"Agreed." Cloris beckoned a member of the waitstaff over to our table.

"Yes, ma'am?"

"When you serve the desserts, make sure everyone is served a sampling of each of the eight croquembouche."

He nodded, then headed back to convey the instructions to the other staff members.

As the croquembouche were divided up and served, Cloris rose from her seat to address the room. "We know some of you are disappointed. This was an extremely difficult challenge, and unfortunately, every entry had problems. Yes, two of the croquembouche collapsed after the end of the competition and prior to the judging. However, the outcome ultimately came down to taste. We believe when you bite into your desserts, you'll not only understand our decision but agree with us."

For the most part, they did, although the four women eliminated continued to grumble, Wanda the loudest. "Suck it up," Hildy told her. "You weren't competing for a Nobel Prize. It's a stupid baking contest. Besides, you deserved to lose. What were you thinking, using extract instead of lemon juice and zest?"

With her lower lip trembling and her cheeks deepening to a shade of purple that clashed with her vintage yellow and orange madras plaid shirtdress ball gown, Wanda somehow managed to level a piercing glare at Hildy before pushing away from the table and fleeing the room.

"Harsh," muttered Cloris. "Not what you'd expect from a retired psychologist."

"Unless her practice espoused tough love," I said, "but I wouldn't think tough love involves embarrassing a person in front of her peers."

Puzzlement clouded Cloris's features. "I thought she was a corporate psychologist. Not that I have a clue as to what that is."

"Beats me. I'm just a former art teacher and current women's magazine crafts editor."

But with my curiosity piqued, I once again accessed the website of the New Jersey chapter of the Stitch and Bake Society, this time to learn more about Hildy. "Says here she owned a company that administered and evaluated psychological tests for prospective employees of Fortune Five Hundred corporations."

"Impressive. But was she a practicing psychologist?"

"Not according to her bio. At any rate, these women could all stand a trip to the nail salon to have their claws trimmed."

"Agreed."

Dinner broke up a short time later. As the stitchers and bakers exited the ballroom, I noticed plates of mostly uneaten croquembouche remained on every table. "So, do you think Marlene chose every challenge?" I asked Cloris as we followed the women from the room.

"I'd bet money on it. Didn't Rhetta tell us Marlene chose the cookie challenge? And she dictated what we'd present at our workshops."

"True. From what we've seen so far, it looks like she controlled every aspect of the conference. I wonder what's in store for the remaining bakers tomorrow."

She shrugged. "My guess is it's bound to be more difficult than croquembouche."

We climbed the rotunda staircase and made our way down the hall to our rooms. As I went to insert my keycard, I noticed my door wasn't latched shut. Had I forgotten to pull it completely closed earlier? Had housekeeping slipped up after performing the evening turndown service? Or did something more sinister await me on the other side of the door? I wasn't about to take any chances. With one hand I placed an index finger to my lips while my other hand reached for Cloris's arm and rushed us back toward the staircase. No way was I about to walk into that room without backup.

We found Justin in the lobby. "Stay here," he said when I told him someone might be in my room. "I'll check it out."

Minutes later he returned, a deep frown furrowing his brow. "Both rooms were tossed," he said. "You'll have to check to see what's missing. Did either of you leave any valuables in the rooms?"

"There's nothing of value in either room," I said. I knew we wouldn't find anything missing because the item the thief wanted was snug against my hip. However, I wasn't going to divulge that information to Justin. "Do you know if any other rooms were searched?"

"All the other doors are locked. As far as I know, no one else has reported a problem." He eyed the computer bags both Cloris and I carried. "Do you think someone was after something on your computers?"

Something *on* our computers? I eyed Justin warily. Had Beckwith paid him to search our rooms? "Like what?"

He shrugged. "Some people have all sorts of personal stuff on their computers. A stolen laptop could lead to identity theft."

"This is my work laptop," I said. "I'm a crafts editor. The only files anyone would find are articles and craft projects for upcoming issues and the slide presentations for this conference. And that's assuming the thief could figure out my password, which I doubt."

He turned to Cloris. "And you, ma'am?"

"Same for me, except I'm the food editor. The thief would find nothing more than recipes, along with the slide presentations for the conference."

"Plus," I added, "all we'd have to do is access the Find My Computer feature on our phones, and we'd be able to locate the laptops and the thief."

I didn't mention the additional thought bouncing around in my brain—that the thief may not have planned to take the laptop, only download the files. He'd still be out of luck, though, since I'd powered down Marlene's computer before we left for dinner. Then again, he may have known her password.

"Of course," said Justin. "I've read that most thieves get caught because they're stupid." He shook his head. "First Mrs. Beckwith's house was ransacked, then Rhetta's apartment, now this. I'm not looking forward to filing a report on another Chateau break-in. Mr. Beckwith is going to have a cow."

Given what I'd discovered so far on Marlene's computer, more than likely, Beckwith was already in labor birthing twin bovines— if not triplets. I also had a feeling that the more I dug, the more incriminating evidence I'd find.

But what made Beckwith suspect either Cloris or I had Marlene's laptop?

TWELVE

"Maybe Beckwith saw us with Rhetta and figured she might have given the laptop to one of us," said Cloris after we returned to our rooms and began straightening up the mess. Cleanup was swift, though, the thief having left nowhere near the havoc he'd wrought at Marlene's home. Then again, the two rooms with adjoining baths contained little to search other than the items we'd gotten from Spa de la Mer Violette. Fifteen minutes later I had slipped into a pair of pink silk pajamas and matching fuzzy socks from the spa boutique and wrapped myself in the Beckwith Chateau's complimentary plush white robe. Then I propped myself up against the bed's numerous decorator pillows to continue my search through Marlene's laptop.

This time I started with her text messages. Luckily, Marlene had the ability to send and receive texts from either her phone or her laptop and hadn't deleted older messages.

Given the temptation, I wondered if she had ever realized the extent of Rhetta's devotion. It became immediately obvious to me that Marlene's personal assistant had never deliberately invaded her privacy, no matter how easy it would have been to do so. If she had, she would have uncovered far more information and possible evidence of criminal activity than she'd divulged to us.

I called to Cloris through the open door adjoining both rooms. "I can confirm Marlene and the doctor definitely had a relationship that crossed professional physician/patient boundaries."

Also garbed in pajamas and robe, Cloris stepped into my room. She curled up in one of the cream and Wedgewood blue striped upholstered club chairs that flanked the room's fireplace. "Please spare me the details," she said, stretching her legs onto a matching ottoman and flipping open her own laptop. "But while you're traveling that voyeuristic route, I'll do an Internet search on Hargrove."

"Good idea."

"Hmm," she said a few minutes later.

I had already exited out of Marlene's text chain with Hargrove, having read enough to sear my eyeballs and turn my stomach. However, I couldn't quite figure out who was manipulating whom in the relationship and to what end. Both Marlene and Hargrove appeared to have hidden agendas. "What have you found?"

"Dr. Chadwell Hargrove is a fourth-generation medical doctor but not the brightest tongue depressor in the stack."

I raised an eyebrow. "It says that?"

"Not in so many words. You have to read between the lines. His father, grandfather, and great-grandfather all graduated from prestigious medical programs—Harvard, Columbia, and Vanderbilt. Chad the Fourth attended medical school in the Caribbean. My guess is he didn't get in anywhere else, even with the help of family money. The Hargroves are loaded."

"Loaded enough to hold a Beckwith Chateau membership?"

"Probably," said Cloris, "but doubtful. They hail from Boston. Besides, wouldn't Rhetta have known if they were members?"

"True," I said, "but if Vernon hired him, my guess is there's a connection between the two of them. How else would he have known he could trust Hargrove to do his bidding when it came to Marlene?"

"And did his duties extend to murder?"

"It's looking more and more likely, especially if Beckwith had either blackmailed Hargrove or dangled enough cash in front of him."

"I'll keep digging."

Meanwhile, I began a methodical search of the contents of each folder on Marlene's laptop. Given the information she'd buried in the conference folder, what else might she have hidden elsewhere?

"I found the connection," said Cloris a short time later. "Vernon and Hargrove the Third attended the same prep school. Daddy secured a job for sonny at Beckwith Pharmaceuticals once he graduated from the island med school for mediocre students."

"Probably because he couldn't get hired by any hospital or practice."

"Not if human resources scoured his social media. You'd think the guy majored in frat parties in college, not pre-med. It's no wonder he didn't get into a U.S. medical school."

"Makes you wonder how he graduated med school."

"Probably with a few well-placed bribes. He was never accepted into a residency program." Cloris glanced up from her computer screen. "Can you even practice medicine if you haven't completed a residency?"

"I don't know." I opened another browser on Marlene's computer and typed in the question. "According to Google, it depends on the state. Some states will grant a medical license after med school and an internship."

"Is New Jersey one of them?"

I searched further. "No, and without a license, options are limited to practicing non-clinical medicine such as a clinical research associate, medical science liaison, public health analyst, or pharmaceutical researcher."

Cloris and I silently stared at each other as the magnitude of this set in. As Marlene's concierge physician, Hargrove was practicing medicine without a license. Finally, I asked, "How long had he worked for Beckwith Pharmaceuticals before becoming Marlene's personal physician and gigolo?"

Cloris clicked a few keys. "According to what's posted on social media, about a year."

"Does he mention the position he held?"

"He oversees drug trials."

"Oversees? Not oversaw?"

"There's no mention of him leaving," she said. "Maybe Beckwith hired him for both positions at the same time."

I reminded her that Rhetta had said Hargrove began working as Marlene's concierge physician six months ago. "I wonder if Beckwith knew Hargrove had never practiced medicine when he hired him to keep an eye on Marlene."

Cloris knit her brows together. "I wonder if he cared."

"What's more," I said, "his position at Beckwith Pharmaceuticals would probably give him access to fentanyl and other opioids, along with the ability to doctor the books to hide the missing inventory. I'm guessing Hargrove runs the fentanyl ring—with or without Beckwith's knowledge."

"Certainly takes the Hippocratic oath to an entirely new level," said Cloris. "Maybe Beckwith found out and threatened Hargrove. If he didn't get rid of Marlene for him, he'd turn him over to the Feds. But wouldn't a pharmaceutical company have enough controls to prevent any one employee from stealing large quantities of drugs? Not to mention security cameras positioned all over the place?"

"You'd think, but I suppose an enterprising drug lord wannabe could find a workaround. Besides, we don't know that Hargrove worked alone. There could be an entire drug gang within the walls of Beckwith Pharmaceuticals. Hargrove may be the ringleader or simply one cog in the machine."

"Beckwith could be the ringleader," suggested Cloris.

"An even more plausible possibility."

"So what do we do with all this information, supposition, and speculation?" she asked.

"I'm sending everything I've found so far to Detective Spader, along with possible theories. He'll contact the proper authorities."

"I like the sound of that," she said. "Let the guys with the badges handle the guys up to no good and keep us far removed from all of it."

After a few more hours of surfing through Marlene's laptop and finding no further explosive revelations, I decided to call it a night. I'd only checked out the files in about a third of the folders so far, but I'd reached the point where I could no longer focus my brain or my eyes. I forwarded the relevant files to Detective Spader, along with a lengthy email, then powered down the computer for the night.

Before we turned in, both Cloris and I not only made certain we flipped the security latches, but we also shoved one of the heavy club chairs in front of each door. Someone desperate to get his hands on Marlene's laptop was hiding in plain sight somewhere on the Chateau grounds. Whether it was Beckwith, Hargrove, or someone working for one of them, I wanted to make sure, he didn't pay us a surprise return visit in the middle of the night.

Unfortunately, I found it impossible to relax enough to fall asleep. Every time I closed my eyes, my brain unleashed a torrent of unwelcome thoughts that kept Mr. Sandman at bay. At midnight I gave in to the insomnia, grabbed Marlene's laptop from the nightstand, and continued my search.

Up to this point, I'd found the private investigator's reports with proof that Vernon had paid off doctors to write opioid prescriptions and evidence of a fentanyl ring operating out of Beckwith Pharmaceuticals. I also knew that Marlene was having an affair with her doctor, a man young enough to be her grandson, who wasn't licensed to practice medicine, and who may be involved in the fentanyl ring.

What I hadn't found was what Marlene had planned to do with the information from the hack. Was she blackmailing Vernon? And if so, to what end? She certainly didn't need his money. Besides, Vernon was teetering on the brink of bankruptcy. Was her goal to push him over that brink? Or was she accumulating enough evidence to make sure he was locked up for the remainder of his days? Would she then gain control of Beckwith's various holdings, including the Chateau and country club? Could that have been her endgame?

I found it hard to believe that with what I'd already discovered on her computer, Marlene hadn't buried the answers to these questions in some file. I simply had to locate that file. Because discovering Marlene's intent might also lead to unmasking her killer.

As I opened and scanned various documents, it occurred to me that the answers I sought might lie in some of her email correspondence. Once I completed a perusal of the files in the latest folder, I detoured to her email.

I found three email accounts, one which Marlene used for the Stitch and Bake Society, one for personal correspondence, and one connected to Rx-Consolidated, the corporation that had bought her company. Out of curiosity, I started with that one and was surprised to learn Marlene had held a seat on the Rx-Consolidated board. However, knowing little of the workings of the higher echelons of corporate America, maybe it was customary for the former owner of a company to negotiate a seat on the board of the purchasing company.

My only personal experience with one corporation buying another was Trimedia's acquisition of the former Reynolds-Alsopp Publishing Company. Hugo Reynolds-Alsopp had remained as publisher of our magazines but in name only. He wasn't offered a seat on the Trimedia board and had no say in corporate decisions. Then again, that transaction had been more of a hostile takeover than a mutually desired sale.

The emails in the company account turned up nothing beyond the minutes from board meetings and the company's monthly financial statements. I found no personal correspondence between Marlene and anyone connected to Rx-Consolidated.

I moved on to her personal account, hoping to find emails between her and Vernon. Surprisingly, I found none. If Marlene and Vernon communicated with each other, it wasn't through email unless she had deleted all of them. This seemed unlikely under the circumstances. Emails probably existed. After all, according to Rhetta, Marlene and Vernon rarely spoke. She'd have to communicate with him in some way since they were still married, unless they only communicated through their lawyers. But if that were the case, there should be emails from the lawyers. However, I found none of those in that account, either.

I'd have to redouble my efforts searching through her files. Perhaps Marlene had copied and pasted some of her correspondence into Word documents and squirreled them away in yet another folder.

My eyelids began to droop shortly after two in the morning, signaling sleep would finally take hold. I powered down the laptop, placed it on the nightstand and turned off the light. I was finally drifting into slumberland when I heard voices outside my door.

THIRTEEN

Two men. With adrenaline pounding through my veins, I slipped out of bed, padded my way across the Persian carpet, and placed my ear to the door. Silence greeted me. Had I been dreaming? To be certain, I waited, straining to hear through the thick wooden door, but I picked up no sounds, not even muffled whispers or the creaking of hardwood indicating footfalls down the corridor. After what seemed like an eternity but was probably no more than a few minutes, I returned to bed, only to toss and turn for most of the remainder of the night.

~*~

"You okay?" asked Cloris the next morning as she swept an assessing eye from my head to my toes. "You look like the proverbial morning after the night before."

"What gave me away? My bloodshot eyes? The huge bags under them?" I tried to stifle a yawn but failed miserably. "My inability to stop yawning?"

"How about all three?"

I never could pull anything over on Cloris. "How about you hook me up to a caffeine IV?"

"I'll call down for room service. Go stick your head under a steamy shower."

I took Cloris's advice and headed for the bathroom. The shower helped. I graduated from nearly dead to only half-dead after allowing hot water to sluice over my body for twenty minutes. By the time I'd toweled off and dressed, breakfast had arrived.

Before I told Cloris about my nocturnal adventure, I downed a cup of coffee. Then, as I savored a strip of perfectly crisp bacon, I filled her in on how I came to look like a zombie this morning.

"You may have dreamed hearing voices," she said.

I agreed. "Especially since I heard nothing when I listened at the door."

"I'm glad you didn't do anything foolish."

"Like what?"

"Like shoving the chair aside, unlocking the door, and sticking your head out into the hallway."

I didn't admit I'd thought of doing just that but had quickly come to my senses. What if I had discovered a couple of men lurking in the hall? Ask them if they'd tossed our rooms earlier? That would have planted me firmly in the world of too-stupid-to-live heroines from teen horror movies. I had too much to live for to succumb to such idiocy. I may have gotten myself into some precarious situations throughout the past year but not from acting foolishly.

All I wanted to do was get through the day, making it to the end of the conference without any further incidents, then head home to Zack and my sons, assuming the roads had reopened. The last thing I wanted was to spend another night at Beckwith Chateau. I'd be perfectly happy to leave the investigating of Beckwith and Hargrove to law enforcement professionals.

"Earth to Anastasia." I suddenly realized Cloris was staring at me. "You really zoned out there for a minute. You going to make it through the day?"

I grabbed the carafe and poured myself another cup of coffee. "As long as there's an endless supply of caffeine." I splashed in some cream and added a heaping teaspoon of sugar. I normally drank my coffee sans sweetener, but I knew I'd need a constant sugar rush to make it through today without falling asleep on my feet. Plus lots of protein. And chocolate.

As soon as I devoured my bacon and eggs and drained my coffee cup, I poured a third cup and reached for a chocolate croissant.

Both of our phones pinged an alert at the same moment. With my fingers gooey from chocolate, Cloris was first to grab her phone. "Roads are open," she said.

"And the weather?"

"I'll check." She tapped her screen. "Partly sunny with a high of forty-five today. I don't think we need to worry about icy roads this evening."

At least the weather gods were finally cooperating. We just might get home this evening without suffering through any further storms—literal or figurative.

~*~

Shortly after I stepped into the Bordeaux Room for my morning workshop, Tanner arrived with the cartons of kits. As he transferred them from the luggage cart to one of the tables, I set up my laptop for the slide show that would accompany my hands-on demonstration.

After Tanner finished, he asked, "Anything else you need, ma'am?"

"Yes, you can stop calling me ma'am."

"Pardon?"

"You're making me feel old, Tanner. Please, call me Anastasia."

His cheeks flushed. "I couldn't do that, ma'am. My mother brought me up to respect my elders."

"She must be extremely proud of you, then. How about if we compromise with Mrs. Pollack?"

"Yes, ma'am, Mrs. Pollack."

I shook my head and chuckled. "I'll see you later, Tanner." As usual, he tipped his cap, then departed with the empty rolling cart as the attendees began to file into the room.

"What's in store for us this morning?" asked Jacqueline settling into her seat.

Cloris had joined me and began passing out the kits as I clicked on the first slide. "Hardanger embroidery. Are any of you familiar with the technique?"

"I've heard of it," said Letitia.

"I've seen it in museums but never tried it," said Hildy.

A few others nodded in agreement with both of them.

"It looks hard," said Joy, who sat next to Jacqueline.

"The technique requires both patience and practice," I said, "but once mastered, you'll find it no more difficult than many other forms of needlework."

"Is that a promise?" asked Celeste.

"May I ask what you did before you retired?" I asked her.

"I was the vice-president of a major bank."

"I promise you, mastering Hardanger embroidery will not be

nearly as difficult as understanding countless banking rules and regulations."

"I'm going to hold you to that." She laughed as the room erupted in chuckles.

After the giggles died down, I continued, "Once again, I'd like you to practice on the smaller piece of linen until you feel comfortable enough to tackle the actual project. The secret to Hardanger embroidery is keeping an even tension."

Before beginning the slide presentation, I did a quick head count. "Who's missing?" I asked, coming up one short.

"Wanda," said Hildy. "She's probably still sulking after being eliminated from the baking competition yesterday.

"Has anyone checked on her this morning?"

"No need," said Georgina. "She gets this way sometimes. Eventually, she'll snap out of it."

"Still, maybe one of you should call to make sure she hasn't taken ill."

"She won't answer her phone," said Georgina. "Trust me, we've been down this road with Wanda before."

Such behavior seemed at odds for a successful businesswoman, especially someone who had broken through the glass ceiling at a time when most of her contemporaries remained barefoot, pregnant, and in the kitchen. Then again, most of these women exhibited behavior I wouldn't associate with my preconceptions of groundbreaking women.

However, I didn't press. The other stitchers and bakers knew Wanda far better than I.

I began the slide presentation with a brief history of Hardanger, then segued into working the stitches. The women followed along, alternating their attention between the slides and their stitching. When I got to the part about cutting away the fabric, several women gasped.

"What if I make a mistake?" asked a woman in the front row.

"That's why we're practicing," I said. "Just take your time. Once you get the hang of it, it's not that intimidating."

"Here goes nothing," said Letitia, offering to snip first. She picked up her scissors, held her breath, and trimmed away the first thread. Then the next. And the next. A minute later she'd completed cutting out the small square of exposed linen centered within her stitched blocks. When she released her breath and held up her sample for the others to see, she received a round of applause.

Letitia's bravery instilled courage in the rest of the class, and fewer mishaps ensued than I'd anticipated. Eventually, the women grew comfortable enough with their stitching that they began to chat as they worked.

"I'm beginning to think Beckwith Chateau is haunted," said Jacqueline.

"What makes you say that?" asked Georgina.

"I kept waking up last night, thinking I'd heard noises outside my room, but every time I checked, the hall was empty."

"It's an old house," said Hildy. "They always make noises."

"Noises, yes," said Jacqueline. "I expect to hear pipes banging and wood creaking, but I swear at one point I heard someone talking right outside my door."

So I wasn't dreaming that I'd heard voices outside my room in the wee hours of the morning. Cloris and I exchanged a quick look.

"Come to think of it," said Hildy, "I did, too. Around three this morning. I thought I was dreaming."

"Could have been the housekeeping staff," suggested Letitia.

"What could they possibly be doing up here at that hour?" asked Hildy.

"Nothing," said Jacqueline. "That's why I'm suggesting the place is haunted."

"Don't be ridiculous," said Letitia. "You were probably both dreaming."

"Unless Marlene's ghost is seeking revenge on whoever sabotaged her," said Arla. She paused, then added, "Or killed her."

The other women turned to stare at her. Georgina was the first to recover her voice. "That's absurd. What makes you think someone killed Marlene?"

"What makes you think someone didn't?" Arla countered.

"I thought she died in her sleep," said a woman seated in the third row.

Hildy stood, hands on hips, and glared at Arla. "Are you accusing one of us of killing Marlene?"

"I'm not accusing anyone," said Arla.

"Could have fooled me," said Jacqueline.

"It makes more sense than believing in ghosts," said Arla.

"She was joking," said Hildy, coming to Jacqueline's defense.

"Well, I'm not," said Arla.

"So you *are* accusing one of us of killing Marlene," said Georgina. "What proof do you have that Marlene was murdered?"

"I overheard some of the staff whispering about it," said Arla.

"That's ridiculous," said Letitia. "They're just letting their imaginations run wild."

"Really?" asked Arla. She pointed to where Cloris and I stood at the front of the room. "Ask them. I also heard them talking about murder."

The room full of women started lobbing questions at Cloris and me.

"Now what?" asked Cloris.

I held up my hands to silence the room. When they'd finally quieted, I said. "We don't know if someone killed Marlene, and the fact is, we'll never know."

"Why is that?" asked Letitia. "Won't the medical examiner perform an autopsy if murder is suspected?"

"You can't autopsy cremated remains," I said.

Arla gasped. "Marlene has already been cremated? How is that possible?"

"You'll have to ask her husband," I said.

"Maybe he killed her," suggested Arla.

I shrugged. "Feel free to ask him that as well." I glanced up at the clock over the doorway. For once in my life, a ticking clock was on my side. "For now, it's nearly time for your next class. Trust me, you're not going to want to be late for what Cloris has in store for you today. If any of you need to use the ladies' room, you'd better hurry."

Since female bladders wait for no one, the other women hurriedly packed up their stitchery and exited the room.

"Well, Arla certainly let the cat out of the bag," said Cloris. "When could she have overheard us talking?"

"No clue. I thought we were being extremely careful. She's also now got everyone second-guessing each other as to the identity of a murderer."

"Assuming Marlene was murdered, do you think it's possible one of these women killed her?"

I shook my head. "If so, it's got to be something deeper than pettiness over these meaningless competitions."

"Then what?"

I shrugged as I powered down my laptop, then unplugged it from the projector. "Hard to say. Maybe I'll still uncover something on her laptop that will shed light on her death. Or at least offer some alternate theories about who would want her dead. Right now, my money—what little I have—is on her husband or the doctor."

"Or both?"

"Or both."

"There's still the possibility that her death was due to natural causes," suggested Cloris.

"Of course. And unless someone confesses to her murder, we'll never know the truth one way or the other."

"But I'm sensing your gut tells you someone killed her."

"It does," I said. "And I've learned to trust the gut, especially when combined with incriminating computer files and ransacked rooms. Given what Marlene knew, someone had too much to lose."

Cloris changed the subject. "You think some of those women really believe in ghosts?"

I laughed. "Who knows? This group has surprised and shocked me from nearly the moment we stepped foot inside Beckwith Chateau."

"But ghosts?" Cloris's eyebrows disappeared under her pixie bangs. "Jacqueline had to be kidding."

I shrugged. "Maybe, but Hildy said Jacqueline was joking, not Jacqueline. I wouldn't be surprised to learn some of these women believe in paranormal phenomenon and may even have attended a séance or had their fortunes told."

"You'd think women who achieved what they have in their

careers would possess more common sense. You have to be pretty gullible to fall for charlatans peddling nonsense."

I cocked my head and raised an eyebrow. "How many well-educated, successful professionals fell for Bernie Madoff's Ponzi scheme?"

Cloris stared at me for a moment, her forehead furrowed as she connected the dots. Finally, she said, "When you look at it that way, believing in tea leaves, tarot cards, and crystal balls isn't much different from believing someone offering you a deal too good to be true."

"Exactly. Remind you of anyone you know?" I asked.

Cloris stared at me. "Karl?"

I nodded. "I'm guessing he thought the next bet would be the one where he scored a huge windfall and solved all his financial problems. But each consecutive spin of the roulette wheel or bet placed on the ponies only got him deeper and deeper in debt. Gambling? Fortune tellers? Ponzi schemes? What's the difference?"

She placed her hand on my upper arm. "Sorry I brought it up."

"No matter." I hitched my computer case to my shoulder and grabbed my tote, leaving the cartons containing the remainder of Hardanger kits for Tanner to retrieve. "It's time to take our minds off murder and other morose subjects. Let's go wow those women with an imposter cake." I yawned. "After we grab another cup of coffee."

Coffee in hand, we returned five minutes later to find Tanner exiting the Bordeaux Room, my cartons on his luggage cart. "I've already placed your items in your classroom," he told Cloris.

After she thanked him, I asked, "Do you have a minute, Tanner?"

"Sure, what can I do for you, Mrs. Pollack, ma'am?"

I ushered him inside the Avignon Room. While Cloris busied herself setting up her laptop, I continued, "Have any of the staff been talking about Marlene Beckwith's death?"

"Nonstop," he said.

"And the break-ins?"

"That, too. We've never had anything like this happen before."

"What are people saying?"

He eyed me skeptically. "What do you mean?"

"Some of the conference attendees are speculating that Marlene may have been murdered."

His eyes darted toward the open door before answering. Lowering his voice to a near-whisper, he said, "The staff, too. No one really liked her."

"Enough to kill her?"

Once again, he glanced furtively toward the open door. "She made lots of enemies, but if you're thinking someone who works here killed her, I don't think so."

"Assuming she was murdered," I said, "do you have any idea who may have done it?"

"Can you keep a secret?"

"Of course."

"The staff is placing bets. It's divided about fifty-fifty. Some think Mr. Beckwith. Others are sure it's Dr. Hargrove."

"And you?"

"My money is on Mr. Beckwith. Justin said he's on the verge of bankruptcy, and Mrs. Beckwith was loaded. Getting rid of her would solve Mr. Beckwith's money problems, right?"

"How does Justin know this?"

"You wouldn't believe what we overhear working here,

especially from the members sitting around drinking in Dix-neuf."

I took a minute to access my high school French vocabulary from some dark recess of my brain. "Nineteen?"

"It's what they call the bar in the golf clubhouse. Sounds classier than calling it The Nineteenth Hole like most country clubs. I guess they think a French name justifies the membership fees."

I nodded. "Got it."

"That hundred-year-old brandy they serve loosens a lot of tongues."

I would have loved to press him for more information, but at that moment we heard voices in the hallway. Panic filled his face. "I'd better go," he said grabbing hold of the luggage cart. Then he made a beeline for the open door, exiting right before the first group of women entered the room.

As soon as everyone had taken their seats, Cloris deliberately jumped right into her presentation. This prevented any possibility of the women picking up their discussion of Marlene's death.

She began with a slide of a bowl of fruit. "Anyone know what this is?" she asked the women.

"A bowl of fruit, of course," said Hildy.

Cloris clicked to the next slide, which showed a slice taken out of the bowl of fruit. The women gasped. "Not everything is always as it seems," explained Cloris. "These are what's known as imposter cakes, desserts that masquerade as something other than what they are."

The women sat enthralled as Cloris continued, showing slides of what first appeared to be a stack of waffles with butter and syrup, a bowl of spaghetti and meatballs, and a plate of sushi. "Most often imposter cakes imitate other foods, but as you can see, they can mimic anything." She then clicked to a teddy bear, a basket of toiletries, and a grouping of a baseball, bat and mitt. Everything looked real until the subsequent slides showed otherwise.

"Those are amazing," said Hildy. "They must be extremely difficult to make."

"Not necessarily," said Cloris, "as you'll soon see." She then moved on to the second part of the presentation, a step-by-step demonstration of the baker creating a realistic-looking sewing basket, complete with pin cushion, spools of thread, scissors, buttons, and other assorted notions. When she had finished the presentation, she removed the sewing basket cake from the carton where she had concealed it.

"You're not going to cut into that, are you?" asked Jacqueline.

"How else are we going to eat it?" asked Cloris.

"But it's so beautiful! It seems a shame to destroy it."

"It's cake," said Arla.

"I know," said Jacqueline. "But all that work..."

"Either we eat it," said Letitia, "or we leave it out for the mice."

Cloris picked up the cake knife. "Before I cut, would anyone like to snap a photo?"

Every woman in the room whipped out her phone. One by one they made their way to the front table to snap selfies. A few wanted group photos and asked Cloris and me to take them.

When the women returned to their seats, Cloris made the first cut. A few of the women cringed as the knife slid through the creation, but when they saw the rich chocolate cake and sour cherry filling, all began salivating.

I had begun passing out plates of cake when my phone rang. Detective Spader's name popped up on the screen. I turned the screen to show Cloris.

"Go," she said. "I'll finish up here."

I dashed out of the room into the hallway, quickly checked in both directions to make sure I was alone, then entered the empty Bordeaux Room across the hall. After closing the door behind me, I answered the call. "Detective."

"Mrs. Pollack, you still have Marlene Beckwith's laptop?"

I guess we were skipping the pleasantries and getting right down to business. "Yes."

"Good. A Detective Waverly Smith from the Essex County Sheriff's Office will arrive at Beckwith Chateau shortly to pick it up. Don't let anyone see you handing it over."

"Understood."

I was curious to learn more, but knowing Spader, he'd hand me his standard line about not being able to share information from an ongoing investigation. Even if it wasn't his investigation. Besides, I couldn't risk someone overhearing my conversation. It hardly mattered, though. Spader had already disconnected the call.

When I opened the door to return to Cloris's class, I saw Vernon Beckwith standing in the hallway.

FOURTEEN

I refused to make eye contact, but from the corner of my eye I saw Beckwith narrow his gaze and glare down at me from his superior height. I guess he was still peeved at the way I'd spoken to him yesterday. Too bad. At least he wasn't blocking my path. With my head held high and my eyes focused directly ahead of me, I ignored him, strode across the hall, and entered the Avignon Room.

My refusal to acknowledge his presence probably annoyed him even more. I doubt Vernon Beckwith was used to being snubbed by anyone, let alone the middle-aged crafts editor of a third-rate women's magazine sold at supermarket checkout aisles.

I just hoped he hadn't had his ear pressed against the door of the Bordeaux Room. In my mind I quickly replayed my conversation with Detective Spader. Other than when I first answered the call, I didn't remember saying anything that might raise suspicion.

I had checked up and down the hall before darting across the corridor to enter the Bordeaux Room. I'm positive the hallway had been empty. Unless Vernon Beckwith possessed magical powers enabling him to appear and disappear at will, he couldn't possibly have overheard me answering my phone.

Still, I found the man's presence unnerving.

Cloris was passing out the last slices of cake by the time I returned to the room. As they had earlier, the stitchers and bakers decided to adjourn to the Chartres Library to pair their cake with coffee or tea. One slice of cake remained on the front table. "For Tanner?" I asked.

"Of course."

I waited until all the women had exited the room, Then, as Cloris unplugged her laptop from the projector, I lowered my voice to a whisper and told her about Spader's call. "By the way," I added, "Guess who's lurking out in the hallway."

"Beckwith?" she asked. "I saw him. He poked his scowling face in here and looked around. I was tempted to call the fashion police."

Vernon Beckwith had exchanged yesterday's orange, yellow, and green plaid golf pants and tangerine knit polo shirt for a similar getup. He'd paired a lavender knit golf shirt trimmed in lime green piping with plaid pants in shades of purple, navy, lavender, and lime green. "His outfit screamed plaid eggplant. Do you think he suspects Marlene gave her laptop to one of the other women?"

"Why?"

"For safekeeping? Maybe she realized her life was in danger."

"If she did, wouldn't she have hired a bodyguard?"

"You'd certainly think so."

"I would have."

That made two of us. I pondered possible reasons for Vernon's sudden interest in the conference and could come up with none other than the need to track down Marlene's laptop. "If it's true what everyone says about Marlene and Vernon's relationship, he probably has no idea of the animosity between Marlene and the other Society members. He might think she entrusted the laptop to one of them."

"He'd know that Marlene intervened to get Arla into that drug trial. Do you think he was trying to figure out which one of the women was Arla?"

I shook my head. "Not necessarily, especially since we don't know the status of Vernon and Marlene's relationship back then. Marlene may have bypassed Vernon and gone directly to the researcher heading up the trial at the time. It's possible Vernon has no idea Marlene pulled strings to aid Arla."

"So why else would he be nosing around the conference?"

"Because he can? After all, he does own the place. Also, he might suspect one of the other women stole the laptop, and he's trying to figure out which one."

Cloris scoffed. "By intimidating each one with a scowl and a glare? Those women were so focused on the imposter cake, I don't think any of them even noticed him standing in the doorway."

I tried to come up with other possibilities for Beckwith lurking around the conference. "He may believe Rhetta lied to him and that she's stashed the laptop somewhere within the Chateau."

"And she'd leave it hiding in plain sight, sitting out in one of the conference rooms? Doubtful. Why wouldn't he think the doctor has it? Isn't that what Rhetta suggested when Beckwith accused her of taking it?"

"He must know the doctor doesn't have the laptop," I said, "either because they're in cahoots, or he's already searched the doctor's residence."

At that moment Tanner entered the room, causing us to cease our discussion of Beckwith. "Anything you ladies need?" he asked. "Besides a winning lottery ticket, I mean?"

Cloris picked up the plate and handed it to him. "Even though you won't share your nonexistent lottery winnings with us, Tanner, I'm willing to share my cake with you."

He reached for the slice. His eyes bulged, and he licked his lips in anticipation. "That looks delicious. I'd better eat it here so no one else sees it and expects me to share."

Cloris and I shouldered our computer cases and totes. Before stepping from the room, I turned and said, "Bon appetit!"

Tanner shoveled a forkful of cake into his mouth, smacked his lips and said, "Man, this is good!"

Much to my relief, Beckwith was no longer loitering in the corridor. Cloris and I detoured to the ladies' room before heading to lunch in the Chartres Library. After checking to determine we were alone, she asked, "How is that detective supposed to contact you once he arrives?"

"Not sure. I assume Spader gave him my cell phone number. His only instructions were to make sure no one sees the handoff. I suppose I'll have to sneak him into one of the unoccupied conference rooms and hope nobody notices us and gets curious. Makes me feel like Jane Bond."

"I hate to break the news to you, but you morphed from mild-mannered crafts editor into Jane Bond the moment you discovered Marlys Vandenburg's dead body glue gunned to your desk chair last year."

"Not by choice." At least a female version of 007 sounded sexier than being dubbed a twenty-first century Miss Marple or

Jessica Fletcher. Although, I'm not sure anyone other than Zack would consider this slightly overweight, pear-shaped middle-aged mother sexy. Maybe Zack needs his eyes examined. However, I'm not about to push my luck by suggesting a trip to the ophthalmologist.

We were walking through the rotunda on our way to the Chartres Library when my phone chimed an incoming text. I glanced down at the message, then said, "He's here. I'm to pretend he's my cousin, and he stopped in to get my signature on some legal documents regarding our grandmother's estate."

Cloris eyed me skeptically. "Rather specific, isn't it?"

I shrugged. "I suppose it's always best to have our stories straight in case anyone questions his reason for being here or why I'm ushering him up to my room."

"He suggested that?"

I nodded.

Worry clouded Cloris's features. "Not that I'm paranoid, but how about if I play wing woman? Or bodyguard?"

Somehow, I didn't think Cloris, all of a Size Two dripping wet, would be a match for an Essex County detective who probably bench-pressed double her weight during his daily gym workouts. Still, it wouldn't hurt to have a witness. "Why don't you head upstairs and leave the connecting door slightly ajar?"

Cloris executed an about-face and detoured to the staircase. I continued toward the main entrance of the Chateau.

As I made my way down the hallway, I saw no unfamiliar man waiting for me near the entrance, only Justin exiting Rhetta's office. His somber expression morphed into a smile when he noticed me. He nodded before continuing down the corridor that led to where the Stitch and Bake Society board of directors had met on Tuesday.

The only other person in the foyer was a woman dressed in tailored brown wool tweed slacks, Ugg boots, and a bulky fisherman knit sweater topped with a caramel-colored cashmere infinity scarf. She looked like she just stepped out of an Eileen Fisher catalog. Standing off to the side in front of the potted plants, she casually glanced around the area as if scoping the place out with the intent to book the venue for a wedding or bridal shower. She wore her blonde hair pulled back in a sloppy bun at her nape and carried a Louis Vuitton briefcase, which I recognized from the iconic overall gold-on-brown monogram print.

The moment she saw me her face broke out in a huge smile. She waved and called, "Hey, cuz!"

I checked my surprise and waved back. Once I was in range, she grabbed me in a huge bear hug and whispered in my ear, "I'm guessing Detective Spader didn't mention I wasn't a guy?"

I laughed as I hugged her back. "Must have slipped his mind."

"Play along," she said. "We have company." She stepped back, lowered her arms to clasp my hands in both of hers, and pivoted me slightly. That's when I spied Letitia and Georgina walking toward us. They stopped a few feet away and settled into chairs in one of the small alcoves near the patio doors. This not only gave them a perfect sightline to us but put them within eavesdropping range. They each then proceeded to remove needlework from their tote bags.

Catching my eye, Georgina held up her sampler and called out, "See? I'm making progress."

I offered her a thumbs-up before continuing with the subterfuge by asking Detective Waverly, "Do you have time for lunch? I'm sure I can make arrangements for you to join me. The food here is to die for."

Waverly quirked an eyebrow at the double-entendre. "So I've heard, but I'm afraid today won't work. I've got to get these papers to the attorney before I head back to the office."

Out of the corner of my eye, I could see Georgina and Letitia hanging on every word of our conversation. "All the other grandchildren have signed?"

She nodded. "Yours is the last John Hancock we need to move ahead on settling Grandmother's estate."

I looped my arm through hers. "Let's go upstairs to my room. We can take care of everything there."

I led her back down the hall, offering a nod to Letitia and Georgina as we headed toward the rotunda and up the steps. Once inside the room, I stuck my head into Cloris's room and said, "Come meet Detective Waverly Smith."

Cloris entered the room, took one look at Waverly, and burst out laughing. "You're certainly nothing like Detective Spader."

Waverly chuckled. "So I've been told."

I removed Marlene's laptop from my computer case and handed it to Waverly. "Good luck," I said. "I have a feeling I only scratched the surface and that there are more hidden files, but I'm happy to let law enforcement take over from here. Vernon Beckwith is hellbent on getting his hands on this baby."

She slipped the laptop into her Louis Vuitton bag. "I'm sure our IT people will be able to find anything else there is to find."

"I'm just not sure you're going to find any evidence that Marlene was murdered."

Waverly raised an eyebrow. "You're convinced she was?"

"What I know is that the doctor acted in a highly unprofessional manner, not to mention that he's not licensed to practice medicine. So he should never have been hired as Marlene's concierge physician.

"Also," I continued, "I find it extremely suspicious that Vernon had Marlene cremated so quickly. However, without a body to autopsy and both her tea and pills removed from her room..." My voice trailed off, and I shrugged my frustration. "It's all conjecture."

She sighed. "Certainly looks that way. We'll do our best. Maybe we'll catch a break, and someone will slip up—if there really was a murder. Meanwhile, from the files Detective Spader sent me, we have enough evidence to issue arrest warrants on some counts and for the district attorney to move ahead with seating a grand jury on the other criminal activity."

I chewed on my lower lip.

"Is there something else?" asked Waverly. "You look like a woman with a question."

"Something has been bothering me."

She waved her hand. "Spit it out."

"Will the evidence be admissible, even though I found it on Marlene's computer and sent it to you?"

"Absolutely, especially since we now have her computer. Besides, the district attorney will likely subpoena the detective Marlene hired to attest to his investigation."

"Even though he hired a hacker to access Vernon's computer? Isn't that illegal?"

Waverly furrowed her brow. "What makes you think the P.I. hired a hacker? There was nothing in what Spader sent me that mentioned a hacker."

I thought back to what I had discovered on Marlene's computer and shook my head. "How else would the investigator have gotten hold of the information on Vernon's computer?"

"There are many possibilities," she said, ticking them off on her fingers. "First, it's possible Vernon's computer isn't password protected, or if it is, it's a common password. You'd be surprised how many people use their date of birth or even the word *password* as their password."

"Pretty stupid of them," said Cloris.

Waverly nodded. "But unbelievably common." She continued with various hypotheses. "Marlene may have snuck the P.I. into Vernon's house while Vernon was at work or playing golf. Or perhaps the P.I. posed as a repairman or a janitor with the cleaning service either the Chateau or the pharmaceutical company employs. Or he cozied up to a disgruntled employee who had access to Vernon's office. Offer someone enough money, and you'd be surprised how quickly they toss aside their integrity—if they ever had any to begin with."

Another possibility sprang to mind. "Or he could have approached someone at the Chateau, someone in Marlene's corner."

"Rhetta?" asked Cloris.

I nodded. "What if Rhetta didn't disclose all she knew to us? What if all along she was helping Marlene expose Vernon, and she gave the investigator access to Vernon's house? You saw that huge keyring she carries with her. I'm guessing she has access to every building on the Chateau grounds."

"If that's the case," said Cloris, "why give you the laptop? Why not just hand it over to the police?"

"Because once she realized she had to hide the laptop, the roads were already closed. She knew if Marlene's laptop went missing, Vernon would suspect she had taken it. We know that after

Marlene's death, someone ransacked both Marlene's home and Rhetta's apartment. That person may have also killed Marlene."

"So Rhetta gave you the laptop to protect her own life?" asked Cloris.

"Makes sense," said Waverly.

If Rhetta had indeed used me. I didn't want to believe she'd jeopardized my safety to protect herself, but what did I really know about her? Nothing beyond what she'd wanted me to know. Either way, I was glad to be rid of the laptop and eager for the conference to conclude at the end of the day.

Beckwith Chateau, for all its old-world splendor, was too full of deceit and questionable individuals. I was beginning to feel like I was stuck in a Gothic novel and wouldn't be surprised to learn of some crazy person locked away in a hidden attic room. Maybe those were the voices I'd heard last night.

FIFTEEN

We waited long enough to make it appear that I had been busy signing legal documents, then Cloris and I escorted Waverly back downstairs. Georgina and Letitia were still camped out in the alcove, stitching away on their samplers.

Waverly continued the ruse. Once we arrived at the Chateau entrance she said, "Let's plan to do a family dinner next week. I'll call you to set up a date."

"Sounds great!" She and I exchanged another hug.

Then Waverly turned to Cloris and said, "So nice to meet you, Cloris!" before she exited the Chateau.

I breathed a huge sigh of relief as Cloris and I entered the Chartres Library and queued up at the buffet for lunch. A moment later, Georgina and Letitia lined up behind us.

"Do you know what the final baking challenge is?" asked Georgina, directing her question to Cloris.

"I have no idea," said Cloris.

Letitia turned to me. "What about you?"

"Why would I know if Cloris doesn't know? She's the baking judge."

Letitia cocked her head and studied me as if trying to determine whether I was telling her the truth or not. "You seem to have gotten very friendly with Rhetta. I thought maybe she told you."

Even though she was nearly twice my age, I channeled one of my Mom Looks at her. "If she had—which she hasn't—it wouldn't be fair to spill the beans ahead of time, now would it?"

She shrugged. "You can't fault me for trying." When I raised an eyebrow, she quickly changed the subject. "By the way, your cousin is stunning."

Maybe I'm overly sensitive, but comments like that have always annoyed me. They seem to imply that my looks are somewhat lacking. I pasted a smile on my face and said, "Yes, she is, isn't she?"

"Is she a model?" asked Georgina.

"No." The line had inched forward, and I turned my attention to the servers behind the buffet, hoping to put to rest any further discussion regarding my *cousin*.

"An actress?" asked Letitia.

So much for trying to end the discussion. I pulled my attention away from the buffet and turned to face both women. "Why are you so curious about my cousin?"

"She looked familiar to us," said Georgina. "We thought maybe we had seen her on television. Is she a reporter for one of the local networks?"

Cloris jumped into the conversation. "You probably think she looks familiar because she bears a striking resemblance to Scarlett Johansson."

Letitia wrinkled her brow, turned to Georgina, and asked, "Do we know who that is?"

Letitia bobbed her head, causing her jet-black dyed pageboy to bounce. "Of course. She's been in all those Avenger movies, remember?"

"As Pepper Potts? I thought that was Gwyneth Paltrow."

"Gwyneth Paltrow is Pepper Potts. Scarlett Johansson plays Black Widow."

Georgina's face lit up with recognition. "Oh, yes! Her."

"That, too," said Letitia.

Once again, Georgina's face filled with confusion. "She was also the voice in *Her*," explained Letitia. "That strange movie where the guy falls in love with the voice on his phone."

Georgina nodded. "I remember now."

I gaped wide-eyed and open-mouthed at the two of them. Never would I have pegged Letitia and Georgina as fans of the Marvel Universe. Letitia blushed. "It's our guilty pleasure. We were both huge comic book fans back in the day. Don't tell anyone."

I laughed. "They won't hear it from either of us." After all, if pressed, I'd have to admit that I, too, always looked forward to the next release in the franchise, even if I had grown up more a Supergirl fan.

Hopefully, that put an end to the conversation. I finished choosing items for my lunch—a chicken and asparagus pasta salad with a side of spring greens with raspberry vinaigrette and a slice of sourdough bread—then followed Cloris to a table for two in an out of the way corner. The last thing I wanted was to have Georgina and Letitia join us for lunch and continue to ask prying questions about my *cousin* Waverly.

"Thanks for the rescue back there," I said to Cloris after we'd taken our seats.

She chuckled. "They were rather persistent, weren't they?"

"I'll say! You really think Waverly looks like Scarlett Johansson?"

"Not in the least."

"Then why—?"

"She was the first blonde actress who popped into my head, probably because I saw her on one of the late night shows recently."

I furrowed my brow as I nibbled on the sourdough and replayed the conversation in my head. "I wonder, were they simply acting nosy, or had they really recognized Waverly?"

"Does it matter?"

"It could. Cops are interviewed on TV all the time. What if Georgina and Letitia recognized Waverly from a recent investigation that made the news?"

"Or they may have stood behind her at the supermarket. It doesn't matter because they now realize she only looked familiar because of her resemblance to Black Widow."

"Not that she does."

Cloris popped half a cherry tomato into her mouth and shrugged. "Hey, I planted a seed that sprouted a diversion. It worked. That's all that matters. Don't drive yourself crazy."

I frowned as I stabbed at a piece of rigatoni on my plate. "Easier said than done."

"This place is making you paranoid."

"With good reason, considering everything that's gone on since we arrived."

Cloris glanced at her phone. "Cheer up. T-minus seven hours

and we can say goodbye to all the drama from the Stitch and Bake Society members as well as Beckwith Chateau."

"It can't come soon enough. We've certainly earned comp time from this assignment." Not to mention hazard pay. Hopefully, Naomi would come through for us by convincing the pencil pushers we deserved a few extra Benjamins along with that comp time.

We were finishing our lunch when Jacqueline approached our table and asked Cloris, "Do you know what the final challenge is this afternoon?"

Cloris exhaled the kind of huge sigh reserved for mothers of overtired toddlers in need of a nap. "Even if I did know, what advantage would it be to learn half an hour before the start of the competition?"

"I'm just curious," said Jacqueline, copping a defensive attitude.

"You'll have to wait like the rest of us," I said, forcing a smile.

"As far as we know," added Cloris, "Rhetta is the only person with that information."

This wasn't exactly true. During my post-midnight surf through Marlene's computer files, I'd hit upon the list of baking challenges for the competition. I'd also discovered proof that Marlene had indeed worked to tip the scales in her favor. She'd kept a detailed record of her multiple attempts until she'd perfected each dessert. As yet, I hadn't had time to share this information with Cloris.

Jacqueline crossed her arms over her chest. "And Marlene. I suppose none of us should be surprised that she tried to rig the competition. I guess there really is something to Karma."

"Assuming she chose the challenges," said Cloris. "You have no proof that she did."

As far as we knew, Rhetta had only shared that tidbit of information with the two of us and only the first challenge. The Society members who believed otherwise were only speculating.

Jacqueline wasn't buying it, though. She offered up a Lucille-worthy harrumph, then turned her back on us and exited the room.

"T-minus how many more hours?" I asked Cloris.

"Too many."

I cupped my hand against the side of my mouth and lowered my voice to a whisper. "By the way, Jacqueline is right. Marlene did cheat."

Both of her eyebrows disappeared under her bangs as they soared toward her hairline. "How do you know that?"

I proceeded to fill her in on the files I'd discovered that documented Marlene's test bakes. Cloris continued to stare bugged-eyed at me as she shook her head and muttered, "Unbelievable."

~*~

With nearly an hour before the start of the final baking challenge, we decided to grab our coats and walk the grounds for a bit of fresh air as well as a much-needed break from the stitchers and bakers. The sun had returned, and the mercury had crept up high enough to hint at the imminent return of spring in a few short weeks. A closer inspection of some of the garden beds revealed tiny green crocus shoots beginning to push their way through the dark loam.

Apparently, others were equally eager to head outside after yesterday's storm. As we strolled through the desolate winter gardens surrounding the Chateau, we found ourselves repeatedly accosted by groups of stitchers and bakers. In order to escape being waylaid further, we decided to wind our way along the path that led to the golf course and clubhouse.

Now that I'd rid myself of Marlene's laptop, I felt as though I had the weight of the world off my shoulders—both literally and figuratively. Lugging around one laptop was bad enough. But two? I reached across my body and massaged my aching shoulder. "You think Naomi would spring for a session at Spa de la Mer Violette before we head home tonight?"

Cloris looked at me as if I'd sprouted a second head, one with pink and purple hair and rainbow freckles dotting my face. "Since she has to account to the Trimedia tightwads for every penny she spends, I'm guessing chances are slim to none."

"I was afraid you'd say that."

"Hey, I'm sure Zack will be more than happy to massage your aching shoulder, not to mention any other parts of your body this evening."

I smiled. "Definitely something to look forward to."

As we strolled along the shrubbery-bordered brick path leading to the clubhouse, we discovered additional paths branching off to the left and right, probably leading to some of the various cottages that dotted the estate. "Want to see where this one leads?" asked Cloris after we'd passed several.

I shrugged. "I'm game if you are. It's not like we're expected at the clubhouse. Besides, I'd rather not bump into Vernon Beckwith if he happens to be holding court there."

"I'll second that. Let's explore."

We hung a right and continued walking. This particular path quickly left the low-lying shrubbery behind as it meandered through a more densely wooded area. Every so often a break in the trees exposed a glimpse of the golf course off in the distance.

"This place is enormous," I said. "It's hard to believe we're only a few miles from the urban sprawl of Newark."

Instead of answering, Cloris gasped as she grabbed my arm and pointed through the trees. I expected to find a deer staring at us. I quickly shot off a silent prayer that I wouldn't discover a bear or a coyote. I didn't expect to find a pair of shoeless, stocking-clad feet sticking out from a pile of forest debris.

SIXTEEN

With Cloris grabbing my arm, we crept closer. "I have a really bad feeling about this," I said. The torso and body were completely covered, making me doubt we'd stumbled upon a hunter taking a siesta or a golfer searching for a ball that had sliced a hundred yards off the green.

Once we stood over the body, I knelt and gingerly touched one ankle, hoping to feel a pulse, but rigor mortis had set in. "She's definitely dead," I said.

"She?" asked Cloris. "How can you tell?"

"I can't. Not with a hundred percent certainty. I suppose it could be a short, slightly built guy partial to pedicures."

Cloris pulled a face. "Point taken. But who is she?"

I shook my head. "This is obviously a crime scene. Whoever she is, she didn't bury herself in the woods. We can't disturb anything."

I pulled out my cell phone. Thanks to the marvels of modern technology, since Waverly had called me, her number was now stored in my phone.

"Have you uncovered something else?" she asked after answering.

"A body," I said. "And this one was definitely murdered."

Through the phone line I heard Waverly suck in her breath. "Spader wasn't kidding. You really are New Jersey's version of Jessica Fletcher."

"Believe me, I'd love nothing better than to give up the title. I certainly don't go looking for dead bodies."

"Where are you?"

After I gave her our location, she asked, "Can you identify the victim?"

"Not unless you want me to disturb the crime scene."

"No! Don't touch anything!"

After the multitude of murders I'd come across the last year, I was certainly aware of law enforcement's standard operating procedures. However, Waverly didn't really know the extent of my involvement in those cases. "I'm familiar with the drill, Detective. As you've pointed out, this is not my first rodeo."

"Right. I'm on my way. I should be there in less than five minutes."

"You're on the grounds?"

"We are."

We? Had Waverly already obtained a search warrant? Was her team currently executing that search at either Vernon Beckwith's or the doctor's cottage?

While we waited, Cloris and I stood guard over the body, hoping no wild animals showed up before the cops. I wasn't game to fend off a hungry fox, wolf, or coyote when my only available weapon was a nearby mold-covered branch, which I was loath to pick up, and a few stones no bigger than baby potatoes.

I had expected the calvary to arrive along the same route Cloris and I had trod, but they headed toward us from the opposite direction. The path we were on most likely led to one of the cottages targeted by the search warrant. My guess was they had taken the service road to that residence, bypassing the Chateau altogether.

Smart move. None of the Stitch and Bake ladies would be any the wiser. It was even possible neither Rhetta nor any of the other staff were aware of the police presence on Beckwith property—which was most likely intentional.

Once Waverly stood inches from us, her team gathered behind her, she flipped open a small notepad she held in one hand. With pen poised over a fresh page, she zeroed in on me. Without any preamble and in all-business mode, she asked, "This is how you found the victim? You didn't move or touch anything?"

"I placed a finger on her ankle, hoping to feel a pulse, but she was stiff and cold."

"Nothing beyond that?"

I shook my head.

She turned to Cloris. "And you?"

Cloris tilted her head toward me. "I leave dead bodies to Nancy Drew here."

Waverly directed her team to begin processing the crime scene, then ushered Cloris and me a few feet farther away from the body. Positioning us with our backs to the CSI activity, she continued her questioning, jotting occasional notes. After a few minutes, one of the team members called to her. "We're ready, Detective."

"Let's go," she said.

Cloris's eyebrows shot up. "Go where?"

"To see if either of you recognizes the victim."

I glanced over my shoulder. The crime scene team had carefully removed the decaying leaves and muck that had covered most of the body. I didn't need to get any closer to identify the victim, still dressed in the vintage yellow and orange madras plaid gown she'd worn when she stormed out of the ballroom last night.

Cloris followed my gaze, then sucked in her breath when recognition hit. "Wanda," she choked before clapping a hand over her mouth and turning away.

"Wanda?" asked Waverly. She jotted a notation, then poised her pen. "Last name?"

Cloris and I both shook our heads. "You'll have to ask Rhetta," I said, then added, "or one of the conference attendees."

"But why would anyone want to kill her?" asked Cloris.

"Maybe she was in the wrong place at the wrong time," I said, "and either saw or heard something she shouldn't have."

"Something about Marlene's death?"

"It's possible," said Waverly. "Do you remember the last time you saw the deceased?"

I told Waverly about the results of the croquembouche competition and Wanda's meltdown over being eliminated. "When Wanda didn't show up for the workshop this morning, some of the other women mentioned that she often goes off in a snit over some perceived injustice or other but eventually gets over it."

"No one seemed concerned," added Cloris.

I crossed the short distance to stand over the body. If she hadn't been found buried in the woods, one might assume she died a natural death. Before heaping wet forest muck over her body, someone had taken the time to arrange her in peaceful repose with her hands folded under her breasts and a serene expression on her face. Just like Marlene, minus the forest detritus.

Waverly walked up alongside me. "I see wheels spinning. What's on your mind?"

I stared at her. "You're really interested in my opinion?"

"Spader trained me. I respect his judgment. If he values your insights, that's good enough for me." Then she nudged me with her elbow and grinned. "Besides, we're family, right? Family sticks together."

I smiled at the compliment, even though her statement certainly didn't apply to all families. After all, Waverly had never met Lucille.

"Well?" she prodded.

I nodded and plunged ahead with my observation. "Assuming Wanda decided to mope about in the gardens last night, what happened to her shoes and coat? It certainly wasn't warm enough to go without either."

One of the techs heard my question and looked over from where he was methodically sifting through the forest floor near the victim. "Working on finding them but so far nothing nearby."

"The killer may have taken them," said Cloris. "Don't they do that sometimes? As a trophy?"

"That's often the M.O. of a serial killer," said Waverly, "but anything's possible."

I wondered how many murders makes for a serial killer. Were two enough? "Marlene was in a similar position in her bed," I said. "Too bad there's no way to prove how she died."

Waverly muttered something indiscernible under her breath that I took as an expression of frustration. I couldn't get past the fact that Vernon had something to hide. Why else would he have had Marlene cremated so quickly? One look at Waverly told me the same thought ran through her head.

"If the killer lays out his victims with care," I said, "could it be because he regrets having to kill them?"

"But if that were the case," said Cloris, "how do you explain the rage of trashing Marlene's home afterwards?"

"Maybe the killer and the trasher are two different people," I said.

Waverly raised an eyebrow. "Good observation, assuming Marlene was murdered. We have no proof and never will unless someone confesses."

"How often do you get those Perry Mason moments?" I asked.

"Not even once in a blue moon."

"That's what I thought. So, what happens now?"

"We proceed with our investigation and see where it leads."

"The final round of the baking competition is set to start shortly," said Cloris, checking her phone. "Are you planning to cancel the remainder of the conference?"

"When does the event end?"

"After dinner this evening."

Waverly mulled this over for a moment, then asked, "What's the schedule for the rest of today?"

"The competition will last upwards of three hours," said Cloris.

"Dinner is at six o'clock," I added, "followed by the awards ceremony. The women are on their own for about an hour in-between, but for the most part, they're getting ready for dinner."

"They're all staying at the Chateau? None are commuting back and forth each day?"

"We drove home the first night," said Cloris, "but stayed last night due to the road closures. As did everyone else."

"I don't remember seeing any of the other women leaving after dinner Tuesday night," I added. "I was under the impression all the attendees were staying at the Chateau for the conference. You'd have to confirm that with Rhetta, though."

Waverly glanced at her team, then pointing to a grouping of rhododendron bushes several yards away, said, "Wait for me over there." Once Cloris and I had trudged through a carpet of dead leaves to the designated area, Waverly gathered her team around her. They conversed out of earshot for several minutes before she placed a call. When she finished talking into her cell phone, she beckoned us back.

"Here's what we're going to do," Waverly said. "I don't want the conference attendees made aware of Wanda's death just yet, not until we've had time to finish here, search her room, and question the staff. We should be able to accomplish that during the competition. Afterwards, we'll interview all of the women before dinner."

"You think one of the conference attendees killed Wanda?" asked Cloris. "They're all in their seventies and eighties. And many of them are quite frail."

"We didn't notice any evidence of a body being dragged through the brush," I added. "I can't imagine any of those ladies having the strength to carry Wanda a few inches, let alone hundreds of yards."

"It's unlikely one of them is our killer," said Waverly, "but nothing is impossible. Nevertheless, we still need to interview them. Someone may have overheard or witnessed something that will help in the investigation." She paused for a moment before adding, "Or one of them could be an accomplice."

As a reluctant amateur sleuth, I had neither majored in criminal justice nor attended the police academy where Accomplice 101 was probably part of the curriculum. I searched my memory for all the interactions I'd observed between Wanda and the other women. Was there bad blood between her and one of the other conference attendees, enough to provide a motive for murder?

As I pondered this, I shot a glance at Waverly's team and performed a bit of mental arithmetic, adding up the staff and attendees, then dividing that number by the small group of crime scene investigators currently combing through the woods. "That's a lot to accomplish in such a short period of time."

"There are more investigators currently on the grounds executing search warrants," said Waverly. "They should be finishing up shortly. I've called for backup. Along with more detectives, I need officers posted at the exits to prevent anyone from leaving the property." She shrugged. "This is nothing compared to some crime scenes we've handled."

That didn't surprise me, given Newark was the county seat of Essex County. I didn't have to imagine what Waverly and her fellow detectives came across on any given day. I saw reports of them on the evening news each night. I just never expected that what goes on in the dark underbelly of the city would make its way onto the grounds of one of the most exclusive country clubs and conference centers on the East Coast.

"And if it takes a bit longer than anticipated," Waverly continued, executing an additional shrug, "they'll just have to postpone dinner for an hour or two."

She glanced at her watch, which I took as a sign for us to leave. "We'll be in the Rouen Conference Center if you need us," I said.

Waverly nodded, but before making her way back to her team, she gave us one final instruction. "Remember, not a word of this to anyone."

"T-minus how many hours?" I asked Cloris as we traipsed back toward the conference center.

"Still too many."

I stopped walking and pulled out my phone.

"What are you doing?" she asked.

"Accessing the chapter's website. I'm curious about Wanda's background. Her behavior struck me as incongruous with that of a successful executive."

Cloris nodded. "Given her advanced age, we can't even chalk it up to the hormonal rollercoaster of menopause."

I pulled my attention from the screen and focused on Cloris. "You're not going to believe this."

"Don't keep my in suspense. Spill!"

"She's known as the Fast-Food Franchise Queen. She owns hundreds of restaurants from California to Maine."

Cloris peered down at my phone. "Seriously? Wanda? I wouldn't have guessed that in a million years."

"That makes two of us." I continued to scroll down the page. "She stepped down two years ago and turned the day-to-day operations over to her oldest daughter." I chewed on this for a moment, then added, "Which could be code for having been forced out when she started exhibiting irrational behavior."

"Being overly emotional isn't irrational," said Cloris.

I pocketed my phone, and we continued walking toward the conference center. "It is if you're the CEO of a multi-million-dollar enterprise, and your emotions are causing you to make poor decisions that affect the bottom line."

We arrived at the Rouen Conference Center to find the Stitch and Bake ladies already milling about the baking stations of the four remaining contestants. They'd divided up, silently announcing their support of either Team Letitia, Team Georgina, Team Jacqueline, or Team Arla.

"Arla doesn't have much of a fan club," said Cloris, jutting her chin toward Arla's station.

I was surprised to see that only Celeste had joined Arla. "Is it any wonder, given her vocal defense of Marlene?"

Still, I've always had a soft spot in my heart for the underdog. Not that I condoned Marlene's behavior. I had found her arrogant and obnoxious, a user who always had to get her own way. The more I had learned about her, the less I thought of her.

At one time I'd viewed life in terms of either black or white. However, as I'd matured, I'd come to realize everything in life is composed of many shades of gray. Few people in this world are devoid of all redeeming qualities. Marlene had gone out of her way to save her friend's life. For that act alone she deserved some credit, no matter her multitude of less-than-sterling qualities.

Even though I had to remain impartial, a part of me hoped Arla blew the other contestants out of the water. Or in this case, out of the kitchen.

Rhetta soon entered, followed by the few remaining stragglers who immediately made their allegiance known by heading for their contestant of choice. With a quick wave to Cloris and me, Rhetta stepped to the mic. After tapping it twice to make sure it was live, she said, "Good afternoon, ladies. Welcome to the final round of the baking competition."

Applause erupted throughout the room. Rhetta waited until it had died down before continuing. "As homage to the Stitch and

Bake Society, for your final bake you must create a three-tier cake decorated in a needlework theme. Each tier must be a different flavor with the three flavors coming together in a compatible flavor profile."

Murmurs filled the room, but I heard no complaints. I studied the faces of each of the four finalists. All nodded and smiled. "They seem happy," I said.

"They should be," said Cloris. "This is a far less intimidating test than yesterday's croquembouche contest, assuming they're decorating skills rise to the challenge."

"Doesn't that seem odd to you?"

"What do you mean?"

"Wouldn't you expect the final challenge to be the most difficult of the three?"

Cloris furrowed her brow. "You have a point. I wonder what Marlene was thinking."

I shrugged. "I guess we'll never know."

Rhetta continued, "Your finished cake must be at least two-feet high."

That immediately wiped the smiles off the faces of each of the contestants. A rumble of groans filled the room.

"Aye, there's the rub," said Cloris. "They're going to have to create a structure much more complex than a simple three-tier cake."

Rhetta finished by saying, "Each of you may choose one person to assist you. The remaining conference attendees must take seats around the room to watch and not interact with the finalists. You have three hours, starting..." She paused for dramatic effect before adding, "now."

The four finalists quickly conferred with their chosen

assistants, sketching out rudimentary ideas on the large pads of paper at each station. Then all eight of them began scurrying around the room, grabbing equipment and ingredients from the storage shelves and industrial refrigerator.

"At least Arla has someone to assist her," said Cloris.

"Hopefully, Celeste has decent baking chops," I said. With the various skill levels I'd observed so far, both in needlecraft and baking, nothing was a given. Arla's one champion might be either an asset or a liability, depending on her baking and decorating expertise.

After initiating the competition, Rhetta made her way to where Cloris and I stood. "I'm guessing you'll be glad to see the conference end," I said.

Her mouth turned up in a wry smile as she rubbed her temple. "I'll be happy to see the drama end. All of it. Not just the conference drama. I'm used to multitasking, but the stress of the last few days has really gotten to me."

I didn't doubt that. The job description for personal assistants and concierges wouldn't normally include dealing with dead bodies. Currently, Rhetta only knew of Marlene's death, which may or may not have been from natural causes. Little did she realize one of the walking paths now led to a murder scene.

I wish I could say something to prepare her for the additional traumatic news that would soon hit her, but Cloris and I were under strict orders to keep our lips zipped. Instead, I said, "Any chance you have some vacation time coming to you?"

"I do. I'm thinking a relaxing cruise to the Bahamas is in order."

Cloris and I exchanged quick side glances.

Rhetta noticed. "Something wrong?"

"I recently returned from a cruise," I told her. "It was anything but relaxing."

"In what way?"

With everything that had happened the past three days, the last thing I wanted to do was freak Rhetta out with a tale of cruise ship murders. Instead, I shrugged and said, "Lots of unexpected family drama that resulted in a less than relaxing vacation."

"That's too bad," she said.

"It certainly was," I agreed, punctuating my statement with a rueful smile. "But I'm sure your cruise will be wonderful. Send me a postcard."

"Absolutely! In fact, I think I'll jump online and book that cruise right now." She spun on her heels and headed for the exit. "I'll be back in time to end the competition," she said, raising her arm over her head to offer us a backward wave.

Cloris and I watched Rhetta bounce out of the convention center. "She's definitely going to need a vacation once she recovers from the next whammy about to hit her," said Cloris.

I heaved a huge sigh. "My thoughts exactly."

We then turned our attention to the baking competition's four finalists. A palpable tension had settled over the room, and as Cloris and I began visiting each of the stations, we caught snippets of hostile conversations between the finalists and their helpers. We were visiting Georgina's station when an ugly exchange erupted behind us.

"Fine," shouted Celeste. "Do it yourself. I quit!" She yanked her apron over her head and tossed it onto the counter where it landed in a bowl of whipped meringue.

A collective gasp filled the room, which then grew silent except for the whirring of the stand mixers. Everyone's attention focused on Arla.

Her face purple with rage, she cried, "You did that on purpose." Then she plucked the meringue-soaked fabric from the bowl and hurled it at Celeste. "You planned to sabotage me all along, didn't you?"

Sidestepping the apron, Celeste said, "No, Arla. I felt sorry for you because no one likes you. Silly me. Now I know why. You're as overbearing and obnoxious as Marlene was. No wonder the two of you were friends." She then spun on her heels, grabbed her coat, and stormed out of the conference center.

Arla stood hands on hips, watching her leave. "Good riddance," she cried to Celeste's back. "I don't need your help." She then turned to the remaining attendees seated around the perimeter of the room. "I don't need anyone's help."

Cloris and I stepped away from Georgina's station and out of earshot of the contestants. "I haven't experienced this much catty drama since junior high school," I whispered. "It's as if along with their retro outfits, these women have reverted back to their mercurial teenage temperaments."

"It's going to be a long three hours," said Cloris.

"Especially for Arla. Any chance she'll finish on time?" I asked. Knowing Cloris's culinary skills, I had no doubt she'd whip up an award-winning confection in record time. But Arla?

"I doubt it." Then she surprised me by adding, "I'm not sure I could complete such a complex challenge by myself in the allotted time."

We returned to making our rounds of the baking stations. The tension continued to escalate. After about fifteen minutes, I whispered to Cloris, "Do you think we should let Rhetta know what's going on?"

She considered the question for a moment, then said, "Probably. Why don't you do that? I'll try to prevent a war from erupting here."

I slipped into my coat and trekked back to the Chateau. As I entered the rotunda, I saw Celeste heading for the staircase. She juggled a cup of tea in one hand, a plate of cookies in the other and stopped when she saw me.

After offering me a rueful smile, she said, "I suppose I shouldn't have lost my temper back there, but that woman is insufferable."

"What did she do to set you off?" I asked.

"She was treating me like a child. Nothing I did was right as far she was concerned. She didn't even like the way I separated eggs. Can you believe it? What difference does it make as long as you don't get any yolk in the albumen?"

"None that I can see," I said.

"Precisely! When she loses, she'll have no one to blame but herself."

"You think she'll lose?"

"Without a doubt. She won't finish in time and will be eliminated."

I nodded. Exactly what Cloris had predicted.

"Anyway," said Celeste, indicating her snack, "I'm going to take these to my room, curl up with a good novel, and enjoy some alone time before dinner."

"Then I'll leave you to it," I said, resuming my way toward Rhetta's office.

No one answered when I knocked on Rhetta's door. I tried the nob, and finding the door unlocked, pushed it open as I called her name. She didn't answer. I crossed the room, walking around her desk to leave her a note, and nearly tripped over her body.

SEVENTEEN

I dropped to my knees and checked for signs of life. Rhetta's breathing was extremely shallow, but at least she was pulling some oxygen into her lungs. I grabbed my phone and called Waverly once again, figuring a CSI team might include at least one person with medical training. Being already on the grounds, they'd get here sooner than an ambulance.

Waverly answered on the first ring. "Please don't tell me you've found another body."

"Unfortunately, yes, but she's still alive," I said. "It's Rhetta. She's unconscious in her office."

The door flew open, and Waverly rushed in. My mouth dropped open. "How in the world—?"

"I was on my way to speak with Rhetta." Waverly joined me on the floor to assess the situation, at the same time placing an emergency call for an ambulance.

A whirlwind of activity filled the next few minutes. The detective drew me away from Rhetta as some of her team administered what aid they could while awaiting the ambulance.

"Do you have any idea what happened?" asked Waverly.

"None. I came to give her an update about the competition and found her this way. The door was unlocked." For the first time since arriving, I scanned the room. Nothing appeared out of place, and I saw no evidence of a struggle.

"Do you know if she has a medical condition?"

I shook my head. "Sorry. I only met her two days ago, but she seemed perfectly fine twenty minutes ago when we spoke in the conference center. Although..."

"Yes?"

"I did notice she rubbed her forehead. I think she may have been trying to fight off a headache. She mentioned that the stress of the last few days had gotten to her. I didn't think anything of it because I've been feeling the same way."

Waverly grabbed a pair of disposable gloves from her jacket pocket, pulled them over her hands, then began opening desk drawers. She found Rhetta's purse in one and rummaged through it. "Looking for something specific?" I asked.

"Drugs. Either prescription or illegal."

"Illegal? Seriously?"

"If she's OD'd, we can administer Narcan."

I stared at her. "I don't think Rhetta is a drug addict."

Waverly leveled a stern gaze at me. "Coming from the woman who barely knows our unconscious victim? How many encounters have you had with addicts?"

I conceded the point. "None."

"I didn't think so. In my experience, they're often very good at covering up their habit."

Once again, I found myself questioning what I really knew

about Rhetta. She'd mentioned Marlene took opioids. Had Rhetta, not the doctor, returned to the cottage to swipe Marlene's pills?

I continued to watch as Waverly searched through the office. After combing every nook and cranny from top to bottom and inside-out, she came up emptyhanded. I breathed a sigh of relief. I liked Rhetta. I didn't want to learn she was both a thief and an addict, not to mention a murderer.

Another thought crossed my mind. "Is it possible she's had a stroke or something? I know she's awfully young, but..."

"Not if she has an underlying medical condition. We'll know more once we get her to the hospital."

As if on cue, we heard a siren drawing nearer. A moment later we were joined by two EMTs, and shortly after that Rhetta was lifted onto a gurney and whisked away.

"Now what?" I asked.

"We proceed under the assumption that this office is a possible crime scene." She ushered me into the lobby while her team continued searching for clues.

Aside from the two of us, the lobby was empty, which I found odd. Normally, at least one of the staff stood sentry at the entrance or the reception desk. "Where is everyone?"

"Being questioned."

"Shouldn't someone go to the hospital to be with Rhetta?"

"One of my team followed the ambulance."

"I was thinking of someone she knows. Someone who will be with her when she wakes up." Assuming she woke up. "Should I go?"

Waverly shook her head. "The Beckwith Chateau grounds are a crime scene. No one leaves until everyone is questioned. I want you to go back to the conference center. We'll be questioning the attendees as soon as we finish up with the staff."

"Not everyone is at the center," I said.

"Who's missing?"

"Not missing, exactly. One of the finalists and her assistant got into a shouting match during the baking competition. The assistant stormed off. That's what I was coming to tell Rhetta."

Waverly pulled out her notepad and pen. She flipped open to a fresh page and asked, "Which woman?"

"Celeste. I bumped into her on my way to Rhetta's office. She had come from the Chartres Library and was headed up to her room."

Waverly scribbled something in her notepad, then looked up. "Do you know her last name and room number?"

"No."

She flipped the notepad closed. "I'll check with the Chateau manager."

"There's something else you should know."

She again flipped open the notepad and poised the pen over a blank page. "Yes?"

"Rhetta and Vernon Beckwith had a huge fight yesterday. She accused him of killing Marlene."

Waverly peered down her perfect Grecian nose at me, cocked her head, and raised an eyebrow. "And you know this how?"

"I overheard them."

"Anyone else hear the fight?"

"Cloris and two of the staff, Tanner and Justin."

Waverly jotted another note. "Anything else?"

"I think that's it. Should I head back to the conference center now?"

Waverly nodded, and we parted ways.

Even before entering the Rouen Conference Center, my ears were assaulted with an undercurrent of raucous competing conversations. The cacophony increased the moment I opened the door, with three of the four finalists shouting orders at their assistants and each of the spectators filling the room with vociferous encouragement for their favorite baker. Who knew fewer than two dozen elderly women could create such a racket?

Arla appeared oblivious to the activity around her, continuing to work by herself. Apparently, no one had stepped forward to take Celeste's place as her assistant.

I made my way across the room to where Cloris stood observing Jacqueline as she extruded turquoise fondant from a pasta machine and rolled it to resemble a ball of yarn. Several other yarn balls in various sizes and colors lay drying on a cookie sheet. As she worked, Jacqueline barked orders at Hildy, who loudly objected to each directive.

I sidled next to Cloris and asked, "Having fun?"

She offered me a visual *duh*. "Ever hear the expression *too many cooks*? These are women used to giving orders, not taking them. In my opinion, allowing each finalist to choose an assistant was counterproductive."

"Would they have finished on time without help?"

She shrugged. "Probably not. Instead, they should have either been given more time or a less-involved challenge."

I scanned the turmoil in the room. "Maybe this is exactly what Marlene wanted to happen."

Cloris turned to stare at me. "Of course! Why didn't I think of that? The woman certainly was devious."

"*Was* being the operative word since it may have gotten her killed."

"True. What took you so long? I was beginning to think you'd abandoned me."

I motioned for her to follow me back out into the hallway where we'd have some privacy. "What's going on?" she asked once the door closed behind us.

"Rhetta won't be returning to close out the competition this afternoon."

"Why not?"

As I filled Cloris in on how I'd found Rhetta unconscious, her jaw dropped. Her eyes grew as large as pizzas—and not the personal pan size. "Will she survive?"

I frowned. "I hope so, but since we don't know what happened..."

"Do you think someone did something to her?"

"Again, hard to say. I saw no obvious injuries or signs of a struggle."

Cloris chewed on her lower lip as she glanced back toward the closed door. "Do we say anything to the conference attendees?"

"As little as possible for now. You should call time at the end of the competition. If anyone asks about Rhetta, just say she's been detained."

"That's an understatement."

"Waverly and her team will arrive shortly before the end of the competition. Once time is up, they'll begin questioning everyone about Wanda."

Puzzlement settled over Cloris's face. "Here? All together? Don't the police usually question witnesses and suspects one-on-one? At least, that's the way they do it on *Law & Order*."

I nodded. "I'm sure Waverly and her team have already decided how to handle the interviews. They'll probably commandeer some of the smaller conference rooms in the Chateau. Anyway, let her determine whether or not to say anything further about Rhetta."

"Sounds like a plan."

We returned to the competition and made our rounds, checking out the progress of each of the four finalists. By now all had their cakes in the ovens and had started whipping up their icing or sculpting their decorations, some having more success than others.

"That's not good," said Cloris, eyeing Joy, who was assisting Letitia.

Joy had begun to cream butter and sugar in a stand mixer. "What's wrong?"

"She didn't use room temperature butter."

"Is that necessary?" I didn't bake often, but I don't remember ever letting my butter sit out long enough to warm to room temperature, only until it was soft enough to cut into small pieces.

"It is if she doesn't want broken buttercream."

"Broken buttercream?" Was that even a thing?

"If the butter isn't at room temperature, the sugar won't incorporate properly. The frosting will look grainy instead of creamy and fluffy."

Which explained why my buttercream never looked like Cloris's buttercream or bakery buttercream. I administered a virtual head slap to myself and made a mental note to use room temperature butter from now on.

Sure enough, when Letitia checked on Joy's progress, she exploded, grabbed the bowl, and dumped the buttercream, bowl and all, into the nearest trashcan. "Don't you know how to do anything right?" she shrieked, towering over the cowering woman who barely came to her shoulders.

Joy, exhibiting anything but joy, backed away from Letitia and stammered something incoherent. Her chin trembled as she fought back tears.

"This isn't brain surgery," Letitia scoffed. "My eight-year-old grandniece knows how to whip up decent buttercream."

Losing her battle over her emotions, Joy grabbed a dishtowel and buried her face in it.

"Oh, grow a pair," said Letitia, turning her back on the sniveling woman. "Start over. Do it right this time before you cost me the competition."

"Too bad we can't include attitude in the judging criteria," I said.

Cloris cocked her head and grew thoughtful for a moment before her lips twitched up in a devilish grin. "Who says we can't?"

No further major skirmishes occurred throughout the remainder of the afternoon, only minor ones. However, that did little to alleviate the tension hanging over the room.

"I still don't get it," said Cloris as the clock ticked down to the end of the competition.

"Get what?"

"Why these women act like winning a baking contest is the most important thing in their lives. Given what they've accomplished in their careers, this competition shouldn't even make the list of their top one hundred achievements."

My thoughts had been running in the same direction, but I think I'd finally figured it out. "Maybe it's because they now feel irrelevant. All their lives they've had to fight to succeed. It's like Fred Astaire and Ginger Rogers."

Cloris nodded. "Meaning they not only had to master every

step as well as their male counterparts, but they had to execute them in heels and backwards?"

"Exactly. *As good* was never good enough. They had to be better at everything. They don't know how to live any other way. Their behavior is too ingrained in their DNA at this point. They've earned the right to kick back and enjoy the remainder of their lives, but they're incapable of doing so."

Cloris frowned. "That's one of the saddest things I've ever heard."

I couldn't disagree. I felt sorry for all the Stitch and Bake Society members.

At five o'clock Cloris walked up to the microphone. "Time's up, ladies. Please step away from your creations. We ask that the rest of you remain seated for now."

The spectators erupted in applause. I glanced around the room. No one asked why Cloris and not Rhetta had ended the baking competition, which was fine with us. One less secret to sidestep.

Within seconds, Tanner and Justin arrived with rolling carts to transport the cakes to the Chateau's large industrial refrigerator until this evening's judging. But before they whisked the cakes away, Cloris and I took a final lap around the stations for a closer look at the finalists' efforts.

All four women had completed the challenge with varying degrees of success that showcased the decorating and construction skills of some and the weaknesses of others. Jacqueline and Letitia had draped fondant over their buttercream crumb-coated tiers. Both displayed creases, cracks, and tears. "Fondant is not forgiving," whispered Cloris.

Letitia had chosen crochet as her theme. A rudimentary

fondant figure of a woman seated in a rocking chair and crocheting an afghan was perched on her top layer. The afghan, in a granny square pattern, was draped over the figure's lap and cascaded down the front of the cake. Letitia had attempted to mask her fondant defects with buttercream roses, but the roses were so incongruous with her design that they only served to highlight her mistakes rather than conceal them.

Jacqueline had decided on four cake tiers instead of three. She'd baked the top tier in a large dome pan, carving out the inside to create a basket covered in fondant. The balls of yarn she'd made from extruded fondant were piled within the basket. The yarn basket sat on top of her three other tiers, which she'd textured with impression mats to give the appearance of knitting. However, gaps in the fondant exposed her crumb coat.

Worse yet, according to Cloris she hadn't compensated for the weight of the yarn basket, which was already sinking into the top layer of her cake. "That's a disaster waiting to happen," she said, studying Jacqueline's completed entry. "Her cake won't make it to the judging in one piece."

Arla had attempted to cover her cake in a mirror glaze rather than fondant. Although uniform, the glaze lacked the mandatory shine. She'd chosen a sewing theme with colorful fondant buttons scattered randomly around the perimeter of her tiers. A fondant pincushion, spools of thread, scissors, and assorted notions decorating the top layer.

Georgina had played it safe, covering her three tiers in white buttercream, but each layer consisted of a different patterned cable knit, creating a cake that appeared to be dressed in a sweater. She had also extruded fondant to create three different sized balls of white yarn which perched on her top layer. A pair of tempered white chocolate knitting needles stuck out of the largest ball of yarn, satisfying the height requirement.

We had no way of judging the flavor pairings or the quality of the bakes at this point. That part of the challenge would have to wait until after dinner when we sampled each cake.

As soon as the cakes were wheeled out of the conference center, Waverly entered the room and made her way to the microphone. Cloris and I took this as our cue to slip away. However, as I headed for the door, I noticed Georgina and Letitia, both with bewildered expressions covering their faces, eyeing our progression. No doubt, they'd soon discover why Waverly looked so familiar.

~*~

Cloris and I quickly caught up with Tanner and Justin, who were taking extra precautions to avoid any mishaps while gingerly maneuvering the cake-laden carts toward the Chateau. "Did you hear what happened?" asked Tanner.

We both played dumb. "Something happened?" I asked.

"I'll say!" said Justin. "Someone knocked off one of those old ladies. They found her buried under a pile of leaves in the woods near the golf course."

Cloris shuddered. "How awful! Who was it?"

He turned to Tanner. "Do you remember her name?"

Tanner shrugged. "Wanda, maybe?"

"Do they know what happened to her?"

"They know she was murdered," said Tanner. "Beyond that, they're not saying."

"All the staff were questioned," said Justin, "No one told us anything specific."

"We did see something, though," said Tanner.

"What was that?" I asked.

Justin jumped in to answer. "About ten minutes ago, two cops marched Mr. Beckwith and Dr. Hargrove out in handcuffs."

EIGHTEEN

Justin eagerly continued, "You should've heard them."

"Beckwith and the doctor?" I asked.

"Yeah, the doctor was running off at the mouth, blaming Beckwith for everything."

Cloris's jaw dropped open, her eyebrows disappearing under her bangs. "Including murder?"

"Nah, just kept saying it was all Beckwith's idea, and Beckwith was screaming at him to shut up."

"What else did you hear?" I asked.

"Aside from Beckwith calling the doctor every four-letter word known to man?" asked Tanner, putting an end to Justin's exuberant recap. "That's about it. By then the cops had them each in a patrol car and drove off."

At that point we had arrived back at the Chateau and parted ways with Tanner and Justin. As they proceeded to wheel the cake carts toward the kitchen, I turned to Cloris. "I think we both deserve a glass of wine before dinner."

She shook her head. "Are you kidding? Given the events of this afternoon, we deserve something a heck of a lot stronger than wine. And whatever I decide on drinking, it's going to be a double."

"Make that two," I said as we headed down the corridor to the Chartres Library.

With the stitchers and bakers being questioned by the police, we had the Chartres Library to ourselves except for a few servers who were standing around chatting with each other. As soon as we settled into seats at a table off to the side of the bar, one of the waitstaff broke away from the group and headed toward us. "Good afternoon, ladies." Her nametag identified her as Skylar. Before taking our orders, she placed cardboard coasters and cocktail napkins, both emblazoned with the Beckwith Chateau logo, in front of us. "What can I bring you?"

Cloris ordered a double Manhattan. "With extra cherries," she added. Cloris is the only person I know whose sweet tooth is sweeter than mine. The difference, of course, is that her superpower enables her to consume sweets without adding calories.

Skylar turned to me. "And you, ma'am?" After I ordered a tall Long Island Iced Tea, she scurried off to fill our drink order.

With no other patrons in the room, Skylar returned in less than two minutes. "Did you hear about Rhetta?" she asked as she set the drinks on the coasters. Before either Cloris or I could answer, she breathlessly continued, "Terrible, isn't it? All on top of someone killing one of those little old ladies, and the cops arresting Mr. Beckwith and Dr. Hargrove. Do you think one of them tried to kill Rhetta?"

"I suppose anything is possible," I said. "Do you know why they were arrested?"

She shook her head. "No one knows. At least no one I've talked to. And then there's Mrs. Beckwith," she continued. "Some of the staff think she was murdered, too. We're all really freaked out. The biggest scandal we've ever had here was a few years ago when several pro golfers were caught cheating during a PGA tournament."

I didn't care about golf, but I did care about Rhetta. "Does anyone have an update on Rhetta's condition?"

"Last I heard, she'd regained consciousness and was doing well enough to speak with the Chateau manager. He said the hospital is running tests, and they plan to keep her overnight for observation."

"So, they don't yet know what caused her to pass out?" asked Cloris.

"Doesn't sound like it from the little he told us." Then she changed the subject. "You ladies want anything to go with those drinks? Maybe a shrimp cocktail? Some crackers and warm brie?"

"We'll have both," I said.

"We will?" asked Cloris as Skylar departed.

I pointed toward her double Manhattan as she took a sip. "I'm expecting dinner will be delayed, and it's not wise for either of us to drink this much on an empty stomach. Not with the possibility of a killer still lurking on the grounds."

"You don't think either Beckwith or Hargrove killed Wanda?"

"I don't see a possible motive, do you?"

"Not unless we're missing something. What about Rhetta? Do you think Beckwith tried to silence her?"

"I think that's much more likely. The man has anger management issues, and we already know she accused him of killing Marlene. However, Rhetta wasn't attacked, at least not from what I could see."

"What about poison?"

I shook my head. "Usually not a weapon of choice for men."

She rolled her eyes. "Your knowledge of murder amazes me."

I scowled into my drink. Unlike golf, I'd had a lot of firsthand experience with murder lately.

Before Cloris could respond, my phone rang. "Rhetta," I told her, glancing at the display. After swiping to accept the call, I asked, "How are you?"

"Better now," she said. "I understand you found me. You may have saved my life, Anastasia."

"Do you remember what happened?"

"No, the doctor thinks someone may have drugged me, possibly with that date rape drug, ro-something or other?"

"Rohypnol."

"Yes, that's it. They're going to run more tests."

"Do you have any idea who could have drugged you?"

"No clue."

I thought back to when I had found Rhetta on her office floor. I didn't remember seeing a water bottle or coffee cup on her desk. Waverly had searched for pills, but I'm sure she would have noticed an open beverage container that might have contained a suspicious substance. "You don't remember eating or drinking anything?"

"The last thing I remember is leaving the conference center after the start of the baking competition. But why would someone want to drug me?"

"Maybe you saw or heard something you weren't supposed to."

"Like what?"

"Have you spoken with the police yet?"

"The police? Why? Because the doctor thinks I could've been drugged?"

"Yes, about that and there was another incident here. They could be connected."

On the other end of the phone, I heard Rhetta suck in her breath. "What now?"

I hesitated, not sure at first how much to tell her. However, when I had discovered Rhetta, Waverly had been on her way to speak with her about Wanda's murder. With the staff already interviewed and the conference attendees in the process of being interviewed, I saw no point in hiding Wanda's murder from Rhetta. She had a right to know, now more than ever.

I took a deep breath, exhaling the news. "There was another murder. Cloris and I discovered Wanda's body while we were taking a walk after lunch."

"And you didn't tell me? How could you keep that from me?"

"We were under police orders not to say anything until they first spoke with the staff and the other Stitch and Bake ladies. One of the detectives was on her way to your office when I found you."

Silence greeted my pronouncement. "Rhetta? Are you still there?"

"Y-yes. I...how did Wanda die?"

I explained how Cloris and I had found her. "She was in a similar pose as Marlene."

"That adds credence to someone having killed Marlene, doesn't it?"

"It looks that way, but with Vernon having had Marlene cremated so quickly, the police only have our word for how she looked at the time."

Not that I hoped there'd be a next time, but if I ever again stumble across another dead body, maybe I should snap some photos before the killer has a chance to destroy evidence—or the victim.

Rhetta's voice grew animated. "Vernon had to have killed Marlene. Or the doctor did it on his orders. I'm sure of it." Then she emitted a strangled cry.

"Rhetta? Are you okay?"

"I'm...I...oh, Anastasia, what if Vernon tried to kill me because he thinks I know more than I do? After all, I pretty much accused him of killing Marlene."

The thought had occurred to me. "Did you have any interaction with Vernon earlier today?" What if Beckwith had doctored Rhetta's water bottle at some point, and she didn't drink from it until returning from the conference center? But if that was the case, what happened to the water bottle? Vernon and the doctor were arrested before Rhetta became ill. He wouldn't have had a chance to remove the evidence after she succumbed to the drug.

"He has to be behind this, but why Wanda?"

"Maybe she, too, had seen or heard something she shouldn't have, possibly after she stormed out of the ballroom last night. No one remembers seeing her later last night, and she never showed up for either workshop this morning."

At that point I heard another voice in the room. "I have to go," said Rhetta. "They need to draw more blood, but before I hang up, I need a favor."

"Anything."

"Would you and Cloris announce the winners this evening? I won't be released from the hospital until tomorrow."

"Of course."

"The awards for the baking and needlework competitions are in the closet in my office, top shelf. There's also a master list of the needlework entries that match the numbers with the entrants' names. I've spoken with the Chateau manager. He told me he locked my office after the police finished up. He'll let you in."

"Consider it done," I said, then added, "You take care, Rhetta."

"I will, and thanks again for everything you've done." With that, she disconnected the call.

"Talk about dedication to the job," said Cloris. I was filling her in on the part of the conversation she hadn't heard as we headed to the Chateau manager's office.

"Especially considering someone may have tried to kill her," I added.

"Do you think it was Beckwith?"

"If he's completely paranoid and trying to cover his tracks? It's possible."

"You don't sound convinced."

"I'm not."

"Why? He owns a drug company. I'm sure he has access to all sorts of deadly substances."

"But he'd also have a vast knowledge of pharmaceuticals. Whoever drugged Rhetta doesn't."

Cloris stopped short and turned to confront me. "All right, Sherlock. I'll bite. How do you know that?"

"Just a hunch but you rarely hear of someone dying from a date rape drug. Beckwith would have chosen something he'd know would work. Whoever poisoned Rhetta either only wanted her temporarily out of commission or was sending her a message."

"Which leads us back to Beckwith."

"Unless we're dealing with an inept would-be killer with some other motive."

Cloris threw her arms up in the air as we resumed walking. "You're making my head spin."

Once we arrived at the manager's office, I paused before knocking and added, "Anyway, given the events of today, a couple of meaningless baking and needlework competitions would be the last thing on my mind."

"Ditto."

However, once we had retrieved the awards and I had a chance to scan the master list of needlework entries, I knew the members of the Stitch and Bake Society would feel quite differently tonight, despite the murder of one of their own. "This is not going to go down well," I said, showing Cloris the names of the women who had created the needlework we'd chosen for first, second, and third place.

~*~

Shortly before six o'clock Cloris and I headed toward the Grenoble Ballroom. We found a sign on the closed door, announcing dinner would be delayed an hour. With time to kill, we arranged for Tanner to bring our belongings to my car, enabling us to make a speedy getaway once the conference ended. We were walking back to the Chateau when Zack called.

"How has your day been so far?" he asked.

There was something in his tone that cautioned me this was anything but an innocent question. After all, he knew he'd see me in a few hours. So why was he calling now to ask about my day unless he had an ulterior motive?

"Uhm...interesting?"

"I can imagine."

I heaved a sigh. "All right, what have you heard?"

"You mean besides the arrests of both Vernon Beckwith and your suspicious doctor?"

"I was going to tell you about that this evening. I don't even know what the charges are at this point."

"Were you also going to tell me that another woman was murdered?"

"Of course."

"Good to know."

"How did you find out?"

"It's all over the news." He paused before adding, "And so are you."

I groaned. "What? How? I haven't talked to anyone other than the police."

"Then someone informed the local media. Would you like me to read you the Breaking News headline from ABC? I wrote it down."

"Do I really want to know?"

I suppose he figured I did because he immediately continued. "*Westfield, New Jersey's Own Jessica Fletcher Discovers Body of Retired Fast-Food Franchise Queen Wanda Reeves.*"

At least they hadn't referred to me as Miss Marple.

~*~

With the needlework and baking awards in hand, Cloris and I made our way to the ballroom minutes before seven o'clock. Most of the women had already arrived and were gathered in small groups. They swarmed us the moment we entered the room.

"You have some explaining to do," said Letitia, pointing a finger at me. "That woman wasn't your cousin. She's a detective."

"Why the deception?" asked Georgina as the remainder of the

women entered the ballroom behind us and joined the others circling around us.

"Are the two of you working undercover?" asked Celeste.

One of their members had been murdered, and what was uppermost in their minds was why I had deceived them into thinking Waverly was my cousin? I glanced sideways at Cloris. She turned toward me, her expressive eye roll leaving no room for interpretation.

Addressing the crowd of women, I answered Celeste, "No, we're not working undercover."

"Then what the heck is going on?" asked Hildy, assuming an aggressive hands-on-hips pose.

"And how does it relate to Wanda's death?" asked Celeste.

"You'll have to ask the detective about that. I have nothing more to say on the subject."

"Well, that sounds suspicious," said Jacqueline. The rest of the group nodded in agreement.

Out of the corner of my eye, I noticed the waitstaff had entered the ballroom and were beginning to set the salad course at each place setting. I latched onto Cloris's arm, extricated us from the mob of women, and hurried to our table for two. Even after we had taken our seats, the stitchers and bakers stood in place, glowering and grumbling, for a few seconds longer before finally breaking up and heading to their tables.

Throughout dinner Cloris and I suffered the slings and arrows of outrageous glares directed our way. "They're insufferable," I said. "Did you notice how Wanda's death was mentioned more as an afterthought?"

"Ignore them," said Cloris, spearing a piece of perfectly broiled Chilean sea bass and popping it into her mouth. "Enjoy your dinner. We'll be on our way home shortly."

"Easier said than done." I looked down at my plate and realized I'd spent the past few minutes pushing my food around without taking a single bite. Maybe the Long Island iced tea and appetizers I'd consumed in the Chartres Library had filled me up.

Or maybe my lack of appetite had more to do with my stomach being tied up in knots from an attack too reminiscent of the constant bullying I'd sustained at the hands of the mean girls in junior high. Either way, I found myself unable to eat, which didn't bode well for carrying out my duties as a cake judge.

I pushed my plate away. "Also," I continued, "none of those women asked about Rhetta. I've come across some self-absorbed people over the years, I even have the misfortune of living with one of them, but this group is Lucille to the nth degree."

The only thing setting the members of the Stitch and Bake Society apart from my mother-in-law was that all these women had retired with large nest eggs. If Lucille had lived the life of a successful capitalist instead of a diehard communist, I wouldn't now be stuck with her as a permanent houseguest.

"You're probably right," said Cloris, "but you should hold off on jumping to any conclusions until we announce the winners. It's possible they don't know about Rhetta."

"You think that's possible with the way the staff gossips?"

She shrugged. "When you found Rhetta, they were all baking their buns off in the conference center, and the staff was being questioned by the police. I'm not sure there would have been an opportunity for gossip to spread from one group to the other."

"Except for Celeste," I reminded her. "She may have seen or heard something after she stormed out of the conference center."

But the more I thought about that possibility, the more I

discounted it. "No." I shook my head. "Celeste couldn't have known. She'd gone up to her room before I arrived at Rhetta's office."

Perhaps I did need to give the women the benefit of the doubt—at least where Rhetta was concerned.

"You're the expert on police procedures," Cloris continued, "Would the detectives have mentioned Rhetta while they interviewed the conference attendees?"

"I'm not *that* much of an expert."

"You're the one with hands-on experience. I get all my law enforcement knowledge from television and the movies."

"I really don't know," I said, "but my gut tells me the interviewing detectives probably wouldn't have mentioned Rhetta because at the time all signs indicated she had suffered a medical episode, not that she was the victim of an attack. There was no obvious connection between the two incidents."

"Except that at least one part of that assumption is no longer true. Wouldn't the doctor have contacted Waverly when the tests showed Rhetta had been drugged?"

"Either Waverly or someone on her team. However, I'm guessing by the time the detective received that information, the interviews had concluded."

Cloris eyed me skeptically. "Okay, Svengali, how do you know that?"

"Look around. All the women are not only dressed up for dinner, but they've also reapplied their makeup. Some have even redone their hair from the way they'd worn it earlier in the day. That takes time."

Cloris scanned the room. "Valid point. I never would have thought of that."

"You're right, though," I said. "I shouldn't haul out the tar and feathers until we see how our stitchers and bakers react to Rhetta's absence during the awards ceremony."

"And if that conclusion you jumped to is correct," said Cloris, "make sure you grab two brushes. I'll help you spread the tar and dump the feathers. I find these women as irritating as you do."

I looked out across the room. Many of the women had already finished their dinner. Any moment the waitstaff would clear their plates and roll in the carts with the four finalists' cakes. I girded myself for the fireworks certain to follow.

NINETEEN

A few minutes later, when the doors to the kitchen opened and two of the waitstaff rolled in the carts, gasps of dismay filled the ballroom. As Cloris had predicted, Jacqueline's cake had not stood up to the weight of her fondant yarn basket. Not only had the basket ripped apart the top tier, but it had destroyed the first two tiers as well. Chunks of cake surrounded the yarn basket, which had toppled over, split in half, and spilled the yarn balls onto the cart.

"Well, we know who's *not* going to win," said Celeste.

"And so it begins," I whispered to Cloris.

"I told you so," said Hildy, pointing a finger at Jacqueline. "You should have listened to me and inserted dowels to support your structure. But you always think you know more than everyone else."

Jacqueline turned crimson. She shot daggers first at Celeste, then Hildy, but to her credit, she remained in her seat. Maybe she was worried she'd meet with the same fate as Wanda if she stormed out of the ballroom. Or given her ego, perhaps she thought she still might win.

The room had grown pin-drop silent, the other women holding their collective breaths, waiting to see how Jacqueline would respond to Hildy's taunts. Finally, she answered back with a shrug. "What do I care? It's nothing but a stupid contest. At least I made it to the final round. Unlike you, Hildy." Then she picked up her coffee cup and took a sip as if nothing had happened.

By this time the two waiters had set the carts in front of our table and stepped aside. Even though Cloris and I had already visually assessed each cake at the end of the competition, we rose and stood in front of the carts for a second look. With our backs to the conference attendees, we made one final assessment of the completed challenge cakes.

Neither Cloris nor I deviated from our earlier evaluation. Hands down, Georgina's entry literally took the cake. Her tiers were level, her decorating skills flawless. If I didn't know better, I'd think she'd enrobed her cake in an actual knitted sweater.

Cloris turned to face the room. "Unfortunately, only three of the cakes meet the challenge. I'm sorry, Jacqueline, but we have to disqualify your entry."

"As it should be," said Hildy, smirking at Jacqueline.

Cloris and I exchanged a slight shake of our heads as we returned to our table. Once seated, she indicated to the waiters they could begin serving samples of the remaining three contenders.

Of the three cakes, Arla had chosen the most unusual flavor combination, going with an orange pistachio tier, a mango macadamia tier, and a pineapple pecan tier. But she'd tied the three cakes together with a maraschino cherry marshmallow filling that was even too sweet for my sweet tooth.

Letitia had gone a more traditional route, creating a flavor palette reminiscent of Neapolitan ice cream with chocolate, vanilla, and strawberry cake tiers. She used a strawberry filling and strawberry buttercream for her crumb coat. Unfortunately, the thick layer of fondant covering her cake left a slightly bitter aftertaste in my mouth.

Georgina had chosen lemon, blueberry, and raspberry for her three tiers with a filling of white chocolate ganache and feuilletine that added a crunchy texture to her cake. Her Italian buttercream frosting was light, fluffy, and not overly sweet.

Cloris and I quickly came to a mutual agreement regarding the ranking of the three cakes. We had also decided ahead of time that I'd present the needlework winners first while the women ate their dessert. I stood to make the announcement. "I want to commend all of you on your craftsmanship and creativity, which made it difficult to narrow down the three needlework finalists."

A smattering of applause filled the room, then died down. I took a deep breath and plowed on. "Third place goes to the cross stitch and beaded wedding sampler stitched by Wanda Reeves."

Silence greeted my announcement. Then one of the women toward the back of the room rose to her feet and began clapping. Soon others joined in until everyone was on their feet and the room was filled with loud applause.

When the room once again grew quiet, I continued, "Second place goes to the silk embroidered peony bolero jacket by Marlene Beckwith." Only Arla rose to her feet to applaud. The others glared, which made Arla set her jaw, lift her chin, and clap even louder.

I braced myself for the final announcement. "And the first-place winner is the smocked baptismal gown trimmed in handmade lace and created by Arla Shoenfeld."

A low rumbling of complaints arose around the room as Arla made her way toward me to receive her plaque. I had expected a more vocal protest from the other women, given their animosity toward Arla. However, knowing she was also one of the three baking finalists, maybe they were reserving their outrage for when Cloris announced those awards.

Once she stood in front of me, I handed her the plaque and shook her hand. "Congratulations, Arla."

"Thank you." She turned to face the audience, as if planning to make a statement. I held my breath, awaiting fireworks, but after scoping out the room, she silently returned to her seat.

With the crisis averted, I handed the remainder of the awards presentation over to Cloris. "Ladies," she said as she stood, "this last challenge was not easy."

"Neither was the previous one," said Joy.

"Thanks to Marlene," added Celeste.

The room filled with murmurs of agreement.

"Nonetheless," continued Cloris, "that three of you were able to complete the challenge is a testament to your baking skills. Please join me up front."

After the three women made their way to our table, Letitia and Georgina clasped hands, wishing each other good luck. Arla stood apart from them. Cloris then rattled off the competition results in rapid succession as I handed each woman her award. "Third place goes to Letitia Cramer, second place to Arla Shoenfeld, and first place to Georgina Malloy."

While the stitchers and bakers swarmed Georgina with congratulations, Arla returned to her seat to retrieve her needlework plaque. Cradling both awards in the crook of her arm, she strode toward the ballroom exit, her eyes straight ahead, her head held high. She arrived at the exit at the same moment Vernon Beckwith stuck his head in the room. The two silently glared at each other for a moment before he stepped aside to allow her to pass.

"Looks like Beckwith posted bail," I said.

Cloris glanced toward the doorway in time to see Beckwith retreat. "That's too bad."

"Our work is done here," I said. "You see any reason why we can't grab our coats and leave?"

"None. Although it would have been nice if at least some of those women had thought to thank us. After all, they wouldn't have had a conference without us."

I watched as the gaggle of stitchers and bakers exited the ballroom, all chatting among themselves and completely ignoring us. As we followed a short distance behind them, I said, "I've had an epiphany."

Cloris cocked her head and arched an eyebrow. "Do tell."

"After spending three days with those women, I've concluded they're all carbon copies of Marlene—stubborn, egotistical, narcissistic, and manipulative."

She nodded. "Agreed. But you forgot to include overly competitive."

"That, too. No wonder they all hated Marlene. But not because they objected to her iron-fisted control of the organization."

"Then why?"

"Because every one of them wants that control for herself."

I was wrong when I surmised that these women were happy to

sit back and let someone else do all the heavy lifting now that they were retired. They were total control freaks. None of them could stand not running everything their way.

Realizing that also made me rethink Marlene and Wanda's deaths, as well as the attack on Rhetta. Was it possible Vernon Beckwith had nothing to do with those incidents?

I paused at the bottom of the staircase. The other women had headed down the hall toward the Chartres Library. Beckwith was nowhere in sight. The rotunda was empty except for Cloris and me. "This may sound completely crazy, but what if one of the Stitch and Bake ladies orchestrated the murders and the attempt on Rhetta's life?"

"To what end?"

"Jealousy? Revenge?"

"All three incidents?"

"If I'm correct, Marlene's murder was premeditated. The other incidents were cleanup operations."

"Cleanup operations?"

"Due to a loose end left hanging or because the killer suspected someone saw or heard something."

"I suppose that makes sense. However, these same suppositions can also be applied to both Beckwith and the doctor."

"True. And they're still both at the top of my suspects list. This is merely an alternate theory."

I still believed that Wanda was killed because she had the misfortune of winding up in the wrong place at the wrong time. The same probably held true for Rhetta, only not necessarily perpetrated by Vernon Beckwith.

Cloris mulled this over as we ascended the staircase. "Not by herself. None of those women have the upper body strength to haul Wanda into the woods. She'd need an accomplice."

"Agreed."

"It's an interesting theory, Sherlock. You might want to run it by Waverly."

"I plan to."

~*~

Fifteen minutes later Cloris and I were in my Jetta driving on Rt. 280 on our way toward the Garden State Parkway. By the time we'd gotten on the road, we'd escaped the heaviest of the bumper-to-bumper evening commuter rush, but traffic was never light, no matter the hour, on New Jersey's major roadways. Still, the stress of the last three days lessened somewhat with each passing mile I put between us and the Beckwith Chateau.

It would have decreased even more except for the testosterone-driven bozos who insisted on weaving in and out of lanes, constantly cutting off one another. "Jeez," I said, "you'd think we were driving on the Indianapolis Speedway."

Cloris snorted. "We aren't? Could've fooled me."

I gripped the steering wheel, my eyes continually darting from my windshield to my side and rearview mirrors. "I'm looking forward to that comp time we're due."

"We certainly deserve it after suffering through the conference from Hades." She let loose a long sigh. "Honestly, Anastasia, I don't know how you do it."

I stole a quick glance away from the traffic to look at her. "Do what?"

"Deal with all those dead bodies you find. How many is it at this point?"

"Too many."

"One is too many for me. I don't know that I'll ever be able to scrub my brain of seeing Wanda buried in a makeshift grave of dead leaves."

Dead leaves. That's when the mother of all OMG moments smacked me in the face. I gasped.

"What's wrong?"

"Justin."

"What about him?"

"Justin killed Wanda. Or at least moved her body into the woods."

"How could you possibly know that?"

"He told us she was found under a pile of leaves in the woods near the golf course."

"She was."

"But the detective who interviewed him never would have divulged such detailed information."

"And you know that how?"

"From the aftermath of all those dead bodies I keep finding. I've had enough interactions with Detective Spader and other law enforcement professionals to learn a few things along the way. Anytime I ask a question, it's always, 'I'm not at liberty to divulge that.' Or 'That information is on a need-to-know basis.' They never tell you more than they want you to know. The only way Justin would know how Wanda was found would be if he was at the crime scene."

"Maybe it slipped out during questioning. Or he overheard some of the officers talking about the murder. Why on earth would Justin be involved?"

"Why not? Someone was. Especially if one of our not-so-sweet little old ladies is a cold-blooded killer. Or like the doctor, he could also be doing Beckwith's dirty work."

"You can include that nugget of inspiration when you call Waverly."

Our conversation had diverted my attention to the point that I nearly missed the exit ramp onto the Garden State Parkway. Luckily, I was in the right-most lane and only needed to make a quick swerve onto the ramp to avoid driving past it. As I slowed around the curve, I heard screeching brakes and a blaring horn. Glancing into the rearview mirror, I noticed another driver had also nearly missed the exit, but it appeared he'd cut off a vehicle as he darted across the road.

He then proceeded to drive so close that if I had to tap my brakes, he'd rear-end me. In driver's ed we had learned to maintain a car length between vehicles for every ten miles an hour of speed. This guy either hadn't gotten the message or thought driver safety didn't apply to him. Forget two-and-a-half car lengths distance on the twenty-five mile per hour exit ramp curve. He wasn't even two-and-a-half inches from my bumper.

As soon as I merged onto the Parkway, I shifted one lane to my left to get away from him. He followed. I waited until I saw enough of a break in the lane to my right and moved back. So did he.

"What's going on?" asked Cloris.

"I'm not sure. I hope we're just dealing with a jerk who's had one beer too many."

"Or?"

"Or we're being followed."

Cloris twisted around in her seat. "I can't tell what kind of car he's driving other than it's a huge SUV. If you can put some distance between us, I'll try to catch the plate number."

"Easier said than done." I checked my sideview mirror and saw that a space had opened between the two cars immediately to my left, enough room for me to switch lanes but not for my tailgating buddy to follow behind me. As soon as the first car moved ahead of me, I slipped in front of the second car.

Unfortunately, seconds later the car behind me decided to switch lanes and moved to his left, at which point my tailgater returned to his tailgating ways. "I think we have a problem," I said.

"Maybe he'll give up after he's satisfied he's made his point."

"And what point would that be?"

"That he's a macho man?"

"More like a Neanderthal."

After checking my mirrors again, I decided on another lane switch, waiting for an opportunity to ease my car between two others. He responded by cutting off the car behind me, leaving no doubt in my mind that whether the guy was toying with me or had a more nefarious agenda, Cloris and I were in serious trouble.

I took one hand off the steering wheel, slipping it under my seatbelt and into my coat pocket to retrieve my cell phone. I activated Siri and said, "Call Detective Spader." Then I passed the phone to Cloris and repositioned my hands at ten and two o'clock.

After three rings, just as I thought the call would go to voicemail, Spader finally answered. As was often the case when I called, he dispensed with any greeting and instead said, "It's been a long day, Mrs. Pollack. Please don't tell me you've found another body."

"You're in luck, Detective. No bodies. At least not yet."

He heaved a sigh. "What's that supposed to mean?"

"I'm being followed." I quickly explained the situation.

"Exactly where are you?"

"On the Parkway heading south. We just passed the Vauxhall

exit."

"Who's with you?"

"Cloris, my coworker. I have to drop her off before I head home."

"Don't. Here's what I want you to do." He then laid out his plan.

TWENTY

Spader instructed me to refrain from any further lane switching and maintain the speed limit. "He may just be a jerk playing cat and mouse. If you don't react, he'll get tired of the game and eventually give up on you."

"What if he doesn't?" For all I knew, I was the unlucky target of road rage by a guy consumed with 'roid rage, a potentially deadly combination. The other possibility? The guy had followed us from the moment we departed Beckwith Chateau, which might prove an even deadlier reality. I voiced my fears.

Spader heaved a heavy sigh that I interpreted as regret over having answered his phone. "Given your track record, Mrs. Pollack? My guess is he'll continue following you. Either way, I want you to take the Westfield exit and head directly to the police station."

"Town or county station?"

"Town. Turn onto Park Drive. I'll make sure there's an empty curb spot for you to pull into in front of the entrance."

"Then what?"

"Stay in your car with the engine running, doors locked. I'm going to position several unmarked vehicles along your route. They'll follow as you pass. Additional officers will be stationed at either end of Park Drive. If you were followed, we'll snare him."

"It's dark out. How will they identify my car?"

"By the description and plate number I've pulled up on the computer and will send to them."

"That was quick."

"That's why they pay me the big bucks."

"Right." Spader's plan sounded great until my brain continued losing itself down that *what if* path. Like, what if the guy following us pulled up alongside my car once I park, and what if he has a gun, and what if he starts shooting at us?

What if he sprays bullets indiscriminately? I didn't want to be responsible for the loss of any Westfield law enforcement lives. Or innocent bystanders. Or people living in nearby homes. Or those who happened to drive down Central Avenue, Broad Street, or Park Drive at the worst possible moment.

Who knew how much weaponry this guy had in his car? He hadn't waved a gun at me—yet. At least not that I'd seen. But that didn't mean he wasn't packing an arsenal.

What if he doesn't wait until I park at the police station? What if he pulls up alongside me at a red light on Central Avenue and opens fire? I rattled off all these *what ifs* in rapid succession, barely taking a breath between each.

"Stop with the *what ifs* already!" hissed Cloris from the seat beside me.

I white knuckled the steering wheel as I stole a glance in her direction. She looked as if she'd prefer to take her chances bolting from my car as we travelled at sixty-five miles an hour down the Garden State Parkway, rather than occupy my passenger seat a minute longer.

"Sorry!" But I was scared, too. If this past year had taught me anything, it was that *what ifs* often manifested themselves into extremely bad outcomes.

"You still there, Mrs. Pollack?"

"We're all still here, Detective." I glanced into my rearview mirror. "Cloris, me, and a possible Freddy Kreuger clone on my tail."

"Breathe," said Spader. "Nice deep breaths."

I tried but only succeeded in a shaky shallow breath that resulted in a hiccup. Hey, he wasn't the one with a possible killer out to get him. "Is car yoga your new thing, Detective?"

When I first met Detective Samuel Spader last year, he had one foot in the grave. No exaggeration. Grossly obese and addicted to both cigarettes and alcohol, his chances of living to retirement hovered in the slim-to-none range. Since then, something had caused him to take stock of his unhealthy lifestyle. In the last several months Spader had dropped both a ton of weight and his tobacco habit.

"Only when I don't have a goat," he said. "I'm guessing there isn't one in your car?"

"Gee, I knew I forgot to pack something." When Spader choked on a chortle, I added, "Tell me you're not into goat yoga."

Rather than confirm or deny, which made me suspect he'd gone full Zen, he moved the conversation back to being about me. "I've seen you get through much worse, Mrs. Pollack. If anyone can handle a situation like this, it's you."

"He's right," said Cloris. "Stop panicking and do your thing."

I shot her a side eye. "My thing?"

"Your Nancy Drew thing. It's time to save our butts."

Wasn't that why I'd called Spader? Protecting the citizenry is part of his job description, not mine. As a women's magazine crafts editor, I don't get paid nearly enough for all the numerous times I've found my derriere in danger lately, not to mention being sucked into solving more murders than the average suburban homicide cop. "You do realize Nancy's a fictitious character, right?"

Spader chuckled. I refrained from pointing out the obvious seriousness of the situation to both the detective and my not-so-helpful best friend.

"I can see you're in capable hands," he continued. "I'm going to hang up now. I have gears to set in motion. Remember, Mrs. Pollack, deep breaths."

He disconnected before I could respond.

Cloris reached across the console and squeezed my arm. Instead of a deep breath, I sighed. I'd already driven past the Kenilworth exit. We'd hit Westfield in three miles, about three minutes at our current rate of speed since I'd slowed to fifty-five miles an hour. I hope Spader's troops had enough time to take up their positions.

I was traveling in the second lane from the right. As I approached the Westfield exit, I didn't bother with a turn signal. I waited as long as possible before scooting onto the exit ramp, then slowed around the curve. A quick peek into my rearview mirror told me I hadn't shaken Freddy. My tail remained right behind me.

Once on Central Avenue, I reduced my speed by thirty miles an hour. At Raritan Road I slowed for a red light. A row of cars sat in the turn lane to my left, another row of cars filled the lane on my right. Freddy stuck closer to me than my glue gun. I stole a glance in my mirror as I braced for the sounds of gunfire. When none came, I released my breath, swiping my sweaty palms on my slacks before resuming the death grip on my steering wheel. As the light turned green and the car in front of me entered the intersection, I lifted my foot from the brake, eased down on the gas pedal, and followed.

At the intersection of Central and Terminal Way, I shot through a yellow light. Freddy raced through the intersection as the light turned red.

"He's definitely tailing us," said Cloris, staring at the passenger side mirror and stating the obvious. "The car behind him stopped at the light. Do you think it was one of Spader's guys?"

"Most likely." But as soon as we drove over the train bridge and entered Westfield, another car pulled behind Freddy. "With any luck, we've picked up a replacement."

"Are we having any luck so far today?"

I shrugged. "We're still alive."

"There is that."

We continued down Central Avenue until it ended at a red light on Broad Street. As soon as the traffic light turned green, this would all be over, one way or another, within a minute. The light changed, and I turned right. A block later I hung a left onto Park Drive.

The short street that bordered Mindowaskin Park on one side and the police station on the other was dark and quiet. Cars, both marked and unmarked, lined the right parking lane in front of the police station entrance except for one empty slot.

Spader had thought of everything. The parking space was large enough for me to nose in, avoiding parallel parking that would have forced Freddy to stop behind me. No telling what he would have done if that had happened. He slowed to a crawl as he moved alongside me, then floored the gas.

"I guess he realized where he was," said Cloris as Freddy sped down the street.

He didn't get far. The moment he drove past me, one of the parked vehicles pulled out and with lights flashing, raced behind him. At the far end of the street, blazing headlights and red and blue flashing lights suddenly filled the roadway. Freddy had nowhere to go. He swerved to the left to avoid crashing into the roadblock, jumped the curb, sped across the park lawn, and crashed into Mindowaskin Pond.

~*~

Guns drawn, a dozen officers jumped from their cars and ran toward the pond. Minutes later two of them forcefully dragged their kicking and screaming suspect across the street toward the police station entrance. When they cut directly in front of my car, my headlights spotlighted the waterlogged and pond scum-covered reprobate who had terrorized us for the last forty minutes.

I yanked open the car door, jumped out, and shouted, "Justin!"

He ceased struggling and turned his head, squinting into the bright headlights, which I'm sure blinded his view of me. No matter. He knew who had called his name. "Why?"

"We saw you with that cop. You could've ruined everything."

"So you were doing Beckwith's dirty work?"

He sneered. "Hell, no!"

"Then who?"

Another sneer. "You think I'm that stupid?"

Spader sidled up next to me as the two officers resumed

dragging Justin into the police station. "Nice try."

"Really? We still don't know who's pulling the strings. Justin certainly isn't the brains. He's not even that good at being the muscle."

"You got him to admit his involvement, even after we'd read him his rights. That's a start."

I shrugged. "I suppose so. He does seem good at spilling the beans, whether intentionally or not." I mentioned Justin's comment about Wanda's body. "I was going to call Waverly when I got home."

"I'll let her know. She's on her way here. From what I just witnessed, I don't think it's going to be too difficult to get Justin to talk."

"You'll make him an offer he can't refuse?"

Spader chuckled. "My Marlon Brando impersonation is a bit rusty, but something like that. Go home, Mrs. Pollack."

Easy for him to say. My brain wasn't done *what iffing*. "What if Justin had an accomplice who had followed him?" I hadn't seen any evidence of another tail, but my concentration had been focused on one car. I glanced down the street. Was someone waiting for me once I turned back onto Broad Street?

"A patrol car will follow you to your house. Once you're inside, hug your kids, then pour yourself a glass of wine, and put your feet up. We'll take it from here."

Although I conjured up an annoying image of Spader patting me on the head, I mentally forgave his condescending attitude. He'd come a long way in our quasi-working relationship, and I knew he genuinely cared about my well-being. "As much as I'd like to comply, I first have to drive Cloris home."

"Not a problem. I'll let the patrol officers know." He then

ushered me behind the wheel, closed the car door, and gave the roof a pat.

Cloris turned to me as I released the parking brake and eased away from the curb. "You did it again. It's almost as if the universe heard you and dropped Justin in our laps."

"Better than having him use us for target practice or ram us into a wall."

"Naomi definitely owes us hazard pay for this gig. My contract says nothing about having to deal with homicidal maniacs. I'm sure yours doesn't, either."

"And yet I keep finding myself confronted by them. I won't rest easy until I find out who ordered Justin to come after us. And why."

"I was afraid you'd say that. The why is easy, though. They think we know something."

"But what do they think we know?" I pondered this as I drove down Broad Street toward Springfield where Cloris and her husband now lived, having downsized to a townhouse after their daughter went off to college. Only a Westfield patrol car followed behind me.

"We know someone killed Wanda," said Cloris, "and we suspect someone killed Marlene."

"But we don't know why or if the two deaths are related. And don't forget what happened to Rhetta. Someone also tried to kill her. Or at least put her out of commission."

"How can these incidents not be related?" asked Cloris. "It's all too coincidental otherwise."

I shrugged. "Until we know the identity of the killer or killers, that's all speculation. The murders might be connected to drug trafficking or something entirely unrelated to Beckwith

Industries."

"Or something else related to Beckwith Industries." I watched from the corner of my eye as she rubbed her temples and let loose a huge sigh. "It's enough to make your head spin."

When I pulled up in front of Cloris's townhouse, she turned to me and said, "You and I are taking a sick day tomorrow."

I raised an eyebrow. "We are?"

"Absolutely. We're not wasting one of our comp days to recover from our unfortunate encounter with those vicious women of the Stitch and Bake Society, not to mention those horrible people connected to Beckwith Chateau."

"Not all of them were horrid, just Vernon Beckwith, that smarmy Doctor Hargrove, and Justin Whatever-His-Last-Name-Is. I do like Rhetta and Tanner."

"Agreed. Let's go somewhere for a nice lunch."

We decided that we'd both email Naomi this evening so that we could sleep in tomorrow morning. "We'll tell her we think we're incubating a bug of some sort," said Cloris, "and we wouldn't want to expose everyone at the office. How can she not agree when our main concern is the health of our coworkers?"

"Devious. But I like it."

I waited until Cloris had let herself in through her front door before pulling away from the curb and heading home. Westfield's finest followed close behind me.

~*~

I arrived home to find Zack waiting at the front door. As relieved as I was to see him, I had no time to fall into his arms. I gave him a quick kiss, then waved my thanks to the two officers sitting at the curb. "I suppose you're wondering about the police escort," I said.

"Not really." He handed me a glass of wine and ushered me

inside.

That could only mean one thing, which I voiced as I shrugged off my coat. "Spader called you?"

"He did."

"Then you know what happened."

"Only the Cliff Notes version. I'm waiting for the unabridged edition."

I glanced around. "Where is everyone?"

"The boys are doing homework in their room."

"And Lucille?"

Zack shrugged. "Your guess is as good as mine. Probably off somewhere plotting an insurrection."

I tried to remember the last time I'd seen my mother-in-law and realized it was before the start of the conference. "Has she been gone since Tuesday?"

"As far as I know. Neither the boys nor I have seen her in days."

"Maybe we should contact Harriet."

"Maybe you should stop stalling and tell me what happened."

"But—"

"Wherever Lucille is, I'm sure she's fine."

"I suppose. If she weren't, I would have been notified."

"Exactly."

"Unless—"

Zack's stern countenance stopped me from finishing my thought. Lucille was known far and wide by not only New Jersey law enforcement but every jurisdiction up and down the East Coast and many beyond. If she were lying unconscious in a hospital bed—or worse—a database search would reveal her identity, and I'd be notified.

I handed Zack the wine glass. There was something I had to do first. "Be right back."

I headed down the hall into the boys' room. Zack followed, watching from the doorway as I hugged each of my sons.

"You okay, Mom?" asked Alex, pulling his attention from his laptop.

"Never better. I just haven't seen my special guys in a few days. I've missed you."

"Missed you more," said Nick. "I got stuck with laundry duty."

I tousled his hair. "And your future wife will praise me for teaching you the fine art of housekeeping."

"Yeah, right."

Zack jumped into the conversation. "Even confirmed bachelors do laundry, dude. Get used to it."

Nick looked from Zack to me, shrugged, and muttered what sounded like, "Whatever," before turning his attention back to an algebra problem.

Zack and I returned to the living room where I collapsed onto the sofa. "Unabridged version," he prompted, handing back the wine glass and grabbing the one he'd left on the coffee table.

"Right." I drained half the glass before beginning the tale of Justin. Or at least as much as I knew. Which, in all truthfulness, wasn't much. Yet.

TWENTY-ONE

"Can I assume you've left all things Beckwith permanently behind?" asked Zack as he topped off my glass.

"Trust me, I have absolutely no desire to set foot in Beckwith Chateau ever again." I took a sip of the Chardonnay, then added, "The investigation is in the hands of capable professionals. Spader didn't think he and Waverly—"

"Waverly?"

"Waverly Smith, the Essex County detective."

"Right. From the press conference."

I cringed, remembering Zack's account of my cameo during the event, but instead of mentioning it, I plowed ahead. "Spader expected they'd have no trouble getting Justin to finger the puppet master pulling his strings."

Zack took a slow sip from his glass, as if mulling over a thought or two or twelve. Then he finally said, "Good to know."

"As a matter of fact, I wouldn't be surprised to learn they're already on their way to make an arrest in the murders of Marlene and Wanda."

"You still think Marlene Beckwith was murdered?"

"Definitely. Especially after someone killed Wanda. It's too coincidental otherwise."

"Is there any evidence at all to suggest Marlene Beckwith didn't die of natural causes?"

I shook my head. "Unfortunately, none. Not even circumstantial. Beckwith made sure of that when he had her cremated before an autopsy could be performed. And either he or someone else removed any possibly incriminating evidence from the room before trashing the place."

"Which would have contaminated the crime scene."

"Exactly. Not that there's even officially a crime scene when it comes to Marlene's death. The police were never called to investigate. That quack who calls himself a doctor declared she died from underlying health issues, and there's nothing to prove otherwise at this point."

Zack shrugged. "Sometimes a cigar is just a cigar."

"I've heard that. But cigars always leave a residual stench. And there's something that really stinks about all this."

"You think Vernon Beckwith is behind the murders?"

"At first. But when I accused Justin of doing his dirty work, his response was so filled with contempt that now I'm not sure."

"Contempt for Beckwith?"

I nodded. "I just don't see Justin killing for a man he obviously hates."

"What about the doctor?"

"You mean Hargrove, the not-quite-a-doctor? Maybe. He had as much to lose as Beckwith. If Justin drugged Rhetta, he may have gotten the Rohypnol from Hargrove." I yawned. "Anyway, the entire mess is someone else's problem. I need a good night's sleep."

Zack graced me with a look that turned my insides into hot fudge sauce. "I know how to make certain you get one."

I offered him my hand. He pulled me to my feet and into his arms. "I was hoping you'd say that."

An hour later, as I drifted off to sleep, I remembered to mention that Cloris and I planned to play hooky the next day. "We figure we deserve a girls' day after suffering through the conference from Hades."

"Not to mention a murder, a possible murder, and a poisoning."

"That, too."

"Sleep in. I'll make sure the boys don't disturb you in the morning. I'm heading into the city for an early meeting, but I'll be home by late afternoon."

With that, I allowed Mr. Sandman to take over.

~*~

My cell phone woke me the next morning. The display read eight-thirty and showed an incoming call from Rhetta. I cleared my throat to remove the frogs before answering. "Hello?"

"Anastasia?" She hesitated. "I didn't wake you, did I?"

I lied, like I always do when someone calls and wakes me up before my body wants to start the day. Stifling a yawn, I said, "No, is everything okay? Are you still in the hospital?"

"I was released this morning."

"You're not back at work already, are you?"

"I'm taking a few days off. Doctor's orders."

"Good. You need time to recover."

"The thing is, though, I had ordered floral arrangements as a thank you for you and Cloris. They were delivered to the Chateau after I was taken to the hospital."

"That was so sweet of you, Rhetta."

"It's hardly enough, given what you went through. Would you be able to swing by today to pick them up? I'd deliver them to you, but the doctor told me not to drive for at least the next week."

And here I thought I'd set foot in Beckwith Chateau for the last time. Once again, the universe was enjoying a huge belly laugh at my expense.

Since Rhetta could easily have one of the staff deliver the flowers to Cloris and me, I figured there was more to this request. Given that I may have saved her life, I assumed she wanted to thank me in person. "I'm meeting Cloris at noon, but I can leave early and swing by to pick them up ahead of time. Does eleven-fifteen work for you?"

Rhetta hesitated. "That late? Any chance you can come earlier?"

"How much earlier?"

"Uhm...now?"

Maybe I should have been honest and admitted she'd woken me up. "Not really." I sighed. So much for enjoying a leisurely morning. "How about in an hour?"

"You couldn't leave now?"

"I'm not even dressed yet. Besides, it's rush hour. Even if I get out of here in the next ten minutes, it's going to take me nearly an hour to get to West Orange."

She didn't respond right away, and for a moment I thought the connection had gone dead. Finally, she said, "I understand. Thank you, Anastasia. I'll see you soon." With that, she hung up without saying goodbye.

I scrambled out of bed and into the bathroom. Zack had left a note taped to the mirror: *Ralph fed and in his cage. Mephisto walked and fed. I'll be home no later than 5, boys by 6. Enjoy Hooky Day!* He signed the note with a Zorro-like Z inside a heart.

I sighed. I still didn't know what a guy whose genes swam around in the same primordial pool as the likes of Hugh Jackman and Pierce Brosnan saw in a slightly overweight, pear-shaped widow with enough baggage to fill a cargo plane, but I was glad he saw more than enough to stick around. I never could have survived the last year without him. Every so often the universe tosses me a measly crumb. But when it came to Zachary Barnes, the sun, moon, and stars had all aligned to present me with an entire bakery.

Daydreaming aside, I wasn't thrilled at the prospect of toting two floral arrangements in my car. Knowing Rhetta, I was certain she'd picked the biggest and best the florist had to offer. I have allergies. Some flowers and certain fillers commonly used by florists cause me respiratory problems. If the arrangements contained either lilacs or eucalyptus, I was in trouble. If they contained both, I'd need a gas mask.

I considered calling Rhetta back and telling her to donate the flowers to one of the local hospitals or nursing homes, but I didn't want to hurt her feelings. Besides, I needed to see for myself that she was okay. I shuddered to think what might have happened if I hadn't gone to her office when I did.

After a rushed shower, I tossed on some clean clothes, compliments of Nick's laundry stint, and gulped down a quick breakfast of toast and coffee. Twenty-five minutes after Rhetta's call, I was inching my way through a merge onto the Garden State Parkway. Not that I expected otherwise. It's a rare occurrence when the GSP isn't clogged with bumper-to-bumper traffic, day or night.

At least the weather was cooperating. No ice storm or blizzard today, not a cloud in the sky, and a balmy forty-two degrees according to my dashboard display. I also didn't have Justin or anyone else other than morning rush commuters on my tail.

When I arrived at the Chateau, I pulled up to the main entrance and parked. As I stepped from my car, a staff member I didn't recognize exited the Chateau and greeted me. His uniform strained at the seams of arms and a chest that looked like he spent all his free time pumping iron. The polished brass nameplate on his lapel identified him as Cash. "No need to park my car," I said. "I'll only be a few minutes. I'm picking something up from Rhetta."

He tapped the visor of his cap. "Take your time, ma'am. Your car won't be in the way. We have no events scheduled for today." After closing the driver's side door behind me, he ushered me up the steps and into the Chateau.

The place appeared eerily deserted without the hustle and bustle of all the Stitch and Bake ladies, who had apparently already departed the Chateau. Other than Cash, I saw no staff in the foyer and heard no activity coming from any of the areas down the various halls. Although, I expected the chambermaids were hard at work on the upstairs guest rooms.

"I'll call Rhetta for you, ma'am."

"She's not in her office?" Even though Rhetta had said she was taking a few days off, I assumed the flowers had been delivered to her office and she planned to meet me there.

"No, ma'am. If you give me your name, I'll tell her you're here."

The *ma'ams* were really beginning to grate on my nerves. I realized Cash was being polite and showing respect, but that word always made me feel ancient. Even my mother, a woman a generation older than I, bristles at the appellation. I forced a smile and said, "Anastasia Pollack."

He nodded, stepped behind the reservations desk, and picked up a phone. After a brief conversation, he said, "She's in her apartment and asked that you meet her there."

I remembered Rhetta saying her apartment was above the carriage house, but I had no clue where to find the carriage house. I didn't remember passing a structure that could have served as a carriage house when I'd walked around the grounds. "I'll need directions."

"No problem, ma'am." He led me back outside and opened my car door for me. As I slid behind the wheel, he directed me toward the carriage house. "You can't miss it. It's a massive stone structure around the second bend past the conference center."

"Thank you, I know how to get to the conference center."

"Then you should have no trouble finding the carriage house. You access the apartment from the steps on the side of the building."

I drove down the road the bus had used to shuttle us to and from the Rouen Conference Center. The grounds were as deserted as the Chateau. I passed no workmen or delivery trucks. Given the events of the last few days, perhaps someone had made the decision to give most of the staff some time off.

Or more likely, with impending bankruptcy and a looming criminal case, Vernon Beckwith had laid off as many people as possible. I knew nothing about inheritance law or how a criminal indictment might impact the disbursement of funds. However, I would imagine under the circumstances, Beckwith wouldn't be getting his hands on any of Marlene's money anytime soon—if ever.

A long cobblestone driveway ran up to the carriage house, which was built in the same style as the Chateau. I parked close to the exterior staircase that led to the apartment above and hauled myself up the winding stone steps. Depending on the size of the floral arrangements, I anticipated a devil of a time carrying them back downstairs. Hopefully, I could wrangle Cash into lugging them for me.

The top of the stairs opened onto a covered patio. Two large planters with miniature evergreens flanked a scaled-down version of the Chateau's main door. Someone had spared no expense on a building originally meant to house several horses and buggies and living quarters for the coachman or caretaker.

I looked around for a doorbell but found none. So I grabbed the heavy brass knocker attached to the center of the door and gave it a couple of whacks.

A few seconds later Rhetta swung open the door. She wasn't alone. Celeste stood behind her. One hand gripped Rhetta's upper arm. The other held a gun to her head.

TWENTY-TWO

"I'm sorry, Anastasia," said Rhetta, choking back a sob as her eyes brimmed with tears. "I had no choice."

"Shut up," said Celeste. She wrenched Rhetta's arm as she waved the gun at me. "Get in here. Now."

I had no idea how good a shot Celeste was, but I wasn't willing to risk my life or Rhetta's by trying to flee across the patio and back down the stairs. Reluctantly, I took a step farther into the room. That's when I noticed Tanner standing in the shadows.

I gasped. "You're involved in this?"

He shuffled his feet and offered an uncomfortable shrug. "It was never supposed to get to this point. We only wanted him to acknowledge us."

"No," said Celeste. "She had to pay for destroying your lives—yours, your brother's, and your mother's."

"Did she, Aunt Celeste?"

Celeste was Tanner's aunt?

"She took your father away from you and denied you your

birthright, Wyatt. Yours and Parker's." She waved the gun around. "All of this is rightfully yours."

"I never agreed to murder."

"Grow up," said Celeste, practically spitting the words. "You do what's required to get the job done, even if it sometimes gets messy."

"The ends justify the means?"

"Always. Haven't you learned anything? Results are all that count in life."

I bit my tongue, wanting desperately to challenge that philosophy, but I knew I had to allow them to keep talking to incriminate themselves. Hopefully, I'd remain alive long enough to make the information count and bring some justice for Marlene, Wanda, and Rhetta.

"But now Parker's in jail," said Tanner. Or Wyatt. *Is Justin really Parker? And Tanner's brother?*

"Because your brother is a stupid hothead who acts without thinking. He can rot behind bars this time for all I care."

"If he talks, you'll wind up there with him."

"And you as well, dear boy."

"I didn't kill anyone."

She scoffed. "You think that matters? You're an accomplice. But don't worry. If you do as I tell you, you'll be fine."

"How do you plan to accomplish that?"

"Once these two have their tragic accident, I'll make sure your brother and Beckwith take the rap for Marlene and Wanda."

The door opened, and Cash, no longer wearing a Chateau uniform, entered the apartment. Neither Celeste nor Tanner expressed surprise at seeing him.

"What took you so long?" asked Celeste.

"I had to change out of that monkey suit," said Cash, his coatless muscle-bound physique now fully exposed under a too-tight long-sleeve black T-shirt despite the March temperatures. "I don't know how you put up with wearing it for so long, bro," his comment directed toward Tanner.

"Never mind that," said Celeste. "Did you finish the task I gave you?"

He dusted his hands. "All done. Just as you requested."

"Good. Get her phone."

Cash ripped my purse from my shoulder and rooted around inside. "It's not here."

"Check her pockets."

He tossed my purse onto a nearby chair, then yanked my coat from my body. He pulled my car keys from the first pocket and tossed them beside my purse. In the second pocket he finally found my phone. "Got it."

Celeste held out her free hand for the phone, then turned it off and dropped it into her blazer pocket. "Bring the car around. We have more work to do." She grabbed a plastic bag from a nearby table and tossed it to Tanner. "Tie them up for now. We'll finish after dark."

"No," said Tanner, dropping the bag at his feet. "This has to end. No more killing."

Celeste sighed. "I'm afraid you're right, Wyatt. This does have to end." And with that, she fired a bullet into Tanner's torso.

I gasped.

Rhetta screamed.

"That's one more body you'll have to dispose of," Celeste told Cash.

He shrugged. "No problem. Leaves more for me." He stooped

alongside Tanner and picked up the plastic bag. "Let's get this over with and leave before someone spots us."

"You needn't worry about that," said Celeste. "The grounds are closed for the day. Locked up tight. No staff. No members."

"How'd you manage that?" asked Cash.

She glanced toward Rhetta. "Cold hard steel persuades most people." Then she waved the gun at both of us and said, "Into the bedroom, you two."

Ten minutes later, Rhetta and I were bound and gagged. Shortly afterwards, I heard a vehicle pull away from the carriage house.

Rhetta lay curled up whimpering on the bedroom floor. Since I had no way of calming her, I tried to block out the noise. I'd been in too many similar situations lately. Each time I'd managed to figure a way out before the bad guys came back to kill me. I had to do it again.

I began wriggling around with the goal of loosening the clothesline rope Cash had used to hogtie me. I quickly determined that if the guy had ever been a Boy Scout, he surely had failed to earn his knot-tying badge. Thankfully, he was all brawn and no brain. He'd tied me up with slip knots. In no time at all, I'd freed myself, then untied Rhetta.

She continued to lie shaking on the floor. "Snap out of it, Rhetta. This is no time for a panic attack. We've got to get out of here before they return."

She stared wide-eyed at me but nodded and allowed me to help her to her feet. I clasped both of her hands in mine and forced her to focus on me. "We're not going to die," I assured her. "Just do what I tell you. Okay?"

When she nodded again, I led her to the bedroom door. We

made our way into the living room and discovered Tanner still lying on the floor. Blood had pooled around him but not as much as I would have expected. My untrained eye decided the bullet hadn't hit any vital organs and perhaps had passed through him, rather than having lodged within his body. When I bent down to check for a pulse, he moaned. "He's still alive. We've got to get help."

"He tried to kill us," said Rhetta.

"No, I don't think so. He tried to save us."

"But he killed Marlene."

"I'm not so sure of that, either. But it doesn't matter. We can't leave him to die."

She stared at Tanner for a moment, then heaved a shaky sigh. "I suppose you're right."

Without our phones, we'd have to drive somewhere to call for help. Not knowing where Celeste and Cash had headed, I didn't want to risk entering one of the other buildings on the grounds. Whatever they were planning, I had a feeling they were holed up somewhere nearby.

I placed my hand on Tanner's shoulder and said, "Hang on, Tanner...uhm...Wyatt." Then I ran back to the bedroom and grabbed a pillow, quilt, and sheet from Rhetta's bed.

When I returned to the living room, I tossed Rhetta the sheet. "Tear off a strip for me."

"Why?"

"We need to stabilize him and bind his wound." I lifted his feet and slipped the pillow underneath.

When Rhetta handed me a strip, I used it to pack Tanner's wound. "We need tape."

"All I have is a small roll of cellophane tape."

"That won't do. Tear another strip."

I didn't want to move Tanner for fear of worsening his injury, but I had no choice. As carefully as possible, I forced my hand beneath him and fished another strip of sheeting around his torso, knotting it tightly over the wound. I hoped I'd helped rather than made matters worse. My entire knowledge of dealing with gunshot wounds came from watching movies and TV. However, the bleeding had lessened to a mere trickle. I took that as a good sign and draped the quilt over him, hoping to prevent shock.

"Now what?" asked Rhetta after I stood.

I glanced around the room, trying to determine if there was anything else that might help Tanner before we left him. That's when I noticed my purse and keys still on the chair where Cash had tossed them.

I stared at the keys.

Rhetta followed my gaze. "Look! They forgot your car keys. Let's get out of here."

When I didn't move, her voice rose in panic. "What are you waiting for, Anastasia? They could return at any moment."

"Something is wrong," I said.

"Everything is wrong!"

"No, either Cash is the dumbest muscle ever, or this is a setup."

"What do you mean?"

I held up a hand to silence her. "Give me a minute."

"We might not have a minute."

"If I'm right, we have plenty of time."

I rewound everything Celeste had said from the moment Rhetta opened the door. She'd planned to dispose of Rhetta and me in some way that would look like an accident. Cash had completed a task for Celeste, a task that apparently hadn't taken him very long since he arrived shortly after I did. In addition, he'd done a lousy job of tying me up, and they'd left my car keys where I'd easily spot them.

"They're not planning to come back for us," I said, donning my coat, "only for Tanner to dispose of his body once it's dark."

"I don't understand."

"Grab your coat and follow me. I'll show you."

Rhetta reached for a coat hanging on a hook by her front door, and I led her onto the patio and down the stone steps. Once at my Jetta, I crouched onto the ground and looked under the car. Just as I suspected, I found a small pool of liquid. "Take a look," I said, once I stood up.

Rhetta lowered her body until she could see under the car. "You're leaking a little oil. What of it?"

"I don't think that's oil. I think it's brake fluid."

"There isn't much."

"Because they didn't want me to lose control until we were off the estate and winding around the mountain."

What little color remained in Rhetta's face quickly drained away. "Where you'd lose control going around a bend and we'd plunge off the side of the road." She stared in awe. "How on earth did you even figure out this was their plan?"

"Recent experience."

Rhetta's eyes widened, and she shook her head in disbelief. "You've lived a strange life, Anastasia Pollack."

"Only over the last year."

"That's more than enough to keep us from dying a horrible death." She scanned the area around the carriage house and beyond. "Now what do we do?"

"We hoof it, keeping to the woods until we've put enough

distance between us and Beckwith Chateau. You live here. Any suggestions?"

Rhetta thought for a minute, then pointed in the direction that took us away from the Chateau. "The compound butts up against one of the county parks with hiking trails. It will take us some time before we can wend our way to a place where we can find a phone, though."

I glanced up at her apartment, my thoughts on Tanner. Hopefully, he'd hang on until we were able to summon help for him. "We have no choice. We can't risk running into Celeste or Cash. Let's go."

When I'd dressed this morning, I hadn't expected to hike through dirt trails still muddy from the recent ice storm. More than once, my foot sank into leaf-covered gunk, sucking off my shoe as I tried to free myself. At one point, I lost my balance but was saved by Rhetta reaching out to grab hold of me.

She wasn't fairing much better. But at least we weren't running for our lives.

The sky had turned overcast. I couldn't see the position of the sun and had no idea of the time. Once I'd gotten a smart phone, I'd given up wearing a watch. But I didn't have my phone now, and I couldn't see the position of the sun.

At one point my stomach rumbled with hunger. Anticipating a huge lunch, I'd only eaten a slice of buttered toast for breakfast. Even when I've run late in the morning and skipped breakfast, Cloris always has some goodies in the break room.

Cloris! She'd be waiting at the restaurant for me. She'd once called in the cavalry when I didn't answer my phone and she'd suspected something was wrong. Did Celeste know I was meeting her for lunch? "Rhetta, when you called me this morning, was your phone on speaker?"

"No, why?"

"Then Celeste didn't hear me mention that I was meeting Cloris later today? And you didn't tell her?"

"No."

I knew I hadn't mentioned the restaurant to Rhetta. I'd had no reason to. "You never heard her mention anything about Cloris?"

"Not a word. She was completely obsessed with you."

"Do you know why?"

"Because you kept asking questions about Marlene."

"And what was her beef with you?"

"I defended Marlene, and she noticed the two of us together quite often."

"But Cloris was usually with us."

"Cloris isn't all over the Internet for solving murders in New Jersey and New York."

I knew I'd occasionally been mentioned on the evening news but..."I'm all over the Internet?"

"You didn't know?"

"I don't make a habit of Googling myself."

"Maybe you should."

And just like that, the pieces fell into place. Celeste was out for revenge and couldn't tolerate anyone getting in her way. "And no one at the Chateau had any idea Tanner and Justin were Vernon's sons?"

"Not even Vernon. They were barely out of diapers when he divorced their mother. According to Marlene, she moved away and remarried. Besides, their names were different. How would any of us have known?"

"But it made no sense that Tanner and Justin wouldn't

confront their father once they were of age. Why all the subterfuge? Vernon may have welcomed them with open arms, regretting abandoning them all those years ago."

Rhetta nodded. "True. Especially since his relationship with Marlene had soured."

"And what about Cash?" Not only had he lacked the military polish of the other staff members, but his uniform also hadn't fit him well.

"He doesn't work here," she said. "I've never seen him before."

"There's something more to this story," I said. "A huge puzzle piece we're still missing."

"What do you think it could be?"

"I don't know, but Celeste is definitely the key."

We continued trekking through the dense woods, eventually stumbling upon one of the park trails and followed it to an empty parking lot. From there we hiked along a narrow, winding road until we found ourselves at the park entrance on Eagle Rock Avenue.

"There's a shopping district about a mile down the road," said Rhetta.

We continued walking, keeping to the trees and out of sight of the main road until we finally had no choice but to transition onto sidewalks. I knew the chances of Celeste and Cash finding us were slim. If my theory was correct, they'd assume I'd already lost control of the car and crashed down the mountain. Still, I couldn't help but constantly dart my eyes left and right and glance over my shoulder.

We ran into the first store we came to and asked the clerk to call 911.

TWENTY-THREE

My first concern was for Tanner. I quickly rattled off the need for an ambulance at the Beckwith Chateau carriage house due to a shooting.

"Is the shooter still on the premises, ma'am?"

"I don't know. Possibly. Please hurry." I glanced up at the clock on the wall behind the counter. More than two hours had passed since I'd first arrived at the carriage house. "He was shot hours ago."

My comment resulted in a battery of questions as to why I'd waited so long to call 911. At least the emergency operator had dispatched the ambulance before subjecting me to a grilling.

I could hardly fault her. For all she knew, I had shot Tanner and was setting up the cops for an ambush.

Sadly, those scenarios happen too often. But when I told the dispatcher I also needed her to notify Detective Waverly Smith because the shooting was part of an active investigation, she stopped treating me like a suspect. It helped that she'd seen the press conference and recognized my name once I repeated it.

The next few hours passed in a blur. Rhetta and I were brought to Essex County Police Headquarters and placed in separate rooms to give our statements. No one would tell me anything about Tanner, whether he'd survived or not. I was informed I'd have to wait for Waverly.

Eventually an officer handed me my phone. I assumed that meant they had Celeste and Cash in custody, but he'd neither confirm nor deny. Again, I'd have to wait for Waverly. However, at this point I was escorted to another room, one that looked more like a private waiting area than an interrogation room.

A coffee pot and a box of donuts sat on a counter along one wall. "Help yourself," said the officer before leaving.

I poured myself a cup of coffee, found a container of half-and-half in the mini-fridge under the counter, and grabbed a donut.

Rhetta soon joined me. "Were you told anything?" she asked, helping herself to coffee and a donut before joining me on a sofa that had seen better days at least a generation ago.

"Only that I'd have to wait until the detective arrived."

"Same here."

Rhetta appeared numb. I couldn't blame her. Near-death experiences had that effect on people. I should know. "Are you okay?"

She took a sip of coffee and made a face. "This is the worst coffee I've ever tasted."

"I know. I'm convinced a cast iron stomach is a pre-requisite for all members of law enforcement. But coffee aside, what about you, Rhetta?"

She offered me a wan smile. "We survived. We'd be dead now if not for your quick thinking. If it had been up to me, I would have jumped in that car and driven off as fast as I could. You've now saved my life twice, Anastasia."

I reached over and squeezed her hand.

While we waited, I called Cloris. At this point I was more than two hours late for our Hooky Day lunch. She had left a series of text and voice messages, each progressively more panicky, the last one stating she was calling Zack.

"It's about time," she said when she answered. "You've aged me twenty years. Where are you? What's going on?"

Before I told her, I asked, "Did you speak with Zack?" I had one missed call from him shortly after Cloris's last text, but he hadn't left a message. If they'd spoken, I wanted to know what she'd said before I called him. I didn't want to worry him needlessly, especially since I was fine, safely ensconced at the police station, and there was no reason for him to worry.

"Of course. After what happened last night, when you didn't show up at the restaurant or answer your phone, I knew something was wrong. In case you've forgotten, you and I have travelled down this road before."

I certainly hadn't forgotten. As a matter of fact, I had counted on Cloris to raise the alarm and muster the cavalry.

"But," she continued, "I couldn't get through at first and had to leave a message for him to call me as soon as possible. He was going to contact Detective Spader and hop on the next train out of the city."

"How long ago was that?"

"About forty-five minutes."

"I'd better call him."

Before I could place the call, the door opened, and Waverly entered—followed by Spader and Zack.

In short order, I was in Zack's arms. Then everyone started speaking at once.

Finally, Spader stuck two fingers in his mouth and let loose an ear-piercing whistle that silenced everyone. He then nodded toward the counter. "The only cop coffee worse than Union County's is Essex County's. And I should know. I've got the ulcer scars to prove it. How about if the five of us head to a diner where we can get some decent joe and talk without interruption?"

~*~

Twenty minutes later we arrived at a diner far enough from police headquarters to avoid any fellow officers popping in and interrupting us. Once inside, we crowded into a large round corner booth at the far end of the room to ensure no other patrons could eavesdrop on our conversation. After coffee was ordered all around and before anyone had time to peruse their menus, I asked the question foremost on my mind. "Did Tanner survive?"

"Thanks to you," said Waverly. "He's conscious and talking. The doctors say he should make a full recovery."

"In time to go to prison?" I sighed. I couldn't help but feel conflicted regarding Tanner. On the one hand, he was obviously involved. How much so, I had no idea. Yet, he did try to keep Celeste from killing Rhetta and me, which nearly cost him his own life. Was it a last-minute change of heart on his part? Would he have tried to thwart her had he known she'd turn on him?

"That's up to the D.A., but Wyatt Beckwith—or Tanner, as you know him—is cooperating. He claims he was railroaded by his aunt and never knew her true plans."

"What about his brother?"

"According to Wyatt, Parker—AKA Justin—has had a troubled past. He spent several years in juvie for burglary, assault, and dealing drugs. I doubt the D.A. is going to be very interested in cutting him a deal, especially since he's refusing to talk."

I glanced at Spader. He'd assured me they'd have no trouble getting Justin to spill all he knew. He bent over his menu and muttered, "So sometimes I'm wrong."

"Did he kill Wanda and Marlene?" I asked.

Waverly shook her head. "Not according to Wyatt."

"Then who did?" asked Rhetta.

"Cash and Celeste. Justin supplied them with the drugs."

"Who is Cash?" I asked. "What's his connection to the Beckwiths?"

"He's Wyatt and Parker's older stepbrother."

"Time out," said Zack. "How about if you back up to the beginning for those of us trying to catch up?"

"Let's order first," said Spader, his eyes still glued to his menu. "I have a feeling we're going to be here awhile, and I, for one, haven't had lunch."

My stomach rumbled loudly in agreement. Four pairs of eyes turned to me. Rhetta tried unsuccessfully to stifle a giggle. Spader tossed me a wink. "That's one vote in agreement."

The waitress returned with our coffees, and once we'd all ordered, Waverly began again. "All of this has been pieced together from what Wyatt said as well as the information I've uncovered in the course of my investigation so far."

Wait! Waverly was going to disclose information from an ongoing investigation? I glanced at Spader, Mr. I-Can't-Divulge-Yada-Yada-Yada. He shrugged. "Her case, not mine."

I turned my attention back to Waverly, but she addressed Spader. "An investigation that wouldn't have been possible without the assistance of Anastasia Pollack and Rhetta Margolis.

Since they were both nearly killed, I believe they have a right to know what led up to everything that went down with Beckwith and his family."

Score one for Girl Power. Spader could learn a thing or two from his protégé. Although, in all fairness, he had started to come around recently—even if reluctantly and even though he had a long way to go. But hopefully, the topic was a moot point. I absolutely, positively did not want to find myself involved in any future murder investigations.

"Starting at the beginning," said Waverly. "Vernon and Caroline Beckwith were married six years when he divorced her and immediately married Marlene. Caroline took their two sons, four-year-old Wyatt and three-year-old Parker, and moved to Arizona where she met and married Harris Ketchum, a widower with a twelve-year-old son."

"Cash?" asked Rhetta.

Waverly nodded. "Two years later Caroline and Harris were killed in a head-on collision with a drunk driver. Celeste Ketchum, Harris's much older sister and only living relative besides Cash, was awarded custody of all three boys when Vernon refused custody of Wyatt and Parker."

"Because of Marlene?" I asked.

"From what we've been able to piece together, but it's all hearsay from some of the other Society members, and most of them are extremely biased against Marlene."

"What about Vernon?" I asked.

"So far, he's remained mum regarding his sons. Anyway," she continued, "being far more interested in her banking career and apparently devoid of any motherly instincts, Celeste left the raising of the boys to a series of nannies and housekeepers.

According to Wyatt, when she did interact with the children, it was to poison their minds against Vernon and his second wife."

"A real piece of work," muttered Spader.

Waverly turned to him and nodded. "When Parker—AKA Justin—turned eighteen, she hatched a plot to help herself to the Beckwith fortune through her step-nephews. The plan was to kill Marlene and frame Vernon for her murder. Wyatt and Parker, as Vernon's only offspring, would then petition the court for control of their father's fortune."

"Would the courts agree to that?" asked Rhetta. "Vernon wouldn't be dead, only in prison for a crime he didn't commit."

"I have no idea," said Waverly. "That's a question for the legal experts."

"But you can't frame someone for murder if you can't prove there's been a murder," I said.

"Exactly," said Spader. "No evidence. No body. No crime."

"But wait," said Zack. He turned to Waverly. "Didn't you state earlier that Wyatt denied knowing Celeste planned to kill Marlene?"

"I did. This came from Cash. Parker might not be talking, but Cash is singing like a canary to save his hide. He claims Celeste ultimately planned to eliminate both Wyatt and Parker after they'd gotten hold of their father's estate. According to Cash, Celeste believed she was entitled to the money for having raised Vernon's sons. She convinced Cash if he did her dirty work, she'd share the money with him."

I executed an eye roll at one more example of Cash being all brawn and no brain. "And he foolishly believed her."

"At first," said Waverly. "He's since figured out that she probably planned to eliminate him as well, which gave him added incentive to turn on her."

"What about Dr. Hargrove?" asked Rhetta.

"Fearing Marlene had died from an opioid overdose, he trashed the crime scene, scouring her home for all the illegal pills he'd supplied her with."

"Along with helping himself to her jewelry?" asked Rhetta.

Waverly nodded. "We found a cache of jewelry in his residence."

"Did he also ransack Marlene's office and my apartment?" asked Rhetta.

"That was Vernon, looking for Marlene's computer. He needed to destroy the evidence she'd collected on his illegal activities at Beckwith Pharmaceuticals."

"But why did Vernon have Marlene's body cremated so quickly?" I asked.

"As strange as it sounds," said Waverly, "it turns out, he really was honoring her final wishes. Marlene's Last Will and Testament stipulated that she be cremated immediately upon her death."

"I can believe that," said Rhetta. "Marlene was both incredibly vain and paranoid. She probably didn't want anyone standing over her casket, making disparaging remarks about her."

Not that many people would have shown up at a viewing for Marlene Beckwith from what I'd learned about her. Besides her loyal personal assistant, she had one friend among the other Stitch and Bake members. And at this point, I was convinced Rhetta's loyalty was most likely derived from what she believed to be part of her job description.

"How did Cash kill Marlene?" I asked.

"Ironically, with an opioid overdose. Hargrove was right to panic. Had there been an autopsy, he probably would have been arrested for causing her death."

"That leaves two major threads still dangling," I said. "First, what about Wanda? Why did Cash kill her?"

"Apparently, when Wanda stormed out of dinner Wednesday evening, she stumbled upon Celeste, Wyatt, Parker, and Cash. They were huddled together on the grounds outside the Chateau."

"Celeste wasn't at dinner?" I asked.

"She'd slipped out at some point. Wanda demanded to know what was going on."

"That was the evening Cloris and I discovered someone had ransacked our rooms."

Waverly nodded. "Wyatt said they were reporting back to Celeste. She had wanted to make it look like Vernon was searching for Marlene's computer."

"How did Celeste know about the missing computer?" I asked.

"Justin mentioned it after he overheard Vernon accuse Rhetta of taking it. He suggested she might have given it to you. One of the boys would claim to have seen him exiting your room. But when Wanda approached them, Celeste came up with a better idea: kill Wanda and frame Vernon for her death."

"What would be his motive?" I asked.

Waverly shrugged. "Beats me. It looks like Celeste wasn't playing with a full deck."

"Later that night, I heard male voices outside my room," I said.

"That was Cash and Justin removing Wanda's body after Celeste poisoned her."

"How?"

Waverly nodded toward Rhetta. "The same way she tried to kill Rhetta."

Rhetta shuddered. "The woman's a serial killer."

"It's beginning to look that way," said Waverly. "And she may have been at it for decades."

"Do you suspect she killed her brother and his wife?" asked Zack.

"No, that was definitely a drunk driver, but there are a series of cold cases around the Phoenix area, including two murders connected to banks where Celeste worked and a neighbor who lived down the street from her. Law enforcement will be taking another look at them now that we've made so many advances in DNA technology."

I leaned back against the banquette and let this additional information sink in. I found it all overwhelming.

Zack placed his hand on my thigh. "You okay?"

I nodded and placed my hand over his. "I have one more question. How did you find Celeste and Cash?"

"That was easy," said Waverly. "They were camped out in the Chateau, enjoying hundred-year-old brandy."

I glanced over at Spader. "If I've learned one thing this past year, it's that most criminals have a hugely inflated opinion of their own intelligence."

Spader laughed. "Mrs. Pollack, you don't know the half of it."

"And with any luck," said Zack, draping an arm across my shoulders, "she never will."

I nestled my head onto his shoulder and said, "Fear not, this reluctant Nancy Drew is retiring her magnifying glass."

Hopefully, I hadn't just given the universe another good belly laugh.

ANASTASIA'S CROSS-STITCH TIPS

Counted cross stitch is worked on Aida cloth, evenweave fabrics, vinyl Aida, and perforated paper. Pre-finished items such as aprons, bibs, towels, and afghans are also available. In addition, cross stitch is possible on ready-wear by using waste-canvas.

Cross stitch fabrics are available in many counts, colors, and fabric blends. The count represents the number of stitches per inch of fabric. Example: 14-ct. fabric has 14 stitches to the inch.

Counted cross stitch is worked from a chart. Each square on the chart represents a stitch. The symbols inside the squares indicate the colors of the stitches as noted in the color key for the design.

Choose a pre-finished item or select a piece of fabric at least 4" larger than the overall design. Most charts give the finished stitching size. You can also determine the finished size of a design by dividing the number of stitches for the height and width of the design by the number of stitches per inch of the fabric. Example: a design measuring 70 stitches high by 98 stitches wide will by 5" x 7" when stitched on 14-ct. fabric. 70 ÷ 14 = 5, and 98 ÷ 14 = 7.

Before beginning to stitch, finish the edges of loose weave fabrics to prevent fraying. You can do this by pulling a few strands of fabric to create a fringe, using a pinking shears, or applying a thin line of anti-fraying glue.

Locate the center of the chart by following the horizontal and vertical centering arrows across and down. To find the center of your fabric, fold the fabric in half top to bottom, then left to right. The folded point is the center.

The number of strands of floss and the size tapestry needle to use will depend on the count of the fabric. Always use a tapestry needle. An embroidery needle might pierce the fabric threads.

5-ct. or 6-ct. fabrics: #20 or #22 tapestry needle; 6 strands of floss for cross stitching and 4 strands for backstitching.

8.5-ct. or 9-ct. fabrics: #24 tapestry needle; 4-strands of floss for cross stitching, 2 strands for backstitching.

10-ct. or 11-ct. fabrics: #24 tapestry needle; 3-strands floss for cross stitching, 1 or 2 strands for backstitching.

14-ct., 16-ct., or 18-ct. fabrics: #24 or 26 tapestry needle; 2 strands floss for cross stitching, 1 strand for backstitching.

22-ct. fabrics: #26 tapestry needle; 1 strand floss for cross stitching, 1 strand for backstitching.

Begin stitching at the center of the fabric to ensure proper centering. Bring the needle up from the back of the fabric, leaving a 1" tail of floss. Holding the tail securely with your fingers, work the first few stitches over the tail to secure it. *Never knot the floss.* To end a thread, run it under several stitches on the back side of the work. Clip close to the stitching.

The cross stitch is made by working across a row with diagonal stitches, then back over the row, crossing the stitches with a reverse diagonal stitch to form an "x". Work all cross stitches in the same direction. The stitches are made over one thread of fabric on Aida cloth and over two threads on most evenweaves. Example: 28-ct. linen is worked over two threads to create a piece which is 14 stitches to the inch.

Some charts have fractional stitches, worked by stitching a partial "x". A ½-cross stitch is one diagonal. A ¼-cross stitch is half a diagonal. A ¾-cross stitch is one diagonal and half the diagonal in the opposite direction.

Backstitching is indicated on charts by heavy straight lines. Work backstitching after all cross stitching is completed. French knots are shown by a dot at the intersection of four stitches on a chart. Work these last.

When stitching is complete, wash in cool water with a small amount of mild dish liquid. Rinse well. Roll in a terry towel.

Gently pat dry to remove excess water. Never wring. Press face down on a towel.

Stitching with Waste-Canvas:
Waste-canvas is a needlepoint-type canvas held together with sizing glue. It is available in several different counts.

Cut a piece of waste-canvas at least 1" larger on all sides than the design area. For lightweight fabrics or knits, apply iron-on interfacing to the reverse side of fabrics. Cover the edges of the waste-canvas with masking tape. Baste the waste-canvas centered onto the garment. Cross stitch the design through the waste-canvas and the garment.

After stitching, soak the piece in cool water to remove the sizing. While still damp, pull out the waste-canvas threads with a tweezers.

Have you ever accidentally stained a favorite piece of clothing? Instead of discarding the garment, use waste-canvas to stitch a design over the spot.

Stitching on Perforated Paper and Vinyl Aida:
Perforated paper comes in 14-ct. Vinyl Aida, comes in 10-ct., 14-ct., and 18-ct. Both are available in a variety of colors. Stitch as you would on Aida cloth, omitting fractional stitches.

Stitching Tips
Environmental laws regarding dyes have impacted the manufacturing of floss, resulting in some floss colors no longer

being colorfast. To remove any dye left in the floss, soak the skeins in warm water before stitching. Roll the skeins in a towel to remove excess water and place the skeins on a towel to dry.

To help keep your place when working with complicated charts, insert the chart in a clear plastic page protector. As you finish stitching an area, cross out the completed section of the chart with a permanent marker.

Another tip for working with complicated charts: baste horizontal and vertical rows of sewing thread every tenth stitch on your fabric to correspond with the darker tenth-row lines on your chart. When stitching is completed, remove the basting threads.

Attach large cross stitch charts to a metal cookie sheet with refrigerator magnets. The cookie sheet will keep the chart flat on your lap while you stitch.

If you find it difficult to work from a chart or book on your lap, try placing it on a music stand at eye level directly in front of you.

Most cross stitchers prefer to work without a hoop. Hoops can leave marks on the fabric which are difficult to remove. If you wish to use a hoop, choose one that is large enough to encompass the entire stitching area. Remove the fabric from the hoop when not stitching. Plastic hoops are preferable to wood or metal. Metal hoops can rust and have sharp edges which can snags and tear the fabric. Wood hoops absorb the oils from your skin, transferring them to the fabric. If you wish to use a wood hoop, wrap it with tissue paper or muslin before inserting the fabric.

Dark colored cross stitch fabrics can be difficult to stitch on because they absorb light, making it difficult to see the holes in the fabric. When working on dark colored cross stitch fabric, place a piece of white fabric on your lap to help see where to place the needle.

Keep a damp sponge nearby when stitching. Run the floss over the sponge before separating the strands to make separating easier.

Another tip to keep floss from tangling while separating the strands is to attach a clip or spring clothespin to one end. As you separate the floss, the clip will spin, keeping the strands from tangling.

If your floss becomes twisted while stitching, it will appear thinner and not cover an area as well. In order to prevent this, work with short strands of floss, 15" to 18" in length. If the thread does become twisted, drop your needle and let it hang down. The floss will unwind itself.

Here's an easy way to anchor your floss when you begin to stitch, but it only works if you are using an even number of strands when stitching. Cut the floss twice as long. Fold the floss in half, and thread the cut ends through the eye of the needle. When bringing the needle from the back of the fabric to make the first stitch, leave a 1" loop. When you bring the needle back down to finish the first half-cross, push it through this loop. Pull taut, and your floss will be secured.

When stitching on perforated paper, use shorter strands of floss and a looser tension to keep the paper from accidentally tearing.

When stitching a piece that has large areas of solid color, stitch the outline of the area first. You can fill the area in without constantly referring to the chart. This is a good technique for projects you want to carry with you because you won't need to bring the chart or book along.

Another good idea for take-a-long projects is to stitch half the cross stitch throughout the project. Complete the stitches whenever you have a few minutes to stitch.

Storage Tips

Store cross stitch books and leaflets in cardboard magazine holders. Separate the books by subject matter, such as Christmas, children's designs, florals, etc., labeling the front end of each holder for quick reference.

A handy way to separate and keep track of different sized needles for various projects is to stick them into small squares of the proper size cross stitch fabric.

Store skeins of floss in the clear pockets of baseball card protector sheets or wrap them on floss cards and store in the clear pockets of coin holder sheets. Keep the sheets in a loose-leaf notebook.

See-through plastic boxes are terrific for storing cross stitch fabric. Purchase one for each of the different fabric types and/or count sizes you have. Label the ends of the boxes for quick reference. Creases can be difficult to remove from cross stitch fabric. To prevent them, store your projects rolled up in the plastic tubes which some cross stitch fabric is sold in instead of folding the fabric. You can also use cardboard tubes from plastic wrap or foil; however, cover the roll with a piece of acid-free tissue paper or white sheet fabric to prevent the cardboard from discoloring your stitching. Store small projects inside toilet tissue tubes.

Keep small scraps of cross stitch fabric, perforated paper, or vinyl Aida handy for small projects such as ornaments, button covers, bookmarks, jewelry, and magnets.

Framing Tips

The easiest way to mount a piece of finished cross stitch is to use acid-free, self-stick mounting board. If not using a self-stick mounting board, center the stitching over a piece of acid-free illustration board or foamcore board. Stretch the edges to the back of the board, securing with acid-free tape.

If you are not framing with glass, boards may be covered with batting before mounting for a padded look. If using glass, place a cardboard shim under the frame between the glass and fabric to keep the glass from sitting directly on the fabric. When fabric is sandwiched against glass, moisture can get trapped inside the frame, causing the fabric to mildew and rot over time.

ABOUT THE AUTHOR

USA Today and Amazon bestselling author Lois Winston began her award-winning writing career with *Talk Gertie to Me*, a humorous fish-out-of-water novel about a small-town girl going off to the big city and the mother who had other ideas. That was followed by the romantic suspense *Love, Lies and a Double Shot of Deception*.

Then Lois's writing segued unexpectantly into the world of humorous amateur sleuth mysteries, thanks to a conversation her agent had with an editor looking for craft-themed mysteries. In her day job Lois was an award-winning craft and needlework designer, and although she'd never written a mystery—or had even thought about writing a mystery—her agent decided she was the perfect person to pen a series for this editor. Thus was born the Anastasia Pollack Crafting Mysteries, which *Kirkus Reviews* dubbed "North Jersey's more mature answer to Stephanie Plum." The series now includes ten novels and three novellas. Lois also writes the Empty Nest Mysteries, currently at two novels, and one book so far in her Mom Squad Capers series.

To date, Lois has published nineteen novels, five novellas, several short stories, one children's chapter book, and one nonfiction book on writing, inspired by her twelve years working as an associate at a literary agency.

To learn more about Lois and her books, visit her at www.loiswinston.com where you can sign up for her newsletter and follow her on various social media sites.

Made in the USA
Las Vegas, NV
09 November 2021